HERE BY
THE BLOODS

HERE BY
THE BLOODS

BRANDON BOYCE

*Based on a concept by Derrick Borte
and Brandon Boyce*

PINNACLE BOOKS
Kensington Publishing Corp.
www.kensingtonbooks.com

PINNACLE BOOKS are published by

Kensington Publishing Corp.
119 West 40th Street
New York, NY 10018

All Kensington titles, imprints, and distributed lines are available at special quantity discounts for bulk purchases for sales promotions, premiums, fund-raising, educational, or institutional use. Special book excerpts or customized printings can also be created to fit specific needs. For details, write or phone the office of the Kensington special sales manager: Kensington Publishing Corp., 119 West 40th Street, New York, NY 10018, attn: Special Sales Department; phone 1-800-221-2647.

PINNACLE BOOKS and the Pinnacle logo are Reg. U.S. Pat. & TM Off.

ISBN-13: 978-0-7860-3520-5
ISBN-10: 0-7860-3520-X

First printing: September 2014

10 9 8 7 6 5 4 3 2 1

Printed in the United States of America

First electronic edition: September 2014

ISBN-13: 978-0-7860-3521-2
ISBN-10: 0-7860-3521-8

For Danielle.

The adventure begins . . .

DRAMATIS PERSONAE

The People of Caliche Bend
Harlan Two-Trees—a young man
David Pardell, Sheriff—the law
Mrs. Pardell—his wife, deceased
Walter Boone—mayor of Caliche Bend
Bennett Whitlock—a prosperous rancher
Merle—owner of the Jewel saloon
Rico—an employee of the Jewel
Big Jack Early—a laborer
Elbert Pooley—a farmer
Polly McPhee—boardinghouse proprietress
Bertram Merriman—postmaster
Doc—the town doctor
Jasper Goodhope—owner of the Dry Goods
Hezkiah Fay—a tailor
Otis Chandler—chemist/druggist
Chandler's son—a stable boy
Frank Wallace—a bank clerk
Mr. Farley—the bank owner
Mrs. Daubman—a widow
Jed Barnes—a drunkard
Brunson Stone—hotelier
Cookie—hotel employee, former slave
Padre—a priest
Madam Brandywine—bordello proprietress
Scratch Gardner—her bouncer
Carmelita—a whore
Maria—a Mexican whore

Visitors to the Bend

Garrison LaForge—a.k.a. The Snowman,
a bank robber
Finn—part of the Snowman's gang
Percy—part of the Snowman's gang
Avery Willis—a gentleman gambler
Genevieve Bichard—his companion
Carter M. Haggerty—a judge
Royland M. Boone—public defender,
Mayor Boone's nephew
The Monsignor—spiritual leader of Heavendale
Silas Townes—mayor of Agua Verde
Jessup—a Kansan gambler

Pinkertons

Captain Mulgrew—the commanding Pinkerton
Bix—his lieutenant
Delmer—the crank-gunner
Casey—a rifleman
The Frey Brothers—Prussian riflemen
Sharpshooters

The Dineh

The Chief—a Navajo
Ahiga—his warrior son
Raven—another son

PART I
THE BEND

CHAPTER ONE

The way the clerk tell it—and the clerk, a churchgoing man name of Frank Wallace who always calls me by my name, never that other word, has no reason to lie—the four men come into the Loan and Trust together at quarter past four, brims pulled low, mascadas covering the rest. Wallace is no fool, sees their Colts drawn for business, but before he can reach for the bell cord or the ten-gauge behind the counter, the voice of the fifth man cuts him cold.

"Leave the scatter gun be." The fifth man steps in from the street and takes his time moving across the plank floor to the window where Wallace stands behind a few steel bars that seemed a lot sturdier five minutes ago. "Farley does not pay you enough to get killed, so do not be pulling on the bell either." The man flashes a snarled grin of neglected teeth stained yellow from coffee and whiskey.

Wallace wishes he had a slug of rye himself right now, because this fifth man is taking no care to conceal his face. That bothers Wallace, as if the man is daring him to remember his pocked jaw, or lake-water eyes, or hair so black you would swear he scalped it from a Chinaman. Or maybe he is saying without saying that remembering his face hardly matters because *it is the last face you will ever see.* That bothers Wallace even more.

"What is your business, then?" Wallace asks, keeping his eyes straight ahead and his voice strong. The fifth man smacks his lips a bit and the four with him grow perceptibly agitated by the question.

"Our business is relieving financial institutions of their fiduciary responsibility. That and blowing holes in them what try to stop us."

"Enough talk." The blue bandana muffles the tallest man's voice, but not the seriousness of its tone. He shoves the leather satchel through the window at Wallace, who takes it and clangs open the till. Wallace does not mind surrendering the hundred or so dollars in his drawer. The concern is that these men are dumber than rope and that he will pay the price for their dumbness with his life.

The real prize, any fool would know, is not the pocket money in the till, but the stout wads of bills, pallets of silver ingots, and bundles of gold coin resting under the protection of seven inches of steel in the safe behind him. And when these goats realize Wallace has not the numbers in his head to open it—only Mr. Farley has those, and he will not be here until five minutes before closing time, when the time lock releases and allows the heavy knob to turn at all—they will surely kill him in frustration. But maybe these men do not know about the safe, even though it squats in the center of the room like a green, pregnant heifer. Wallace hides these thoughts as he loads up the satchel and passes it back through the bars.

"Now open the door," the barefaced leader says.

"You have your money," says Wallace.

"We are not here for your farm boy's allowance! It's the vault we want. Now unlatch that side gate or, I swear it, I'll send a lead slug straight through your eye."

Wallace looks out at four pistols and a sixteen-gauge aimed square at his head. Resigned, he slips off his stool and thinks, *Tuesday is as good a day to die as any other.* The tall one in the blue mascada—a fine silk one, Wallace notes, now that he is closer to it—hovers outside the office door. Wallace keys the latch and turns the knob a twitch. The man in blue does the rest, pushing through into the office and going straight for the safe. The other men come in behind him, the leader entering last. The four hands set to clearing away all the furniture around the vault, upending tables, scraping Mr. Farley's desk to the corner, tossing chairs aside like kindling.

"Time lock," one of the men says.

"I cannot open it. Even if I wanted to," Wallace blurts out, his voice weaker now.

The leader steps up to Wallace. "No one asked you to." A lump of cold fear takes hold in the belly of Frank Wallace. The man is close enough for Wallace to smell the coffee on his breath, the boiled, cowboy kind, the drink of nomads. Beneath that is the dank, wet stench of leather, sweat, and what he believes is Mexican tobacco. But when the man grins again, letting out a half-breath of bourbon-tinged vapor, Wallace knows in that moment that these men have come from the East, riding hard.

These are not broken gamblers, or rustlers in search of a stampede, or even desperate laborers from the mines, sick with boredom and hunger now that the copper has run dry. These men are professionals.

The barefaced man reaches into the burlap sack and comes out with a pound bag of wheat flour, sopped wet with liquid, like the whole lot of it had dropped in a creek without breaking open and got pulled out ten minutes later. Except this is no creek water oozing out of the paper. And that is the thing that bothers Wallace most of all, because the Snowman leaves no witnesses.

"You know what this is?" the Snowman asks through his piss-colored teeth.

"It appears to be a sack of flour," Wallace says. That lump of fear in his belly squeezes the base of his spine, leaving his voice little more than a whisper.

"And do you know the purpose of this sack of wheat flour?" Every soul in two territories knows the bandit's legend. The Snowman—so named for the simple, ingenious *modus operandi* represented by what he now clutches in his weathered, buckskin glove—didn't even have to ask.

About here is where poor Widow Daubiman comes through the bank door that the bandits did not bother, or care, to bolt. Her eyes go big. She lets out a gasp that is more breath than sound and turns her little frame back toward the door. The nearest of the Snowman's men—the stocky one with the gray tasseled topcoat—swoops through the office door and buries his six-inch bowie through her paper skin so hard that Wallace hears her ribs crack before she hits the ground. No discussion. No gunshots. No witnesses.

The Snowman's eyes alone stay on the face of Frank Wallace, still awaiting an answer. "I say, friend, tell me to what end do I carry about this here pound of wheat flour?"

"They say it stabilizes the ni-ni-nitroglycerin." I suspect this is where Frank Wallace loses control of his bladder, but he was not as precise with that particular as he was with the rest of his account.

"I see my reputation precedes me."

The Snowman catches Wallace's gaze flicker toward the far wall, where hangs the notice of the bounty. The Snowman crosses to the posted sign and yanks it down. "Precedes me, and how." He holds the sketch up beside his own visage, inviting the comparison. "This artist has done my nose an injustice. Would you not agree, friend?"

Wallace need not answer. Despite its vagueness, there is not a curve of the rendering, nor a word of the type, that Wallace has not committed to memory:

WANTED
for MURDER and BANK ROBBERY
Garrison LaForge
A.K.A. THE SNOWMAN
$10,000 Dead or Alive
$3,000 for all known accomplices

In truth, the artist had done the Snowman a service, tempering the more pronounced Roman nose—presently huffing at Wallace—with a charcoal retelling of no discernable distinction, but no grotesqueness either. The sketch is blocky and indiscriminate, a product of winnowed hearsay and conjecture. The Snowman leaves no witnesses.

The fear gurgles up Wallace's spine into the root of his skull and digs in behind his eyeballs, drunk-spinning the room. He thinks of the sheriff, one of the few living men ever to see the Snowman's face. And that was in a card game years ago. The sheriff never thought much of the likeness on the wanted notice, but he figured it was better than no likeness at all and ordered a dozen bills printed and posted around town as the governor requested.

Wallace does not like thinking about any of this as he watches the Snowman scoop up the flour sack and carry his trademark explosive toward the safe where the man in the silk blue mascada carefully unwraps the fuses from a square of cheesecloth. The Snowman wedges the sack beneath the front leg of the safe and forms it gingerly into the crevice between the door and side panel that the manufacturer will no doubt reconsider on future models.

There is talk between the men, Wallace says, but the fear grips Wallace's ears now and pummels the words into a flat, meaningless drone. The man in blue inserts the fuses with the precision of a surgeon. *An artist*, Wallace thinks, turning his head toward the customer side, where Widow Daubman bleeds out into an expanding puddle. Wallace looks down at his own puddle and steps out of it.

The commotion of the remaining men draws Wallace's gaze back to the office, where the haphazard destruction of the furniture seems to have taken on meaning. Nearly every stick and cabinet lies piled up against the partition that separates the office from the customers' area, forming a barrier, a shelter, from what is about to happen.

The fiery fuse snakes to life, shooting thin, gray whippets of acrid smoke in its wake. The Snowman appears before Wallace, his mouth moving with understated urgency. "You would be advised to secure yourself." The bandits scamper like schoolchildren around the partition and down onto the floor behind the tangle of furniture. Wallace stands there, unable to digest the one thought that chews through his reasoning brain. *Why am I still alive?*

His other brain, the animal one, tells him to move his legs. Wallace dives into the pile as if it were made of hay instead of oak and iron, clutching himself small behind Mr. Farley's upturned desk. And then everything goes white.

"How about crack us a window," Sheriff says. "Getting a mite close in here."

I lean my broom against the wall of the cell and walk around the desk where Sheriff sits, boots up, spit-shining his badge. Sheriff prefers this time of day, even though it is the hottest. The heat subdues lawless ways, he once told me, or at least sends them under a rock till the sun sets.

I throw open the shutters. The flecks of desert dust dance in the harsh beams of sunlight that cut through the gloom of the station house. Beyond the glass, the big red eye has just started to drop behind the Sangres, pulling the long shadow of the church steeple from one end of Caliche Bend to the other. The big red eye sees all, and at night the little white eye catches the rest. Mamma taught me that, in between her customers. I see best when there is no eye at all, in the dead of a moonless night. That is the Navajo in me.

I jimmy up the window sash and take the air deep into my lungs. A breath of sage rides the September breeze, undercut by the thick scent of horses from the stables and the frying bacon from the hotel next door. Dancing high above it all, like the thinnest wisp of a cloud, is the faint vapor of potassium nitrate.

"They start back up at the copper mines?" I ask.

"Lord, no. Those mines have not been step foot in, nearly two year."

"Somebody burning quick match."

The sheriff pulls his feet off the desk, rubs the stiffness from his knees before rising. "Well, I know better than to doubt your nose, Harlan. Or your ears, or eyes, for that matter. If I were not sure it was equal part Navajo and White Man blood running through your veins, I would swear it was half hawk and half bloodhound." He smiles as he heads over to the window, wanting to take a breath for himself.

I smile too. Sheriff's ribbing never bothers me. He and Mrs. Pardell earned the right through kindness.

"Cannot say I smell any quick match. Perhaps the chemist has concocted a faulty remedy and pitched it out the window." I nod politely. I do not think much of Sheriff's conclusion. So I swallow a little tobacco juice and go on staring.

The thundering boom cobwebs the glass before my eyes. Through the prismed lattice Sheriff and I see the charred, iron cube shoot clean through the back wall of the Loan and Trust and land on the dirt. White smoke rises from where the safe door cleaved from its hinges. The paper money, most of it aflame, flutters through the choking black cloud that billows from the shattered windows. Something wrapped in white, bloodstained cotton lies smoldering on the ground.

"God in heaven." Sheriff's voice trembles like it did when he told me the typhoid had taken sweet Mrs. Pardell, but then it regains its lawman timbre. "Get my Spencer thirty-aught."

I scamper to the cabinet and key it open. Sheriff has his second Colt loaded and holstered before I even free the rifle from the rack. I toss it to him and he catches it without breaking stride for the door.

Frank Wallace opens his eyes and learns that the Snowman's moniker is well earned. The whiteness drifts through the air like a high-country flurry, catching the golden sunlight through the brand-new crater in the back wall. Settling on the shoulders and brims of the bandits, the flour casts each man in a ghostly pall.

The Snowman is on his feet, stuffing the scattered gold pieces into a satchel. He yells something to the man in blue, but Wallace hears nothing—nothing but the constant, high-pitched ringing in his ears. He looks left where the bandit who killed Widow Daubman now slumps against what is left of the woodpile. A chair leg protrudes from the murderer's skull, wet with the pink liquid of brain and blood.

The third bandit hops down through the blast hole and snatches the remains from the scorched, upturned carcass of the safe. The man in blue strides for the front door. Frank Wallace feels the warmth in his left shoulder and looks down at where his arm used to be.

I see Frank Wallace fall out the back of the Loan and Trust as I follow Sheriff Pardell down the boardwalk. Sheriff moves fast when he needs to. "Back inside, Polly!" Sheriff yells without looking. Polly McPhee retreats into her boardinghouse and bolts the door. "You too, Merle, get these drunken fools inside! The bank is being robbed." The drinking men clutter the boards outside the Jewel as we pass.

I hear Merle try to wrangle his customers back to the bar. "You heard the sheriff. Get back inside and I'll buy you cocksuckers a drink." But the promise of a shootout draws men's attention like flies to a dead cow, even under the threat of free whiskey.

A drunken voice yells out, "Send the halfbreed in after 'em, Sheriff. No sense in gettin' you'self kilt." I want to turn around, but do not.

Elbert Pooley's wagon lies jackknifed in the middle of the road. His two mules, spooked by the explosion, strain and whinny against the reins, dragging the wagon in a slow-moving arc. Elbert is down with the mules, holding the bridle of one and trying to grab the other. "Take cover, Elbert. Leave them mules be," I say to him.

"Their legs will snap!" Elbert pleads, trying not to cry. I take the bridle of the bucking mule and calm her.

"Cut 'em free then." I know by Sheriff's tone that this is meant for me and I start pulling at the leather. Elbert stops dithering and gets busy on the other mule. Sheriff takes a knee behind the overturned wagon and peers around at the bank door directly in front of him. I get my mule free, slap her hindquarter, then set about helping Elbert, who is making a mess of it.

"This one here," I say, unfastening the proper line. The mule pulls free and I put Elbert's hand up to her bridle.

"God bless you, son. God bless, you!" Elbert says, leading one mule off with him to chase after the other.

I glance over at the bank, squat down behind Sheriff. "Two geldings hitched up out front."

"And neither one spooked," Sheriff says. "I suspect they have seen this before."

"Not much cover here with this wagon."

"No, but it will have to do." Sheriff turns his head toward me, but not all the way, keeping one eye on the door. "You best go on. Get over to the post office. Tell Bertram to wire the governor's office. Tell him to send marshals. Then go fetch Doc. We are going to need him for sure." Sheriff sees that I do not want to leave him so he says, "I will be all right, Harlan. Now go on."

I stay crouched and run off down the alley opposite the Loan and Trust. At the end of the building I turn left and flank Main Street from the alley behind the chemist's. I enter the post office through the back door, all the while hoping I do not hear a gunshot, or worse, a scream. I arrive at the front of the post office but find no one behind the counter. "Anybody here?" I ask.

"We're down on the dang floor and I suggest you do the same." The voice of Bertram Merriman, the postmaster, sounds far away. I turn toward the window and see Jasper Goodhope on all fours behind the writing desk, still clutching the letters he came in to post. Through the window I have a clear view of Loan and Trust. The upturned wagon is off to the left and I can just see the edge of Sheriff's boot behind it.

"Who is it?" Jasper asks. "Is it the Snowman, you reckon?"

"Don't know." I crouch down to where the glass meets wood. All at once a man kicks up a horse and a second later that same bandit who followed the safe outside comes barreling around from the back of the bank on a palomino he must have had tied up there. Clever thieves. Keep the horses spread out. He is at full gallop when he hits the street. He cuts hard to the left, rushing away from the sheriff. The bandit fires his Colt three times, hitting the wagon twice. He holds the booty in his rein hand. A fine rider. Even better with the gun. Sheriff rises and fires off two shots from his Spencer, but the palomino knows what guns mean and has her rider a hundred yards off before Sheriff can get a bead on him.

I see the door of the Loan and Trust swing open, revealing darkness inside and little else. Sheriff swings the Spencer around toward the door. "You come out slow with your hands where I can see them." Sheriff's voice echoes through the window. Then silence. I hear Jasper Goodhope's heart pounding beneath his clothes. Sheriff rises a little, which I do not like. But he might see something I cannot.

The dark interior of the bank holds no clue, until a muzzle flash barks out from it, biting an apple-size chunk from the wagon's flank. Sheriff falls to his side, hit, but not dead. He regains the Spencer, leans around the side of the wagon, pounds a half dozen rounds into the dark void and through the walls. The Spencer clicks empty and he grabs his right-side Colt. From the darkness comes a single shot that pierces the wagon like it was not there. Sheriff slumps.

Two men charge out of the bank. The barefaced man fires deliberately toward the saloon, discouraging any vigilante sniping. The one covered in blue leaps from the railing and lands in the saddle of his gelding before positioning his compatriot's horse for a similar mount. He calls out to the town, but I swear his eyes fall on me. "Anyone riding after us gets the same." Then he kicks up the gelding and they are gone.

I am already halfway to Sheriff. I turn him over— his green eyes seem to look *through* me. But then they focus, finding me, recognizing me.

Sheriff touches my face for only the second time in my life. "It was the Snowman. I seen him with my own eyes. Snowman, sure as day." He tries to say something else, then stops, exhausted.

"We will get you to Doc's. I swear it." I watch the blood drain from his face. He starts to look through me again, all the way to heaven. I try to lock eyes with him, but I cannot see his face through all the damn water.

CHAPTER TWO

The last of the mourners disappears down the hill trail heading back to town. My Sunday shirt is soaked from shoveling. I take a seat beneath the shade of the big pinyon pine and steal my first smoke of the day. Even with three of us laying into our spades, it took a quarter hour to fill in the berm of fresh earth that holds the sheriff.

The widow was laid to rest earlier this morning, in the churchyard. Padre spoke a good piece beforehand, carrying on about damnation for the offenders and the broken morality of the West. He had to lump his lamentations for Sheriff and widow Daubman into a single go because he knows most rightly that assembling the citizenry of the Bend twice in one day, even if the second time is for their beloved sheriff, is beyond the miracles of the Almighty.

From the churchyard the townsfolk followed the wagon carrying Sheriff's casket—a handsome, cherrywood design donated with respectful condolences from the mortuary in Heavendale—in a slow-moving processional down Main Street and up the half-mile trail to Sheriff's final resting place. The heat stirred a few sighs of vexation, which stern eyes quickly silenced.

All of Caliche Bend had come to honor its fallen lawman. All except Frank Wallace, who remains bedridden on Doc's orders, and Mrs. Wallace, who must be half-deaf herself the way poor Frank shouts everything now. Frank Wallace has come along in the two days since the Snowfall, when the search party, headed by me, found him mumbling nonsense in Big Jack Early's cornfield an hour after dusk. My nose led the way, the smell of charred flesh and urine-drenched wool lighting him up like a beacon.

Frank Wallace is lucky. Whatever shard of metal dismembered him was hot enough to cauterize what it left behind. Otherwise he would have bled out and the smell that drew me to him would have been the same one that attracts the vultures.

Doc worked on him through the night while the padre convened a vigil of the widows that prayed and wailed by candlelight until dawn. When Frank Wallace opened his eyes just before noon the next day, he was, save for his damaged hearing, in remarkable possession of his faculties—so much so that two hours later he was able to holler out his account of the robbery from his bed.

At the mayor's insistence, a man from Western Union was brought in to serve as scribe, scribbling down every word. I and a dozen other folks gathered outside Frank's window to hear the account, while Mayor Boone stood bedside, nodding solemnly at the appropriate junctures. When

Frank Wallace, hoarse and weak of body, finally concluded his narrative, Boone anointed himself official witness by certifying the written record with his signature.

"Well done, Frank. They will hang by this, for certain," Walter Boone said, collecting the ream of parchment the moment the ink had dried.

Tending to personal matters in Santa Fe at the time of the murders, Boone had received the news by telegram at his hotel and returned on the first train. He had not yet been home when he strode out of Frank Wallace's house carrying the pages in his valise. The sight of his steamer trunk aboard the wagon, hastily packed no doubt, confirmed his direct arrival from the depot.

The fine headstone, spared the vicious glare of an unfettered sun by the broad branches of the pinyon, sends its gentle warmth through my waist-coat as I lean against it. I know it is the warmth of Sheriff and of Mrs. Pardell next to him, beneath a fathom of New Mexico dirt. My finger drifts languidly over the stonecutter's work. The Pardell name I have seen enough times to know the letters. But the latest amendment, D-A-V-I-D, chiseled this very morning, marks what can only be Sheriff's Christian name, while the fresh numbers recall a life that began some fifty years ago and ended, by a lone slug from a murderer's forty-four, in 1-8-8-7.

"If I go before my dear Catherine, be sure I am buried here." Sheriff said those words to me after the huge Mexican bighorn gave the place to us. I'd spotted the big male among the ewes, stone still, nearly invisible against the ashy rock slope. His eyes had me in his stare. I nodded just the slightest to tell Sheriff I had something.

"I don't see him," Sheriff whispered.

"He's there," I said, even softer. "Just below that gray boulder." A half minute passed before Sheriff let out a small breath that told me he saw the ram too.

Sheriff brought up the Spencer and fired. The ram buckled, then recovered and skipped off. The ewes scattered. With Sheriff clamoring behind me, I tracked the ram for an hour, following the scant blood drops and faint click of his hooves over the rocks until the animal could run no more. He knelt down and waited for us. When we found him he was still breathing, his eyes open and at peace. This was a few yards from where Sheriff now lies. The big ram wanted us to have this place—we had earned it. He stayed alive long enough to make sure we understood.

I thanked him and with my knife passed him on without suffering. I joined Sheriff at the edge of the overlook. "My God," Sheriff said. "What a view."

As I stare out at it now, the panorama of the landscape appears much as it did on that day three years ago when we discovered it. The whole of the valley stretches in both directions to the horizon. To the south, the white houses and fertile fields of Agua Verde hug the banks of the river. The snaking, emerald water holds its hue even in the full glare of the sun. Clear air makes the town appear much closer than its true distance of twelve miles, but to anyone in Caliche Bend, the bloom of prosperous green that is Agua Verde lies across a dusty, inhospitable ocean of busted claims and broken dreams.

Our neighbors to the north seem equally unreachable. The town of Heavendale, with its mines running rich with copper and turquoise, shimmers regally from its perch atop the foothills of the valley's northward rising edge. Eight hardscrabble miles of high desert separate it from the Bend, which, after crossing, greet the weary traveler with a sign that reads: *Heavendale—Closer to God.*

The Sangre de Cristo range rises like a spine to the west, straight across from me, bridging the whole of the valley and pinning those who live in it behind an impenetrable wall of cragged peaks, perilous ravines, and general misery. The Sangres swallow a man whole. They can wilt the heartiest frontiersman or freeze an entire mule train in its tracks. Billy goats starve in the stingy landscape while the punishing winds have been known to grind adobe huts into dust. Even the strongest Navajo hunters stay away from all but the lowest ridges—and even then, they venture into the Sangres only for a guarantee of a big reward, perhaps to finish off a wounded elk that could feed a village for a week. The Sangres were not put here to be crossed. They are here to be respected.

The valley thrives at its extremities, protects its flanks, and in its barren and forgettable crotch, offers up the Bend. I tune my ears to the sounds of its discontent. I can almost hear the arguments brewing at the meeting hall, where this minute strident voices debate the proper course of action. It is a circus of frustration I will step into soon enough. But for now, my eyes fix on the Sangres.

A wildfire, when it happens, coats the sky for miles in a billowy, ashen cloud. And a controlled brush burn or the clearing of timber leaves a choking thumb smudge of black. But the thin gray string of vapor rising from the pass directly across from me now indicates none of those things. From the Bend I would not see this spindly column of smoke at all. Only here in the foothills—blessed by the sharp eyes the Spirits gave me—am I of sufficient altitude to detect it. Perhaps Sheriff guides me still, or through him, the bighorn. But the meaning of the smoke is clear—a mile or two into the Sangres, in a pass the Navajo call the Gulch of No Place, a campfire burns.

I pull hard on the last of my cigarette and stub it out on the ground. Then I steel myself for the long walk back to town. There will be no sleep for me tonight.

CHAPTER THREE

"It was a fine wagon I lost," Elbert Pooley yells, rising from his chair. "Some fifty dollar! And now a barn full of hay with no way to move it."

"Fifty dollars?" Polly McPhee's lip trembles as if the sum were a personal affront. She clenches the overworked handkerchief in her fingers. "Everything we had was in that bank. What are you going to do about it, Mr. Farley?"

The air of the meetinghouse hangs thick with lamp-oil smoke and rancor. I slip in unnoticed and ease against the back wall. Thirty pairs of eyes fall on Amos Farley and await his answer. A small, plump man unaccustomed to sweat or scrutiny, Farley dabs at his beaded forehead and looks to the mayor for assistance. Finding none, he says in a weak voice, "Most of you had funds with us. The Loan and Trust will do all we can, as well as provide for the needs of Frank Wallace, who so bravely stood up to these barbarians. I have wired the safe company in Chicago, demanding restitution. No response yet, but I assure you I will be most vigilant."

"I lost everything, Amos," Big Jack Early says. "How much you expect to get out of them fellas in Chicago?"

Farley blots his brow again. His voice goes even softer, if that is possible. "Well, typically, in these situations, if the company finds a claim to be valid, they have been known to pay as much as . . . ten cents on the dollar." A wave of indignant gasps, followed by irate cries repeating the paltry amount, erupt from the crowd.

"Fifteen!" Farley offers, "in certain circumstances."

"We'll take the rest out of your end, Farley. Your land is worth plenty!" Otis Chandler yells, to a chorus of approval.

"Order! Order!" Mayor Boone shouts, gaveling the mallet upon the heavy oak table where he sits at the front of the room with the other members of the council. "I will remind all of you that the bandits have not robbed us of our common decency nor our Christian brotherhood toward our fellow man. We are all victims here."

"The town is broke, Mayor. Broke!" Jasper Goodhope says. "And with the mines run dry, there is not a family in here that can hold out more than a month or two."

"What we need is our money back," Bertram Merriman says, "before those bandits gamble and whore it away."

"Or worse, vanish into Mexico with it," a woman's voice rings out.

"We need the Texas Rangers, is what," says Doc, rapping his knuckle on the council's table for emphasis. "This is their job."

"The Rangers do not work on charity, mind you," says Bennett Whitlock, the rancher. "I hired them once, to track down rustlers. I found them petty and most irritating. Paid them two thousand and they never did find my cattle. In a matter such as this—considering the Rangers' commission and the stiff cut Texas would demand for the loan of them, we might be better off holding out for Farley's Chicago deal."

"Might I remind you there is a ten-thousand-dollar bounty on LaForge's head? Let the Rangers have a piece of that," Jasper Goodhope says.

"You think they would risk their necks to go against a killer like the Snowman and then cotton to sharing the reward with the likes of us? You, sir, have not dealt with the Texas Rangers."

"Perhaps, Mr. Mayor," Hezekiah Fay, the tailor, says from the council table, "you could persuade the governor to increase the bounty. Certainly recent developments warrant such an action."

"Hezekiah Fay is right," Bertram shouts. "These bandits are a scourge upon the land."

"Hear, hear!"

"I am more than willing to solicit the help of the governor and I have no doubt His Excellency would provide whatever resources are available. But as to the question of the Texas Rangers, we must not forget the reality. It is a three-day ride from Amarillo. By the time the Rangers get here, the Snowman's gang and our money will be scattered to the wind."

"Then forget them Rangers," Big Jack growls. "I say we form up a posse."

"Hear, hear!" agrees Merle. Then everybody

gets to yelling again, some in agreement, some just to yell.

"I will ride with you, Jack!" Elbert says.

Boone comes down with the gavel again, "And just where do you think you will go riding off to, Elbert?" The question puzzles Elbert. "Yes, it would do our names proud to be the town that brought in the Snowman. Hell! We would all reap the benefits. But without some indication of where we might apprehend this gang, the efforts of a search party would be as bountiful as an orchard of tumbleweed."

"I know where they are." The starchy rustle of wool crunches the air as spines twist to face me. I clear my throat a bit, these being the first words I have spoken aloud in almost two days. Had no reason to do so till now. "In the Sangres, about a mile in. Seen their fire. If I was hiding out, that is where I would do it. Figure their best chance of crossing the range is to wait until just before dawn. That gives us tonight to track them down. Wait longer than that, we take our chances up in the Bloods same as they do. I figure ten, twelve ablebodied men would do the trick." My words hang in the air, just floating there. It is the mayor who breaks the silence.

"Uh, thank you, Harlan." Boone has that tone he always has when he speaks to me, like he is speaking to a child, but a child who makes him uneasy. He turns partly toward the council without looking at them, keeping an eye in my direction. "It is suggested before the council that Harlan Two-Trees lead a team of volunteers into the Sangre de Cristo range this very evening in an attempt to ambush

the Snowman's gang and bring them back to town
to stand trial."

"I ain't staking my life on no half-breed!" yells a
voice I recognize.

"Suicide!"

"You will stay respectful, gentlemen," Boone
grumbles. "The sheriff was a friend to many
people."

"The young fella here could track a coy-yote,"
Big Jack says. "Hell, Harlan, I will ride with you.
Who else?" A long silence follows as a roomful of
eyes avoid Big Jack's gaze. "How 'bout it, Elbert?"

"I suppose I cannot stand by and let my whole
savings vanish into the Bloods," Elbert says. "You
have me." But his voice lacks the vigor of before.

"And how would your wife feel about that,
Elbert? Or yours, Jack?" Boone asks. Doris Early
touches her husband's shoulder, pleading.

"Do not do it, Jack. He will shoot you dead." Jack
deflates a bit. His eyes grow uncertain, as if remembering the accuracy of the shot that killed Sheriff,
or the brutality that dispatched the widow. Elbert
lets his gaze drift down to the floor.

"Your bravery is commendable, all of you," the
mayor says. "But this town does not long for more
widows. This is a job for professional lawmen, not
farriers and farmers—no disrespect, gentleman.
I am not itching to get shot either."

"Professionals? Wait! The Pinkertons have an
office in Agua Verde," Doc shouts, practically
bursting.

"And one in Heavendale. A fine idea, Doc," says
Hezekiah Fay. A murmur of agreement swells through
the room.

"We can inquire of the Pinkertons, of course. They too, will not come cheaply . . . ." Those are the last words I hear as the voices from the meeting-house fade in the distance. The night gets no younger as I walk on alone. I fix up at the moonless sky, another gift from the bighorn.

CHAPTER FOUR

The sheriff's bed is just as he left it, made up clean and proper the way a soldier's would be, but devoid of any woman's adornment, like the way Mrs. Pardell would have touched upon it. His leather holster hangs from the post where he always kept it—where I must have slung it a few days ago. I cannot say I remember.

I hitch on the leather and work the buckle tighter than it is used to. The fit is better than I expect and the two Colts hang within easy reach. I catch my reflection in the mirror. A sheriff's guns do not make me a sheriff.

I slide the footlocker from beneath the bed and, opening it, am greeted by the private mementos of an honest man. What I came for lies near the bottom among the other speculating tools from Sheriff's younger days. The coil of slow-burning fuse is old, but dry and usable. The detonator caps lay scattered throughout the locker. Most crumble in my hands, leaving only three, which I fold into my handkerchief. It would be nice to have more.

The bighorn looks down on me from above the bed—fake, glass eyes holding me in my own doubt. Not doubt over tracking down some bandits— doubt over what comes after, doubt of ever seeing that ram or this house again.

In the kitchen I load the saddlebag with an extra blanket and canteen. I throw in some hardtack, coffee, a tin of sardines, and a few cans of tomato juice. I wipe the table down and leave it clean. Sheriff would not approve of an estate agent leading prospective buyers through an untidy house. I snuff out the lamp and lock the door behind me.

Storm, the stallion, could run down anybody, but a stallion has a bad day every six months and tonight I cannot risk being thrown. The gelding will do fine.

"Easy, Buster," I say, touching the gray of his neck. Buster usually responds as I ask and is too dumb to spook. For the second mount, I take the mule, Strawberry, from the paddock and tie her line to the horn of my saddle.

I put it a quarter to midnight when I lead Buster down toward the road, Strawberry following behind, accepting her fate. She is loaded up with every inch of rope I could find, a few feet of leather cord, and the heavy, old slave irons that Sheriff kept in the barn. A cold wind picks up, whipping down from the mountains. A wind and no moon—perfect for where I am headed—but I find little comfort. I button the topcoat to my neck. Down by the gate I see an orange glow flare brightly and then dim as a man exhales smoke into the night. By his shape and the wide, folded brim of his hat I make him to be the mayor. He has been waiting a good while.

"Whoa," I ease back on Buster and he stops. Boone's chestnut mare snorts, annoyed we have kept her from her barn. "Evening."

"I thought I might find you heading out," he says. "I know he was like a father to you, Harlan, but there is no need to play the hero. We will hire the Pinkertons, sure enough. You heard the folks tonight. Trying to get a consensus out of that lot is like trying to draw blood from a stone."

"I heard a lot of talk 'bout money—'bout what was stole. How much it cost to get it back. I did not hear much about doing what is right."

"I am sorry, son. Sometimes necessity over-shadows justice." Boone takes a long pull from his smoke. "You know these men will kill you, Harlan. I cannot in good conscience allow you to walk into certain death."

"Respectfully, sir, your permission I do not need."

At this he smiles, the whites of his teeth reflecting what scant light there is. "A truth, there. You are your own man, to be sure. What, you are nineteen now?"

"Thereabout."

"Then as one man to another, is there anything I can do to convince you to leave this to the professionals?"

"Calling someone professional does not make it so."

"A truth again. In that case . . ." Boone goes to his saddle and comes back with something folded into wax paper. "Betty put up some biscuits and salt pork for you. You will need all the strength you can muster."

"Obliged," I say, taking the bundle with a nod of gratitude. "Now, if you will pardon me."

"Godspeed to you, son."

"Mr. Mayor."

CHAPTER FIVE

There should be four of them. Five men entered the bank. One took it in the blast. Peering though the branches at the camp, I see three lumps beneath the bedrolls. Maybe one is indisposed, off with a shovel somewhere. In this howling wind he would not go far, though. I wait a half hour, watching them—no fourth man has returned. What internal squabbling reduced their numbers by one I cannot say, but the treacherous five miles leading to this inhospitable clearing offered no shortage of possible burial sites for a traitor's corpse.

I fade back from the trees and into darkness, scaling my soft moccasins down over the rocks until I am fifty yards below the camp. There among the loose boulders I clear out a space of bare earth no bigger than my fist. I reach into my coat and fish out the handkerchief now damp with sweat. Maybe the detonators are ruined. Maybe I am free to head back down this craggy slope, pick up Buster and the mule where I have them tied, and get back to my

bed before this fool mission leaves me blown apart
to feed the coyotes.

But then I remember Sheriff and the voices of
fear in the meetinghouse and figure there are
worse ways to die. The detonators are dry, as is the
slow-fuse, so I will not have to gaze up at that
bighorn though the eyes of a coward tonight. Tying
a foot of fuse to the first detonator, I lower the cap
into the crevice, leaving the tip of the fuse just
below the edge. I take my coat off and lay it over the
opening and myself like a tent. Protected from the
wind, the match lights on the first go, so close to my
skin that it sears me. My eyes turn to slits as I
struggle to adjust to the flare of sudden brightness.
The fuse simmers to life as the flame kisses it. No
turning back now.

Still blinded, explosions of red and yellow blos-
soming beneath my eyelids, I find my way back into
my coat and make my way to the right, guided by
touch alone. Out here, a busted ankle does the
same as a blow to the head. I lead with my fingertips, the rest of me following, one cautious step at a
time, until the shapes of the boulders—and finally
the stars—return to my vision. I check my progress,
some thirty yards, but my line has held true. Not
bad for a blind man. I skirt the camp for another
twenty yards, then hunker down to do it all over
again, only now I shorten the fuse two inches to
allow for the time it took me to paw my way over.
This time I know to look away when I strike the
match.

Two minutes later, the fate of the third and final
cap—and perhaps of me—is sealed when an eight-
inch bit of slow-fuse takes fire. Now speed matters.

Doubling back, I slink among the boulders, their positions burned into my memory by touch and necessity. Just short of the camp I stop, taking a moment to let the air deep into my lungs to calm what is happening inside me. How the bandits are not awoken by the thundering of my heartbeat, only the stars know. Every thump sounds like I am standing at the maw of a copper shaft on blasting day. I say the words in my head.

> *Silent as the snow.*
> *Eyes of a hawk.*
> *Ears of a buck.*
> *Nose of a wolf.*
> *I am Navajo.*

The words always do the trick. I will not be seen until I want to be. It is what comes afterward of which I am less certain. But I cannot think about that now. I glide up to the spot where I was before, behind the branches. The killers have not moved. *Kill them all. It would be easy. Shoot them in their bedrolls.* No. That is not for me to do. Something cold rests in my grip. I look down. I have chosen my knife, but do not remember drawing it.

BANG! The first cap blows, so much louder than I expect, even through the ripping wind. Loud is good. One of their horses, the palomino, I think, lets loose that horrible screech a horse saves for the few times in its life it is truly terrified. The lumps on the ground shudder and become all at once living, dangerous beings. A boot scrapes. Three men stand. The confusion that momentarily stunned their brains is gone before they reach their feet. I should have known. No night is ever fully restful in their line of work. Professionals, spooked by nothing. Just like that, I am the hunted. Someone cocks a pistol. Another chambers a rifle round. Then silence. The men listen, patient for what clues the night will give. And it will always give something. My knife feels as lethal as a pencil. In a full moon, I would already be dead.

BANG! Their heads snap to the center, focused in one direction. A figure points out the spot where the second cap blew. Another man nods. The third does nothing. If they stay bunched together, my plan, what there is of it, falls apart. Their disciplined silence works against me too. I need to hear his voice. The voice of the Snowman.

"Indians?" says the one farthest from me. He is not the Snowman.

"Maybe," says the man with the shotgun before dropping to a crouch. He slinks off down the hill in the direction of the second cap, using the boulders as cover. "Psst," he hisses, "that way." Following his lead, the one farthest from me dashes off to his left and soon disappears down the scarp.

The third man stands alone before me, a silhouette holding a pistol. PAAAPPP! The blast of the final cap shreds the air behind me, so close I can feel the wave against my back. The man turns, facing right at me.

"This one is mine." The sheriff's murderer starts to walk straight toward me. I go stone still. *Invisible.* The Snowman comes to a stop three feet from me, peering with a killer's eyes into the darkness just beyond my head. The smell of coffee and whiskey is just like Frank Wallace told it, but there is foulness beneath it, a fetid effluvium of stench and decay. The Snowman stinks. But I do not so much as inhale. His head angles toward me. He stares right at me, yet does not see. I have lived my life this way. A gust of wind rustles the prickly pear to my right. The Snowman's eyes follow it. He takes a single step beyond me and stops again, the back of his head in three-quarter view to me.

I swing my arm. The butt of my knife handle lands true against his skull. The pistol drops to the ground. I kick it down the rocks. A sound comes out of him as he staggers—a low, stunned moan. He doubles over. I grab him by the head and bring my knee up hard into his ribs. He makes a new sound and stumbles to his knees. From behind I throw my left arm around his neck and pull him up against my knife. Even concussed and disoriented, no man mistakes the cold steel of a blade to his throat. His hands go up. With my knee in his back I drive him onto his belly and lay my weight into his spine.

"Okay."

"Shh," I bring my mouth near his ear. "Your bounty spends the same dead or alive. Make a sound and I will bleed you out right here." Before he even thinks about responding, I yank his hands back and get the shackles onto his wrists. As they click into place I pull him back onto his knees. I grab the oily cloth of his mascada and yank it off his neck. I roll it tight, out of his line of vision. "Say you understand," I whisper.

"I—"

I slip the gag between his teeth, cinching it taut. The knife goes back into its sheath and I come out

with one of the pearl-handled Colts. "Now walk."
A shove gets him shuffling, but he stumbles at the
first down-step and I have to grip the back of his
collar with a stiff arm to hold him up and keep him
moving at the same time. He could make trouble.
He could run. He could plop down onto his butt
and make me have to drag him or kill him. The
blow to the head seems to have numbed him and
rendered him compliant. I am less worried about
him now. It is the other two who will kill me on
sight.

We make slow progress down the hill, negotiat-
ing the loose boulders with difficulty. My eyes do
not leave him. This is the Snowman, the cagiest,
most feared outlaw in the territory. I know not if he
is playing possum. My ears stay tuned to the surrounding night. I rehearse the motion in my head.
There is only one move to be made come trouble
and I will have a split second to make it. The wind
abates for a few precious seconds and I throw my
net of listening as far as it will go. *Ears of a buck*.

The faintest click touches my hearing. I stop. It
could be—but then the scrape. It is a sound I know,
the scrape of a rifle barrel resting on stone, of a
shooter *correcting* his aim. In a single motion I yank
the Snowman back and camp myself behind him
while bringing up the Colt. I squeeze the trigger
before I even have him in my sight. The man peers
down the barrel at me from behind a boulder, his
head and upper torso all I have to work with. I keep
squeezing, correcting with every shot until the
fourth bullet skims the rock surface and the fifth
drops him behind the boulder. "God almighty,
son," groans the Snowman, his body tensed, but far

from panicked. Professional. The strain of his muscles has popped the gag from his mouth. A string of profanity erupts from behind the rock.

"Percy! That you?" It is the voice of the third man, checking on his compadres from off in the darkness to the right. I see him now. His shoulders bounce hurriedly toward the fallen man.

"He shot my ear, the damn bastard," cries the one called Percy from behind the rock. The second man passes behind a boulder. I fix my sight on the spot where his head will emerge on the other side. The brim comes into view and I squeeze. The shot pings off the sandstone, sending the man back behind the rock.

"He get you, Finn?" the Snowman says.

"Nope."

"Well, he is now holding an empty Colt."

I drop the empty Colt from my right hand and cross-draw the other from the left side of the holster.

"Like hell I am." I sound like a kid.

"Never mind," says the Snowman, disappointed.

I aim at the second man, who has reappeared and has his rifle leveled at me. He says, "You wriggle free, I will put him down for you." I tighten my grip on the Snowman and shrink down behind him best I can. The Snowman's ribs vibrate as he chuckles.

"I suspect I will take a bullet in that exchange," he says. "Better you boys follow along where this young 'un aims to take me. You all right, Perce?"

"Yeah. Winged is all. Tell your friend that is bad luck for him."

"The horses run off," says Finn.

"Ah. You best round them up, then. Tend to Percy. You know what to do after that." The Snowman cranes back at me, expels a mouthful of nasty air in my direction. "Your move, young 'un."

I snatch up the fallen pistol and bring the Snowman close. "I have a mule tied up for you down the way. You can choose to sit atop it, or get dragged back to town by a rope. I am not fussed either way."

CHAPTER SIX

We must make quite a picture—two grown men descending the foothills on horseback, mounts tied together, one man seated backward on a mule, trussed up like a Sunday roast, what with all the rope and cord lashed around him. The three feet of line I tied to each of his ankles and laced under the mule's belly eliminates any lingering thoughts of escape while my back is turned. If he tries to slip off Strawberry, tied to her like he is, that mule will trample him if the fall does not break his neck first. I glance back at him every few yards anyway. The eastern sky grows pale.

My canteen empties in three swallows and I bend down to refill it. The cool water from the stream dances over my fingertips. I splash a palmful onto my face and feel the sweat and dirt from a long and active night begin to melt away. A fine, clear morning breaks through the hills. Kneeling over the water, I am grateful that it moves too fast to send back my reflection. I would not want to see it now. It would be someone I might not recognize. Drying my face on the blanket, I feel his eyes on me. He lets out a little laugh. Ignoring him, I unwrap the biscuits and salt pork and set back down on the log. Buster laps at the stream. Strawberry is so tired she lies flat out on her side, snoring. The Snowman's eyes are still on me. He puts a little more air into his snickering so I will look up.

"Something funny?"

"If I was a betting man, and I am, I would wager that was your first time shooting a man. Tell me I am wrong." He starts up giggling again before I even think about answering, which I will not. "I knew it! Well, fear not, son. It gets easier." He sits there pleased with himself, watching me eat, and then adds, "Oh, it is not as though you kilt him. No sense in flogging yourself. Of course, old Finn will make it his life's work to hunt you down and kill you, but I suppose you will, for a day or two, get to enjoy being the fella what brung in the Snowman."

I take another bite and wash it down with the cold water from the stream. The mayor's wife sure knows how to cure a ham.

"Look at me, son." I level my eyes at him. "Nearly all the men what have looked at my face as long as you have are buried in the ground. You are swimming over your head, to be sure."

"I am not the one tied to a tree."

"I should be dead! You had the drop on me. And you should be sitting there with three corpses and a sack full of money what we stole. But for that, you would have to be a killer, and you are not. You also appear to be powerfully disinterested in the loot.

Surely that sum, plus the bounty on three of our heads, would ensure your fortune, security, and longevity. As it stands, none of those three will transpire. So I am left scratching my head as to why they sent you."

"I sent myself."

"You venture up here alone, into the asshole of the world, to track down the most feared outlaw—and I do not overspeak here—the most feared outlaw in the country, with the intent of what? Extracting me from my men, clamping some nigger irons on me, and dragging me back to town—the triumvirate of which are dependent on the miracle that you yourself are not kilt in the process?"

"Something like that."

The Snowman shakes his head, leans back against the tree, and looks at me. "You know," he says thoughtfully, "as far as plans go, yours was noticeably lacking in forethought."

"Was a good man you killed."

"I have killed many. To which do you refer?"

"Sheriff by the name of David Pardell. You will do your part to remember it, or I will spare the rope and gun you down right here!" The pearl-handled Colt finds itself in my hand, balanced steadily at his chest.

"Your past behavior has already neutered that option."

"Good day as any to start." The words hang about for a thick moment, then the Snowman nods, making it known that he believes me. I holster the Colt.

"Is it also part of your plan to starve me to

death?" I think about it, but not too hard, and stick the rest of the biscuit in my shirt pocket for later. Long miles lie ahead. I cross to him, his eyes never leaving me, and kneel beside him to start at the knots. He smells like a barn, a latrine, and a trash heap all at once.

"That sheriff. He your kin?"

"Nope."

He takes a long look at me. "What are you anyway, some kind of Injun?"

"Only the half that tracked you down."

His eyes cast up toward the heavens. "Well, if that does not beat all. Waylaid by some simpleton half-breed."

I snap from the hips and bring my fist up into his jaw. *Fwack!* The blow is clean, solid. I watch his eyes roll back into his head and then flutter back to consciousness. Hacking from deep in his throat, he spits a mouthful of blood into the dirt. The blow tore his teeth up into his tongue. That should cut down on the chatter.

"Damn, son," he says, coughing out the words. "That is one hell of a punch." Another slug of crimson streams from his rank maw. "Might be a killer in you yet." He opens his jaw wide, stretching it. I shove the last of the biscuit into the opening.

"Eat up. Sooner I get you to town, sooner I hear your neck snap." I leave him to choke down the biscuit. His blood will soften it for him.

CHAPTER SEVEN

The Chandler boys see us first. The older one, rolling a hoop down the back steps of the druggist's into the excited arms of his little brother, glances over at the sight of our arriving mule train and, after a pause of comprehension, drops the balancing stick from his slack fingers.

The little one catches the hoop clumsily and lets out a squeal of delight, but his older brother's gape-jawed stare causes him to look our way, and then fall over.

All at once, the boys spring to life, scampering up the steps and into their father's shop like desert mice vanishing into a burrow. A high-pitched voice squeaks from within the whitewashed building. "Pa! Pa! Come look. The half-breed got the Snowman!" Buster hears it too, smart boy. He perks his ears a bit and adds the slightest strut to his step. I keep my eyes straight ahead. Between the two of us, I will let him do the preening.

We come around the front of the druggist's and make the turn onto the top of Main Street. Otis

Chandler himself bundles out the front door to get a peek. The boys, timid now that the corona of intimidation radiating from the Snowman has reclaimed their thoughts, peer out from behind their daddy's thighs.

The wide thoroughfare stretches out before us. Nearly noon, the big yellow eye glares straight down, keeping the shadows short and blanketing the Bend in a listless haze that crackles into vibrancy with every door we pass. Startled bootfalls clamor across the boardwalk—bodies crowd doorways and faces press against windows for a view of the spectacle. I pair each voice with its speaker without the faintest turn of my head.

The post office door jangles violently as Bertram Merriman bursts out of it. "Good Christ Almighty," he says.

"Is that truly he?" Polly McPhee shouts to anyone within earshot of her window.

"It is, most certainly," Bertram announces. "Jasper, go fetch the mayor. I will cable the governor's office directly." The door jangles again as Bertram withdraws to his wires.

Jasper bounds down the steps and trots alongside me, pulling into my periphery. He stares agape at me, then to my captive, then back to me. "You . . . you got him? Holy Mary, you got him!" Jasper sprints off, a town crier. "The Snowman is captured! Harlan Two-Trees brung in the Snowman!"

The doors of the Jewel swing open, spewing forth a belch of tobacco smoke and stale beer. Jed Barnes, not fully to his drunk yet, pounds the railing and roars, "Lord mercy, half-breed! What you gone and done? Hell, even a broke clock is right twice a day." He falls over himself laughing. He will not call me that again.

"Look upon it, folks. It is I!" The Snowman yells wearily from behind me. Then his voice lowers, tailored for my ears alone. "Enjoy it, son. I promise you, dark days lie ahead."

"Murderer!" It sounds like Polly McPhee. "God have mercy on your soul!" Polly, for sure.

"Shit, he looks hardly dangerous now," Merle announces from the Jewel. A clutch of children forming the tail of our procession brazenly inch toward the Snowman. One boy holds a branch, pokes the outlaw's leg to see if he is real. Another boy skips along beside me. He touches my boot, gazing back up at me. I throw back a shimmer of a nod that lights his face up, spreading a wide grin across his cheeks through a puzzle of missing teeth. The Snowman lets the little ones get right up on him, sitting nearly comatose as they squeak out their childish taunts. Then all at once he snaps out a fiendish bear growl. "Aaarrrrgh!" Those kids scatter like scared rabbits and oh, how that makes him laugh.

Elbert Pooley clamors up, licking his lips expectantly. "Did you get the money, boy?" When I offer no answer he glances back at the Snowman, then to me again. "How did you do it, Harlan? Is them others kilt?"

Half the town, it seems, trails behind us. Strawberry, never a mule to shy from attention, acknowledges the unmistakable significance of the rider with which she has been entrusted by trumpeting a glorious whinny and then emptying her bladder.

Big Jack Early appears to my left, his double-barrel twelve gamely clutched in his meaty fists. Merle takes up a similar position on our right, wielding his archaic, bolt-action ten with grim-faced officiousness. Elbert, damned if he will be left from the proceedings, draws both pistols and dashes out ahead of me, putting himself on point. The Negroes stoking the grill fire behind the hotel forsake their duties and stare in amazement.

Through it all, a curve of pale white skin draws my eye. Her raven hair tumbles down her bare shoulders and frames her chestnut eyes perfectly above lips that part with tacit approval. She is the new girl at Madam Brandywine's. Her eyes fix on me and do not let go. Carmelita, the well-seasoned professional, leans over to the young girl and says, nodding in my direction, "I would let him throw me down for free." Noticing the unwavering gaze of her smitten charge, Carmelita adds, "Ay, Maria, put your eyes back in your head."

Hezekiah Fay, the tailor's measure draped around his neck, stands in his doorway and begins to clap his hands. Soon a roar of applause swells from the throng behind us and makes no sign of abating. A second crowd clusters at the door of the sheriff's as the station comes into view. I pull back on Buster and he stops in front of the door.

"Where you want us, Harlan?" Big Jack says as I dismount. I head straight for Strawberry and set to work on the ropes. "Help with them lashings, Jasper." Jasper Goodhope does as Big Jack commands, unraveling the bowlines that bind the Snowman's legs. Elbert moves over to the door and holds it open, still wielding the pistols unsteadily.

The crowd pushes in. "Give them room, now," Jack admonishes.

The ropes and leather straps drop to the dirt. I grab the killer, one hand on his collar, the other on his belt, and heft him off the mule onto his feet. Standing among them, a legend in shackles, the Snowman has an unnerving effect on the people. Grown men backpedal out of the way as we climb the steps. Women crinkle their faces and bury their noses into handkerchiefs as the stench of him takes hold. His clothes will have to be burned. Why that is the thought that enters my mind as I open the cell door and push him inside I cannot say. Perhaps it is the sudden, jittery silence of the crowd that makes me think of it. It is not until I step out of the cell, clang the heavy door shut, and deposit the key into my pocket that their vigor—in the form of an exultant, full-bodied cheer—returns.

I turn to face them and the first man I see, standing before me like Moses, is Mayor Boone. A wide smile reddens his cheeks. His thin fingers find my hand and press into my palm. "Well done, son. I never had a doubt."

Outstretched hands descend on me, eager to shake mine. Ruddy, cheerful faces fill my vision. "Three cheers for Harlan Two-Trees!" cries a voice from somewhere in the packed station house, and three cheers from a grateful town obediently rattle the rafters. I shake every hand offered me. More questions come my way than have ever been asked me in my life, and I am too numb to answer any of them. No one seems to mind.

CHAPTER EIGHT

A fiddler's lively tune filters through the open window, accompanied by the long shadows of the waning day. "Tonight, very busy," she says with a touch of trepidation. Drunken voices pass one another in merriment as I hear the saloon door bang for the hundredth time in an hour. Men piss in the alley below us into what, by the sound of it, must be a deepening puddle.

"I suspect so, with all the work the door of the Jewel is getting."

Maria rolls over toward me, smiling, the under-curve of her breast landing gentle on my forearm. "You want to go again before you go?"

She glides the comb through her hair, watching me in the mirror as I work my way into my boots. Her thin white gown drapes open to her waist. I pull a ten-dollar gold piece from my pocket and set it on the edge of the vanity.

"I said you no pay. You catch the bandito."

"You keep it. The next fella might not think you are worth it." My finger graces her neck as I kiss the top of her head. "He would be wrong." A little smile returns to her face, easing, for a moment, her worries of the night ahead.

"You ever scared?" she asks.

"If I were not, I would fear I was already dead." I put on my hat and give a nod. The bathtub sits in the middle of her little room. An oily film clings to the surface of the cooling water, thickly browned by the sweat and filth of my previous ordeal. "Thanks for the bath," I add.

"Thanks for washing," she says.

CHAPTER NINE

"Sorry to bring up such business after what you have done for the town, Harlan, but circumstances being what they are . . ." Mayor Boone draws a sheaf of papers from his case and slides the lantern over a little closer.

"Sheriff did right by you, son," Bennett Whitlock interjects from across the kitchen table. "This house, the acreage, all the livestock. He left it in your name."

"Plus there was a small savings at Union Bank in Santa Fe," continues Boone. "A few hundred dollars only, but that too will go to you."

"Sheriff was my oldest friend," says the rancher. "I know he wanted you provided for, but folks have been hit hard by this and . . ." Here Whitlock's eyes drift to the floor then back up to me. "With our money still out there, and with the safe company dragging their feet in Chicago—"

"The reward," I say. "That why you come?"

"It is ten thousand dollars," Whitlock says, almost embarrassed by the number.

"I need it not. That money should go to them what lost theirs at the bank. When it come in, that is what I want."

"Sounds as if you had already decided this," Boone suggests.

"Way I see it, one man prospering while the rest of the town starves is in nobody's gain. Them with kids should get their fair shake or close to it, the rest parceled out accordingly." They both sit stunned for a moment, as if a hill whose ascent they were dreading turned out to be a patch of flat ground.

"Well, as if you need any more goodwill thrown your way, God bless you, son. You do the sheriff proud." Whitlock takes my hand as he rises and gives it a hearty squeeze.

"Who watches him now?" I ask.

"Big Jack has the honor. He and his twelve-gauge," Boone says.

"Tell Jack I will spell him come midnight."

"He will appreciate that," the mayor says. "As for these papers, I know you are not a reader. I would be happy to keep them in my care."

"Leave 'em," I say.

"Are you sure? It is the sheriff's official will and testament. As executor—"

"For heaven's sake, Walter, let the boy have his papers," Whitlock says. "You have mightier concerns. Like how on earth do you intend to get that sonofabitch to Heavendale to stand trial? I hardly think our young friend here is up for another mule train."

"Yes, I have been thinking about that," Boone says, turning his gaze toward the window and the rising moon over the pasture. "What if he never went to Heavendale?"

"What are you saying, Walter?" the rancher asks. "We have no magistrate."

"We can send for one. This man committed his crimes in Caliche Bend. And it is in the Bend that justice should be served. Judge Haggerty is an old friend. I have no doubt he would agree to such a reasonable request. We can put him up at the hotel. Hell, he can stay at my place."

"Well," Whitlock says, rubbing his hands together, "I guess with Heavendale and the Bend being part of the same county, there would be no issue of jurisdiction."

"Oh, it is all perfectly legal. I have already checked. But dammit, that scoundrel should swing!" Boone barks, his face reddening. "And I will be dammed if some freethinking jury in Heavendale should decide it any other way. We cannot leave it to chance."

"This man killed our sheriff, my friend. You really think he could escape the gallows, even in Heavendale?" Whitlock asks.

"Ask yourself how you would feel if he did," Boone says. The mayor turns from the window and slinks into a chummier tone. "You boys ever seen a hanging?"

"Cannot say as I have," Whitlock frowns.

"How about you, son?" Boone says, fixing on me.

"Seen what was left of a lynching once, old Mexican fella. Caught stealing the wrong chicken. Couple farmers made example of him. Left him up in that tree nearly a week. Buzzards finished off what the coyotes could not reach."

I figured Whitlock for a heartier man, but he goes a bit green around the gills at my story.

"Yes, well, we are not talking about vigilantism. We are going to keep everything aboveboard," the mayor says.

"Are we?" I ask.

Boone settles back into his chair and folds his hands before him on the table. "I witnessed a hanging, couple years ago, down El Paso. Fellas, it was the darndest thing. A spectacle! Must have been in the hundreds, maybe thousand, Christian and heathen alike, shoulder to shoulder, like they were watching a prizefight. And the commerce! Drummers of every kind—cigars, ladies' dresses, potions and calmatives. I tell you, if it could be sold, some drummer had a stand set up to shill it."

"Goodness, that must have been a sight," Whitlock says, enraptured.

"Like the circus had come to town." Boone continues. "The saloon was so packed with drinkers and gamblers the proprietor had to turn people away at the door."

"Could you imagine our Merle doing such a thing? Ha! That would be the day." The rancher is right about that. Merle would sooner lop off a toe than say no to a dollar.

"And the hotel? Not an empty bed to be had," Boone says. "Why, I myself stretched out on a cot set up in the parlor and felt lucky to have it. Not that anyone did any sleeping that night, or the night after, for that matter. They were too busy celebrating and carrying on and spending money."

And then, finally, it hits Whitlock. "Ho! Wait a

minute. Imagine such a thing happening here. We could . . ."

"Make our money back. Tenfold." Boone says.

"Oh, hang on, Walter," Whitlock says. "Some folks would. Like Merle, the whorehouse, the hotel, even those with a spare room. But I'm a rancher. How would I share in the bounty?"

"You think a thousand mouths will not be hungry? How does a two-dollar steak sound?"

"Imagine. Two dollars for a steak. I could set up a grill tent right on Main Street! Oh, Walter. It is a fantastic idea. A stroke of genius. You must bring it to the town council tomorrow."

"We do not need a council to tell us what common sense already approves. There is going to be a hanging in Caliche Bend. And a hanging is good for business."

CHAPTER TEN

The little eye, half-open, punches through the night's blackness, gobbling up the stars that dare swing too close. The ground crunches under Storm's easy stride. Up ahead, the orange glow of the station house frames Big Jack's wide shoulders where he stands in the open doorway, awaiting me. I put it dead midnight. "You shoulda seen it, Harlan," he says, plodding down the steps as I tie off Storm. "Me and Elbert blasted him with the fire hose. Had to bathe him somehow and he proved most disinclined to do it of his own accord. Stench was overbearing."

"That why you got the door open?" I ask.

"Well, not entirely. I do not much care for his company. He unnerves me. I admit I was eager for your arrival."

"He is a talker, all right."

"That is the matter right there. He has said hardly a word. Only that he would not wash. And after we put the hose to him, he demands a can of boot polish. You believe that? Fella is sitting in there in a burlap smock, but has the shiniest boots from here to Laredo. There is no figuring his kind, that is for sure."

We move up the steps and I catch the glint of Big Jack's five-point star pinned to his vest. He comments on it before I ask. "Pretty swell, huh?"

"Where you get that?"

"The mayor give it to me. 'Special Deputy Atta-shay.' By appointment of His Honor, the Mayor. Yours is sitting there on the desk. And Elbert's makes three. Merle wanted one too, but Boone figured the fella pouring the whiskey ought not have too much legal authority. Probably good thinking."

"Sheriff wears the star. And appoints the deputies. Sheriff is dead."

"Oh, it is just temporary. A special 'dee-cree,' he called it." Jack hands me the key to the cell and lumbers back down the steps, still gripping his shotgun as if someone aimed to snatch it from him. "Elbert will be in come sunup. And mind his stare, Harlan. It will unsettle you."

The most notorious outlaw in the West cuts a slighter figure when laid out on his back in a ten-foot cell, swaddled in ill-fitting burlap. He does not move when I come in. His eyes stay fixed on the ceiling. I settle in behind the desk and pick up the star. No writing or emblems, just a flimsy piece of tin, cheaply made, like a child's toy. I wonder if Boone keeps a box of them under his bed. In his honor I give it a spin on the desk and watch it fall over itself and sputter to an unsatisfying stop. I toss it into the bottom drawer.

"Will you not wear it?" the Snowman asks, hardly containing his amusement. "The way those two fools fussed and flapped over a five-cent piece of tin, you would swear they had been appointed U.S. Marshals." He sits up on the cot. "I was starting to think you had abandoned me."

"Hardly."

"I suspect you were out reveling in newfound glory, if not rolling in a welcoming bed somewhere. Tell me, did one of them whores toss you a free one?" He laughs at his own joke, lays back again. "Oh, I have learned all about you this night. Those two really can gossip like a couple of old hens. Until today, folks in this town did not think much of the one they call a half-breed." I stand up, but he throws his palms open in an instant. "Easy now, friend, I am only reporting history. I have felt the sting of your overhand right and do not care to suffer it again."

"I am not your friend."

"Fair enough. I see now how bringing me to incarceration took precedent over retrieving the booty. Why, you were still a boy when the sheriff took you in. What, thirteen, fourteen, thereabouts? No wonder you would trek all the way to hell and back, leaving fifty pounds of gold sitting by a campfire. Your quest was personal. I respect that. Cannot say I understand it, but I respect it. And you are quite the tracker, it seems. That is the Navajo blood in you, but you know that. And the way them whores hung their mouths open as you passed— yes, I saw that. The Snowman sees everything—why, from that I deduce that the white man who partook of your mother's services was of a handsome stock indeed. But in a town of churchgoing white folks, you are just the bastard of an Injun whore. Hell, I know how you feel. Once an outlaw, always an outlaw, even when you go straight, whatever that means. And if you got a drop of dark blood in you, that is all the white folks will see. But what I cannot figure is why they seem to take you for simple. I know you are not simple. Surely someone along the way saw to your schooling."

"You talk too much."

"Ah, so it is a matter of education. Reading and whatnot." The Snowman leans back, pondering, like he is gazing up at the stars. "I could see an Injun heathen woman not too concerned with tending to a boy's schooling, but churching types like the sheriff or his wife? That does not figure."

I rise and cross to the door. "Fire hose it is."

"All right, all right," the Snowman says. "I will let it be, sir. There is no need to douse me further. Besides, I doubt the floor could take another soak. Forgive my conjecture." I think about dousing him anyway. So be it if the floorboards rot. "I was intending a compliment—that you are a man of ability. That should be recognized. Appreciated. Even rewarded. Not brushed aside by a backward town full of timid, little cake-eaters. What you should be doing is riding with me."

The laugh snorts out of me in a heavy gust. The last thing I ever thought this sack of horseshit would do is fetch a grin from me. I do not believe I have smiled in three days.

"I do not joke, son. A man in my line could make fine use of a good tracker. And you need to be with those who respect you, where you are no outcast, but a brother. Men would kill to ride with me. Hell, no 'would' about it. I got a gang of men whose hometowns did not deserve them, men who strove toward something greater. I take only the best— them with ice in their veins who can shoot the hair off a hedgehog at full gallop. They are my brothers. And hear me, son—day or night, it is the most fun you will ever have. I swear you have not lived until you have had a whore suck you till dawn on a bed made out of Union dollars."

"From what I seen, your gang is down to two, one of them shot, and both lost in the Sangres."

"Oh boy, maybe you are dumber than I thought. You think I require the full power of my gang to knock over a hayseed bank like this one here? No, son. This is what I am trying to tell you. High up in them Bloods, miles from where you found me, in a little ass-crack of rock even you would overlook, are a dozen of the hardest, most killingest sonsabitches the devil ever made. That is the Snowman's gang. And I assure you, Finn and Percy have reunited with them by now. These are loyal men, son. Now do you *comprende*? I do not fear the gallows because I will never see it. They are coming for me. They will bust me out. And any man raises a finger to stop them will die. And them what stand aside will wish they was dead. I could not stop it now if I tried."

A drop of cold sweat beads on my lip where a smile stood not a minute before. They will do far more than bust him out. The image of the Bend, awash in vengeful flames, stamps itself in my brain. Women scream, raped before the eyes of their helpless, bleeding husbands. The entire town, leveled to ashes. The apocalypse.

"Come with us, son. It is all I can offer you. We aim to cross the Sangres and ride into California, where the gold drips from trees. You are the man to see us through."

My legs spring from the chair and kick open the door. I bring up the Spencer, shattering the night with a lone blast. A handcart, overburdened with firewood, creaks to a stop on my right. A dark figure skitters behind it. The whites of his eyes fall back on me from between the fresh split logs.

"Cookie, that you?" I call in a harsh whisper, knowing damn well it is Cookie, the stoker from the hotel, trudging his midnight load back to the woodshed in time for the hotel's early risers. Cookie pokes his black head around the cart, eyeing me warily.

"What is it, Mister Harlan?"

"Need you to rouse Big Jack and Elbert. Tell them I say come straightaway. There is a dollar in it for you." I fish out the silver piece and flip it to him. His thick hands collapse on it midair. "Do not speak to anyone else. Just tell them to come. Can you do that?"

"Sure thing, Mister Harlan."

"One more thing. Wake up the mayor."

"The mayor? Lawsy! At this hour? He sure won't like it."

"I know. There will be another dollar in it for you if you get him here within the hour."

"I'll get him here, all right, if I have to carry him myself!" Cookie charges off into the night. I stay in the doorway, keeping an ear tuned and an eye on the horizon. I glance back at the Snowman, who shrugs, disappointed.

"Have it your way," he says, settling back in his bunk.

PART II
BLACK TIDE RISING

CHAPTER ELEVEN

There is no mistaking a Pinkerton man. The first six ride into town just past noon, holding their team to a perfect chevron and a tidy, purposeful canter, even after the long trek from Heavendale. Mayor Boone comes out to receive them from the telegraph office where he has been all morning. The lead rider gives the mayor's hand a perfunctory pump without dismounting. He states his name as Mulgrew, but to his men, and to everyone else, he is Captain.

Boone gestures to the station house. Mulgrew tips the brim of his bowler once and in an instant the whole crew swings out of their saddles and ties off before disappearing into the station.

Fifteen seconds later Elbert shuffles out, scratching his head at the speedy ignominy of his dismissal. The Pinkertons have it from here, and thanks to a barrage of furious and convincing telegraphs from the mayor, the governor has agreed to foot the bill. "Santa Fe can ill afford the blood of an entire town on its hands, nor the humiliation of seeing its most infamous inhabitant go from captive to fugitive," Boone said to me an hour ago, after securing the assurance he wanted from the governor's office. Now I watch this transfer of authority from the door of the Dry Goods, where two dollars got me a fresh box of bullets for the Spencer.

"Real-life Pinkertons. Right here in the Bend," Jasper says, rubbing his hands into his apron. "Never thought I would see that." The heinous, high-pitched cackle I have grown to detest rips from inside the station house. I turn to Jasper, who looks back at me, fear-eyed.

"What this town never seen before is just beginning," I say, tearing open the box.

"Got a couple more cartons back there if you want 'em." Jasper says, pointing toward the stockroom. I finger the last round into the magazine and tuck the half-empty box into my pocket.

"Nah, I best not clean you out."

"Nobody in town carries a Spencer but you."

"Set 'em aside for me then," I say, stepping down off the boardwalk into the street. "If I come back for 'em, we are in trouble."

"That all you brought?" The Snowman's incredulous voice peals from the open windows of the station house. "Take more'n six Pinkertons to fend off a whole gang of Snowmen!"

By four o'clock, six has swelled to a dozen. Captain Mulgrew installs his best marksman in the church bell tower, the highest structure in the Bend, while two more sharpshooters roam the roof of the hotel, one training his gaze on the street below, the other on the mountains to the west.

I make four more Pinkerton men, all in the same black waistcoats, smoking what smells like the same tobacco, posted at each corner of town. The captain himself bunkers down in the station house, with four grim-faced deputies stationed outside.

The last man, the only one in shirtsleeves, stands sentinel in front of the jail and dabs his brow with the very rag he has been using to wipe down the ominous Gatling gun perched next to him. The lowering sun catches the glint of the long, lethal barrels, polished beyond comprehension and plainly visible from anywhere on Main Street. The placement is intentional. The Pinkertons want everyone to know who, and what, is in charge.

Elbert cannot take his eyes off the Gatling as we maneuver the handcart toward the station house. "They say it can cut down a whole tribe of savages," Elbert says. Then, remembering, "Oh, sorry, Harlan."

"I reckon it cuts down just about anything you aim it at," I tell him.

The handcart creaks under the weight of the freshly filled sandbags that burden it. Grunt work, this is. The mayor called it a favor.

The breathy cry of the afternoon train echoes across the sagebrush, marking the imminent arrival of the judge from Heavendale. Boone himself drove his hansom to collect his esteemed friend from the depot.

We bring the cart to a stop just short of the front steps. The Pinkerton nearest me looks over, snorts, then goes back to staring out at the horizon. Elbert starts to haul the sandbags onto the ground, but I turn toward home. "All yours, gentlemen," I say, walking off. Elbert looks at me, confused. I hitch the Spencer higher up onto my shoulder. It will not leave my side until the Snowman is in the dirt.

The station door swings open and I hear the captain address me. "I do not recall dismissing you."

I turn back to him. "I do not recall being hired."

The captain flies off the doorsill and closes the distance in a heartbeat. "You uppity red heathen," he spits through a snarl of gnashed teeth. "I will beat you like a dog." His arm comes up, the black-jack clutched in his fist.

The sight of the Spencer leveled at his forehead stops him cold. The four Pinkerton men draw their pistols. The veins in the captain's neck throb with rage. I hear the faint click as the sniper in the bell tower beads on me. The scuffle of feet on the hotel's roof follows soon after. Seven guns to my one.

"You have no cause to come at me, sir," I say coolly. The Spencer holds steady. The Snowman was right. It gets easier.

"The mayor told you to get them sandbags laid up in the windows."

"Mayor asked me to lend a hand while you positioned your men. They seem to have found their posts. And as them sacks are for your protection, not mine, I reckon the Pinkertons would want to handle directly the laying of them, you being professionals and all."

"I assumed you were the mayor's laborer."

It is Elbert, his voice quaking with fear, who offers the correction. "Why, Captain, that there is Harlan Two-Trees. He is the one what brung in the Snowman."

The pulse in Mulgrew's neck subsides. The blood retreats from his face, restoring his previous pallor. He nods, his eyes cast upward, and I know the sniper has stood down. Same for the two on the roof. The captain stows the blackjack and calls over his shoulder to the four, "Casey, you and Bix fortify them windows. Rest of you lay what is left around the crank gun. Pack 'em tight now."

The one called Casey snatches a sandbag from Elbert's trembling grasp. "Give me that, dammit."

"You will pardon me, Captain," I say. "I have horses to tend to."

"Wait, son," the captain says. I turn back to face him. "The Pinkertons are much obliged for your efforts."

"I have no doubt you would have found him too, if so charged," I say, unbothered by the lie. "And the money."

"Yes, the money. Indeed. Well, your sort cannot be expected to think on too grand a scale. The important thing is to bring the scoundrel to justice. Tell me, though, when he spoke of this gang of his, did he put a number to it? We call this *reconnaissance*, you see—"

The sound of his voice drops away as his mouth continues to move. My gaze focuses beyond his shoulder and onto the horizon, where dust blooms like smoke from a torch. Jagged shapes flicker though the unsettled cloud, disrupting nature's rounded curves and betraying the presence of movement, the presence of life. A white dot emerges from behind a gray one, then spawns a dozen more in every shade of brown. Then the dots sprout legs. Horses. I squint, draw my hearing to a focused point. *Eyes of a hawk. Ears of a buck.* The herd swells and contracts, unfussed by the protocol of holding formation—they seem more concerned with hiding their numbers. Their increasing proximity brings forth new colors: a fleck of crimson from a waistcoat, a smattering of black Stetsons. In the center of the herd, a single form, tinged with blue, holds steady as the others swirl about it. The blue mascada.

All at once the sound of the captain's disdainful drawl returns—"Any detail, even minor, could be useful for our investigation as to where they might be holed up."

"Captain," I say, letting the Spencer slide down my arm, "they are far from holed up." The whistle peal from the church tower shreds the air.

"Captain! Riders. From the west," the sharp-shooter yells.

The captain turns and squints into the setting sun. "How many?"

"Twenty, at least," I say.

"Man that crank, Delmer." The one called Delmer, in shirtsleeves, slams in a heavy magazine and chambers a round. I see now he wears an eye-patch—if he earned it in the war, he would have been no more than a boy. His small, wiry frame dances from the munitions cache to the tripod that holds the weapon. He pulls free the locking pins that secured it during transport. The muzzle swings freely at his touch, like a dragon loosening its neck.

"She is hot, Captain."

Two hundred yards out and closing, the riders slow perceptibly behind the tall man in blue. They have human shapes now, and clothes, but not yet faces. They form a fluid and restless mass of bodies, held in the gravitation of a single swatch of azure. The tall man's arm raises from the elbow. All at once the team slows to a trot, then stops altogether behind him.

So much for buried in the hills. He must have broken off from LaForge and the others before I reached the campsite, no doubt to get word to the rest of the men farther up the Sangres, or to plan for the contingency of the Snowman's capture. Yes, there is a clever mind behind that blue bit of silk—a trusted lieutenant, the kind of man you could count on to bust you out of a scrape. I can hear his conspiring brain from here.

"You think they see us?" Casey asks.

"Oh, they see us. And the Gatling." The captain draws his pistol and steps to where all his men, even the itchy fingers atop the hotel, can see him. I drift down to the edge of the station, where the alley leads to the woodshed behind the hotel, and take a position behind the log pile, with the captain and the riders still in view. "No one fires till my signal," announces the captain steadily. "Those horses touch Main Street, we cut them down."

The Gatling man flips up the sights, then gives the adjusting knob a single, calculated click. He settles in behind the gun, smoothly caressing the trigger. I wonder how many Indians he has shredded over the years.

The riders pack tighter as they close within a hundred yards. Then, as if suddenly released from its binding force, the huddled form splinters. The horsemen on the edges set off at full gallop, but not toward the jail that holds their leader.

The men break either right or left, skirting the boundary of the town. Each rider keeps his distance from the horse in front of him, vexing any haphazard potshot from a Pinkerton gun. The Gatling man whirls his barrels around to the left, sending his panicked colleagues to the dirt, until he has the station itself in his sights.

"No, you dang ignoramus," cries Casey.

"Do not fire!" yells the reddening captain. "They are too scattered."

The bandits stream ahead, cutting two lines, one eastbound, the other heading west, until the town is encircled. They stay at their gallops, shouting and mocking our inferior numbers. I hold the man in blue in my sights as he makes the turn toward me, passing within fifty yards. His eyes fix on me, and as he passes, he points two fingers dead in my direction, acknowledging that this is not our first encounter.

"I have no shot, Captain," hollers Delmer, whipping the crank gun wildly from side to side.

"I can see that, Delmer. None of us do," the captain answers sharply. "And they have numbers on us."

"Do we engage, sir?" calls the voice in the tower.

"We do not," the captain says, resigned.

A rider at full gallop makes a difficult target. In this revolving perimeter, a clean shot would be the exception, even for trained marksmen, and the bandits know it. As the lines pass each other in opposite directions, the ring tightens, daring us to shoot. I recognize Finn, raising his rifle tauntingly as he passes. And there is Percy, none the worse from when I winged him, standing high in the saddle, a torch ablaze in his up-stretched hand. Others carry flames too, ready to set fire to the tinderbox town at the slightest provocation. Their incessant hooting proves contagious, like the howl of boneyard dogs.

The Snowman starts up from within his cell. "There it is, boys. Ride on! Ride on!"

I feel the hand on my shoulder. "Not today, son. Not unless they come at us," the captain says, ever proud in defeat. I let the Spencer drop, knowing I could take out two or three of them without a miss. But that might be it for me if they swarmed me afterward. And they surely would.

After a few minutes, their point well made, the man in blue peels off to the east. The rest of the gang fall in behind him. As quickly as they came they are gone, but not without a final flourish.

"Captain! A fire, to the east," barks the sniper, pointing in that direction.

"What is it?" the captain asks.

The sniper peers through his spyglass, focusing though the waning daylight. "It appears to be . . . it's a wagon, sir."

"They torched a wagon?" The captain wonders aloud.

"Boone," I say. "And the judge."

I break for Buster, and then remember that it is Storm, the stallion, I saddled this morning. He sees in my eyes, as I approach, that it is time to run and can hardly contain his eagerness.

The Pinkerton men are barely to their horses by the time the stallion and I have made short work of Main Street. Anxious voices rise and fall from passing doorways as Storm's rhythm churns the dirt below. We bank left after the post office—I smell the smoke through the dusky air. Storm powers up the gentle slope just past town, into the thickening odor of burning oak and singed whitewash. From there, the source of the smoke fills my vision. A quarter mile off, where the trail rises between two cols, a fireball on wheels sways to one side then topples over. Two figures in black, one frailer than the other, do their best to free a pair of panic-stricken geldings from their reins.

To the men's credit, they get the first horse free as I close to within fifty yards. Seconds later, I jump off Storm and start on the lines of the second horse. Boone's little pocketknife does a third of the work of my bowie.

"Savages! Bloody savages!" cries the older voice.

"That line there," Boone barks at me.

"Got it." I do not need to slap the gelding. He is gone the second my blade frees him.

I turn and take in the two men. The judge, old and unfamiliar with labor, sinks down into the grass, trembling. The captain descends the col, followed by Casey and another man. Boone turns his face, sweat-beaded and blackened by soot, toward his assembled audience.

"We try that sonofabitch at nine tomorrow morning!"

CHAPTER TWELVE

Excerpt from *Albuquerque Daily Journal*, September 23rd, 1887:

by J. Webber Standish.
*Reporting from Caliche Bend,
Navajo Territory.*

The trial of notorious outlaw Garrison LaForge, better known as the Snowman, commenced shortly past noon in a cramped public meetinghouse with the honorable Cater M. Haggerty presiding. The trial had been delayed nearly three hours to allow for the prosecutor and public defender, both freshly arrived from Agua Verde this morning, to be apprised of the specifics of the case.

Assisting the prosecution and serving as vice-counsel was the mayor of Caliche Bend, Walter V. Boone,

Esq., who presented the majority of the evidence to the jury. A gifted orator, Mr. Boone's opening remarks lasted nearly ninety minutes and regaled all within earshot the infamous exploits of the dreaded Snowman and the reign of terror, murder, and destruction attributed to him and his associates for the better part of five years across Texas and the territories.

With a gruesome tapestry firmly etched in the minds of the jurors, Mr. Boone soberly laid out the charges alleged against the accused: Armed robbery, unlawful use of explosives to commit a crime, and the cold-blooded murder of Caliche Bend's beloved lawman, Sheriff David Pardell, who was shot dead as the Snowman and his gang made their escape after the robbery of the Loan and Trust. LaForge was also charged with complicity in the murder of Mrs. Harriet Daubman, who unwittingly happened upon the robbery in progress and was executed.

In stark contrast, LaForge's attorney, a newly-appointed public defender only three months removed from the bar, spoke for less than a minute. He asked simply for a fair trial and that his client be given access to a clergyman should he desire it.

The lawyer's name is listed as Royland M. Boone. Public records indicate that Royland Boone is the nephew of Walter Boone, the very man seated at the bench to his right. When the issue of their blood relation was raised by the judge, both Messrs. Boone assured the court that their ability to remain impartial in the eyes of the justice system remained unassailably intact. Satisfied that both men were of the highest probity, Judge Haggerty allowed the trial to proceed without delay—a decision that brought forth hearty cheers from the crowd of vested observers, followed by a swift admonishment for silence from His Honor.

As for the accused, LaForge appeared bored and inexplicably disinterested throughout the presentation of evidence and the scant cross-examination. Heavily shackled by wrist and ankle, with another chain around his waist that never left the grip of Captain Gerald Mulgrew of the Pinkertons, LaForge's only notable reactions were the occasional smirk and a single, vocal outburst during the testimony of the second and final witness, for which Haggerty threatened to remove him from the proceedings altogether.

Only two witnesses were called in

the trial. The first, providing the cornerstone of the prosecution's case, was Francis Wallace, the duty clerk at the Loan and Trust and a man believed to be the only survivor of a "Snow-job." Mr. Wallace, severely injured in the crime, entered the courtroom courtesy of four broad-backed Pinkertons, who carried him in his bed, complete with quilts and linens, and deposited him before the judge. Despite being bed-bound, even in court, Mr. Wallace wore a Sunday topcoat and gave his harrowing account of the crimes with a stoic dignity—laudable for a man who lost an arm in the demolition of the bank vault.

Mr. W. Boone commended his star witness for his detailed account and then thanked God that Providence had allowed Mr. Wallace to speak in his own, well-timbered voice, now that his hearing had returned. Some ladies in attendance wept as Wallace recounted the brutal slaying of the Widow Daubman.

The second witness, Harlan Two-Trees, a nineteen-year-old ("or thereabouts") of Navajo descent, is credited with the daring, if not impulsive, capture of LaForge days earlier in the rugged, inhospitable foothills of the Sangre de Cristo—the

Blood of Christ—mountain range.
The reckless exuberance that inspired
the late-night confrontation bears
testament not to the young man's
savage bloodstock, but rather to the
respectable Christian upbringing
afforded him by his benefactors—and
his admirable loyalty toward them.
The late Sheriff Pardell and his wife,
also deceased, raised Mr. Two-Trees
after his mother passed, leaving
him orphaned at age twelve. "An
understandable, blinding quest for
justice," said Mr. W. Boone of the
young man's actions. Before the one
true God, the soft-spoken Two-Trees
testified that the accused provided an
ominous, unequivocal warning that
his gang of outlaw associates would
bust him (LaForge) from his cell
imminently and raze the town in a
siege befitting the Book of Revelation.

Closing arguments concluded just
before four, with Judge Haggerty
sending the jury into deliberation
with the solemn task of deciding
whether a fellow being shall face the
mightiest penalty of all at the gallows.

Well! The gentleman of the gallery
had hardly enough time to stretch
their legs—indeed the accused had
not even been prepared for transport
back to his cell—when word came
from the foreman that the twelve had

reached a verdict. With the spectators hastily returned to their seats (if not still standing in the aisles) and an anxious, humid hush over the courtroom, jury foreman Bennett Whitlock read the four fateful words aloud: "Guilty on all counts."

Then for a brief moment, the makeshift courtroom transformed into a sort of pirates' den as robust cheers and more than a few unprintable expletives erupted from the exultant crowd. Fierce gaveling from His Honor brought some semblance of order, while several men, clearly already at the whiskey, were escorted out, courtesy of the Pinkertons.

The prosecution asked that the punishment be meted out at the next day's dawn, while the defense asked for the customary delays in hope of a pardon from the governor's office. In the end, it was suggested by none other than Mayor Boone that a compromise be made—the hanging shall take place in three days' time, at noon this coming Friday. A conclusive fall of Haggerty's gavel made it so.

Indeed, the tiny hamlet of Caliche Bend has found itself the unexpected center of attention in New Mexico and soon, as word of the verdict will surely spread, all of the Southwest. For

a town that recently lost its only
lawman, the Bend (as it is locally
known) has a worthy steward of order
in the Pinkerton Investigative Service.
Any prospective perpetrators of
unruliness or deviant behavior should
take heed at the unprecedented
number of private guns now charged
with not only securing the condemned,
but the general task of civic policing.
Your correspondent counted no less
than two dozen of the men in black
guarding the courtroom, observing
from rooftops, and patrolling the
environs. Multiple sources report that
more Pinkerton men from the
neighboring towns of Heavendale and
Agua Verde will be arriving in the
coming days as the population of
Caliche Bend swells considerably in
anticipation of the sentence being
carried out. The Daily Journal will
remain on the scene with regular
dispatches.

"'Dispatches'?" Elbert asks. "I never heard of no
patches like that."

"Means reporting, you blasted dullard," Merle
says, his voice hoarse from reading aloud. He drops
the fresh newspaper on the bar and cools his throat
with a sip of beer. The incessant hammering from
outside, peppered with sporadic orders barked in
rapid Spanish, fights for the attention of those of us

gathered around him. Big Jack picks up the paper
and offers it to me.

"Your name in print. That is something, Harlan.
You will want to keep it for posterity, I reckon."

"Guess I could wipe down a saddle with it," I say.

"Like heck, you will," Big Jack says. "I will hang
on to it, then. Not every day a newspaperman come
to town."

"I hear he stays over at the hotel. He come in
here yet, Merle?" Elbert asks.

"Not yet, but whatever flask he brought with him
will not last forever," Merle says. "He will crave a
drop eventually. And maybe a place to dip his pen.
Either way, the Jewel can accommodate him."
Merle pours a dab of mineral oil onto a chamois
and rubs it into the bar, darkening the wood to a
surprising luster.

I have never seen the Jewel this clean. Or this
empty. But Elbert looked about to pop with excite-
ment when he bounded up to me on the street,
clutching that silly newspaper. He insisted on
buying me a beer to accompany the reading of it.

Merle works his way down toward where I sit.
"Another round, your highness?"

"You quit that, now."

"Not often you darken my door. And never at
eleven on a Wednesday morning."

"I am not alone in that," I say, nodding toward
the surplus of available seating.

"Ha! You just wait," Merle says, pulling an upturned chair from atop a table and setting it on the
floor with a courteous wipe of the chamois. "That is
why I am cleaning it while I have the chance."
Merle could soak the Jewel with lye and never

banish the stale, thick remnants of so much spilled beer, smoke, and vomit enough to appease my nose. "This time tomorrow, you will be stepping over bodies to get to the piss pot." Merle looks back at me, amending his thought. "Well, not you specifically."

Jasper Goodhope bursts through the swinging doors from the street. "You fellas got to see this." I get up from the stool, Big Jack and Elbert following, and push out from the dim environs of the saloon into the bright, clear sunlight.

The sweet scent of fresh-cut lumber from the gallows cuts the day's dry, dusty air. Mexican laborers crawl about the rising structure like ants, laying boards, driving nails, and coating the street between the Jewel and the gutted bank with a golden flurry of sawdust. Somebody must have thought the damage the Snowman caused should be the last thing the swinging bastard sees before the sack goes over his head. I cannot say as I mind the sentiment.

All at once the Mexicans rest their hammers and turn toward the approaching sound of measured horse steps. The rattle of a wagon swells behind it. "There it is!" cries Jasper, pointing down the street at something not yet in view thanks to the scaffolding of the gallows. "I saw it cresting the ridge from the store. Never seen anything like it."

The gilded cornices of the coach bob into sight from behind the stacked woodpile, pulled in crisp undulation by a team of four true black Irish Draughts, a frightfully scarce breed in the territory. The only other time I have seen one was when I was a boy. I recall the Irish Draught huffing beneath the saddle of a visiting Army general who had little use for Indians. The thundering power of that Draught has not waned from my memory. Every elegant, obsidian-coated stride of the four horses restates the power and purpose of their meticulous breeding and the noble fortunes that funded it.

The driver's fine black suit makes him more undertaker than hired coachman. And the gleaming, black lacquered panels of the coach itself support that morbid assumption. But this is no hearse. No corpse could afford such stately and luxurious passage.

"Lordy mercy," Big Jack says, slack-jawed. "That is not any stage I ever seen."

"Not a stage," I say. "Private charter. Out of Santa Fe. Says so on the caboose." I know the others cannot discern the city's tiny flag painted above the fender.

"We will have to trust you on that," Elbert says, squinting. The driver pulls the team to a halt in front of the hotel as every available eye in the Bend looks on. What he does next, not one of us has ever seen. His obedient team halted, the man descends from his seat and unlatches a heavy black box from the sidewall. Placing the box on the ground beneath the door, I see that the oddness of its shape comes from the three steps built into it. He inserts two rods into a pair of drilled holes on the side, snaps a third rod between them, and in a matter of seconds has assembled a tidy staircase.

"Well I will be dipped in pig shit," Elbert says. "A footman. An honest-to-God footman." We move closer, edging down the boardwalk as the rest of the townsfolk similarly choke forward, compelled by their curiosity.

"Must be the king of England," Big Jack offers. The driver, now footman, unfurls a handsome parasol and takes his position attentively aside the stairs before touching the door handle.

"Queen, more likely," I say. No man, no matter how fancy, needs more that his own hat to walk ten yards. The footman gestures back at the hotel, and from within, Cookie appears, scurrying to the coach to receive some instruction from the man. All at once Cookie sets about unfastening the sizable trunks and cases that fill the hold. The coach door opens. A hint of red leather from a fine upholstered bench catches the sunlight. Then the man steps out.

And quite a man indeed. The striking cream-colored suit, impeccably paired to the wide-brimmed hat of the same shade, denotes a traveler cognizant of his rugged surroundings and the sensible tastes of those who inhabit it, while the fanciful buttons and embroidered piping can only reflect what Eastern tailors must call the latest in "European fashion."

Braided epaulets frame his broad shoulders as he strides down the steps. I expect flecks of gray in his beard as he turns back toward the coach, but am met only with the trimmed black whiskers that match the hair peeking out from beneath his hat. He is younger than any robber baron or cattle tycoon, and fitter and more sporting than a man who has earned his fortune behind a desk. Family money must be the answer, the sweat of his father or grandfather. But he carries his wealth with the easy swagger of a man who has known nothing else.

His possessions are the finest in creation, including his reason for the parasol.

A flower—blown from some far-off Eden and rarer than the steeds that carried her across this craggy, sunbaked desert—emerges from the coach. Her tiny ankle dips gingerly to the top step like a child testing the water of an unfamiliar pond. The footman offers his free hand to complement the already extended arm of the gentleman. Delicate, white-gloved fingers enlace the awaiting palms, allowing the lady to forsake entirely the banister assembled in her honor. Whatever effort her male counterpart has made to countrify his appearance has been inversely applied by the woman. In every conceivable regard, from the style and color of her frilly ice-blue dress to the alabaster complexion and graceful comportment of her person, she is altogether and entirely a marvel.

"Christ in heaven," Big Jack says, not realizing that he has removed his hat.

Elbert glances back, his felt bowler similarly pressed against his overalls. "I never seen her kind . . . even in Santa Fe."

I let my eyes drift momentarily from the angel to the assembled crowd of bareheaded men and newly concerned women. Elbert's words had said what we were all thinking: that the choice of ostentatious carriage and accoutrement was less about transporting a wealthy man than it was about being a worthy conveyance for the likes of *her*. No reasonable mind would toss this fair beauty into the back of a hay cart any more than it would a Swiss clock or a pallet of quail eggs.

A man's shoulder jabs me hard, shattering the

peace. "Move it, half-breed." I turn to see Jed Barnes trudging down the boardwalk, hell-bent for the Jewel. The weight of the pearl-handled Colts tugs reassuringly from my hips as I reach for his shoulder.

"Call me that again." I slap the greasy nap of his shirt, feeling the acrid, boozy sweat that no doubt coats the rest of him. Jed Barnes explodes at the touch, spinning back at me with a vicious, slashing arm stroke. I hitch backward. The tip of his blade grazes the loose flap of my jacket.

"Get the fuck off me!" Jed snarls, more concerned at the assault than by who committed it. Then his eyes fall on me, focusing, despite the tremors that ravage him.

"Jesus, Jed." Elbert says. "Get ahold a' yourself."

"I am sick, dammit," the drunk hisses. "I have not had my drink yet." The razor trembles in his grip as his eyes dart from face to face, assessing threat like a cornered tomcat. I finger the fresh cut in the fabric beneath the buttonhole. I look back at him. Jed sees something in my face that propels his feet backward. "Any fool know better than to interfere with a man and his drink. Now you just leave me be!"

Drawing my Colt, I step toward him. Then I feel something thick and sturdy press against my rib cage.

"There a problem here?" I look down and see the truncheon, clutched in the firm, uncompromising fist of the Pinkerton captain. His eyes fix solely on me, keenly aware which man more requires his authoritative gaze. "Or maybe the two of you want to bunk up with the Snowman for the night?"

I let the Colt fall back into its resting place. "No problem at all, Captain," I hear Big Jack say. "Just a little misunderstanding among the locals, is all."

"Locals? Is that what we call them now?" Jed says. "As a God-fearing white man, I think—"

"—that you should be getting on to the Jewel now," Big Jack sternly completes Jed's thought.

The captain considers Jed, then me, then Jed again. "Best be on your way then."

Jed tips his hat to the captain. "Good day to you, sir," he says, letting his eye linger on me for a moment longer before shuffling off down the street.

The captain stows his truncheon and adds in a calm but foreboding tone, "Next time, I bash skulls and we sort it out after. Let there be no misunderstanding on that." He nods, turning away slowly, like a man who need not hurry for anyone.

"Forget old Jed. He is not worth your time," Big Jack says.

I turn back toward the hotel—throbbing with rage—to see the two newest arrivals locked in a stare right at me. Her eyes, little saucers of cornflower blue, melt the anger from me in a watery instant. I want to climb inside them and soothe the faint ripples of fear that, even from this distance, emanate from her, telling me that I have caused her discomfort. Even under the parasol of another man's protection, she is my guest and I have dishonored her. She breaks the gaze, removing from my sight the fairest sprig of color that I have ever seen and may never have the privilege of beholding again.

A shielding caress from the gentleman turns her

away from me and ushers her toward the hotel porch, where the full staff has assembled. The Bend, in its unworthy entirety, watches the couple disappear through the door.

A flicker of familiar raven hair catches the breeze from a window to my left, mingling with the sheer white curtains that flutter from it. Tears leak from Maria's eyes, tears she wants me to see.

CHAPTER THIRTEEN

Hezekiah Fay inspects the tear in my coat and brings it over to his worktable where the light is better. "Gave his name as one Avery Willis of Chattanooga, Tennessee. A professional gambler, by his own admission, and very particular about his clothes." The tailor points to a rack of starched white shirts hanging in the corner, each with identical lettering monogrammed above the right breast—a large W, flanked by a smaller A and D. I know my letters that much.

"He come in here already?" I ask.

"Oh, I believe I was his first order of business after his arrival yesterday. Four shirts of the finest cotton I have seen in some time, laundered and pressed, extra powder. I guess visible perspiration is a liability in the poker business. I informed the gentleman that the hotel would have gladly sent his garments to me, thus saving him the trouble of visiting my shop directly, but he said he did not trust that the specifics of his instructions would survive such a third-party conveyance. I cannot say he is wrong in that assumption." Hezekiah Fay weaves Jed Barnes's handiwork through his fingers, eyeing the sliced fabric skeptically. "You say you caught this on a fence post?"

"Barbed wire."

"Must have been the sharpest barbed wire in the territory. That is good, though. Allows for a cleaner mend." The tailor eyes me delicately, adding, "You know, perhaps a new shirt would be in order as well."

I look down at the gray flannel clinging to my frame. It is my favorite—cool in the summer, warm in the winter, and soft like a baby's diaper. "I just got this broke in. Sheriff give it to me."

"You think I do not recognize my own craftsmanship?" he says, coming around the counter to me. "I made that shirt for Sheriff Pardell nearly twenty years ago. Yes, it is a fine garment—I stand by it. But weaves tend to rub thin over time. Understandably, the sweat of a working man." Hezekiah Fay takes a step back, looks me up and down, and smiles. "Perhaps something a little more reflective of the current fashion. I cut that shirt for his shape, not yours, what with the way you have filled out and all. Nothing makes a man feel whole more than a smart white shirt and a crisp white collar. Why, I think I might even have one or two ready to wear out of here."

"Thank you, but I believe the coat is all."

"Very well. I will have it for you by noon tomorrow."

"I had hoped to wait for it."

"Oh, now son, I am swamped today. Two suits

await my altering and I have the gentleman's shirts to return."

"Thought your boy did that."

"At home with a touch of cough. How his mother coddles him."

What I say next comes out of me before I even think of forming the words. "I could run them shirts over for you." Something about the way I say it brings a little smile to the tailor's face.

"Ah, and you would not by chance be offering your services in the hopes of catching a glimpse of the gentleman's fair, young companion, would you?" That was the word he used too. *Companion.* Not "wife," not "betrothed." I find that most interesting.

Hezekiah Fay fixes on me, expecting a response to a question he never asked. I hold steady, offering no evidence of the butterfly that feels right ready to bust from my ribs. "Very well," the tailor says, taking the shirts from their hanging place. "I would be much obliged for the favor, Harlan." He wraps the shirts in brown paper and hands them to me.

"I convey these over, we are square on the mending?" I ask. Hezekiah Fay puffs a tired sigh from his lips.

"You have your mother's flair for negotiation." He keeps me waiting for a few moments and then flashes another smile. "Room twelve, if you please."

The coarse strap of the Spencer chafes unfamiliarly against my paper-thin layer of flannel. Foot traffic has grown since yesterday. Beleaguered pedestrians negotiate the crisscrossing trajectories of errant horses and creaking wagons that now crowd the street. A cigar drummer has set up his stand just outside the hotel, unpacking his wares and displaying them on a small folding table. "Direct from Havana, Cuba, gentlemen! Ten cents apiece, a dollar a box. The finest in hand-rolled tobacco."

Trunks and traveling cases clutter the receiving room of the hotel. I have to step over some as I enter. Cookie hurries about the luggage, trying to match the piles with their corresponding guests, most of whom—if the line of new and grumpy faces ten-deep at reception is to be believed—have yet to be assigned rooms.

Behind the counter, Mr. Brunson Stone, the silver-haired proprietor, records the names of his new guests into a ledger book, all the while offering sharply whispered commands to any staff member bustling within earshot.

Cookie looks up, the gears of recognition slowed by the swirl of overlapping thoughts taxing his brain. To be fair, I am not a familiar sight inside the hotel. And in my shirtsleeves, with the Spencer slung over my shoulder and a bundle of expensive finery cradled in my free hand, I must look altogether foreign. That makes two of us. More accustomed to laboring near the stoves and woodsheds out back than with demanding customers front-of-house, Cookie finds himself equally out of place in both location and uniform. The ill-fitting bellman's tunic, gaudily appointed with stripes of red and gold to complement the jaunty blue pillbox hat, still holds the dust and awkward creases, having been hastily retrieved from some cabinet. But a flash of yellowed teeth tells me he welcomes the recent course of events. "Lawd, Mister Harlan, these white folks sure tip good. I made six dollars already and only been cussed at twice."

"Better than hauling firewood," I say.

"Sho' is. All this fussin'. Hell, when a Negro swings, ain't nobody paying attention but the vultures." He dabs his sweated brow with a chuckle as I duck up the stairway.

For all the commotion downstairs, the upper floors are eerily quiet, almost funereal. I instinctively silence my walk, floating up the steps without the slightest creak escaping the warped floorboards beneath my feet. I pause at every landing, count the doors in the hallways—four on the first floor, five on the second, four on the third.

The stairwell continues up past the third floor landing to a small half-door, ringed at the top and bottom with a slash of golden light. The roof. I think about the two Pinkerton sharpshooters just on the other side of it who probably do not like surprises. So I ease back down to the landing. An open window sweetens the air made sour by the stretch of musty wool carpet that lines the corridor and the boiled lye soap that infrequently cleans it.

I move down the hall, checking the numbers— 1-0, 1-1. I see the approaching 1 and 2 together and hope I am right. Numbers vex me more than letters. My pulse quickens at the thought of knocking on the wrong door, or worse, confirming, by my own negligence, the gentleman's doubts as he expressed them to the tailor of ever being reunited successfully with his property now in my charge. Then the woman laughs, and my heartbeat leaps.

The door after number 12 stands partially open. Soft voices within that room betray the presence of a man and a woman who believe they are alone. Keep your nose where it belongs, Mamma told me. And here I am, inching down a hallway in a hotel where I am neither staff nor lodger, compelled by a bubbling, dangerous curiosity.

Her front is to me, in three-quarter view, but her attention lies with the unseen man in the room's interior. She brushes the hair from her face, freeing an unguarded smile not meant for my eyes, but one I will cherish forever as if it were. A swallow comes to her delicate throat, expectantly. Words will soon follow.

"You shouldn't have," she says. Her voice lays softly on the ears, like a piper's song.

"The pleasure is mine entirely," says the man, in a voice I recognize. My spine stiffens. He crosses to her, his familiar black suit obscuring all but her eyes. I quell the shock of the discovery, save for a fleeting twitch of my bicep, which clinks the stiff brown paper tucked under my arm. Her eyes fall on me and she gasps. Boone turns his head in response.

"Sorry." The word finds its way out of me as I turn away. I fumble toward the door of number twelve, sensing the two of them closing the distance to the doorway.

"Harlan," the mayor says.

I touch the door at number 12. "I was just . . . I have the shirts for the gentleman."

"There is no trouble, Harlan. Please, I would like to introduce you."

When I turn back, and find the courage to lay my eyes on her, the top button of her hastily fastened collar has returned her dress to full modesty. "Harlan Two-Trees, may I present Miss Genevieve Bichard?"

"Pleased to make your acquaintance, Mister Two-Trees."

"Ma'am." My left hand somehow finds my hat, which I remove completely. "I apologize for the intrusion."

"Nothing of the kind, son," Boone starts in. "Miss Bichard's father is an old business associate of mine. Back in New Orleans. I was just reminding Miss Bichard that when last I saw her, she was this high and cradling a rag doll." Boone flattens his hand aside his thigh, indicating a child's stature. "It is only by complete coincidence that she finds herself here in our little corner of the world."

"If there is profit to be made at the poker tables, no corner of the world is too remote for Mister Willis," she begins the statement fixed on Boone. But then, at the mention of her lover's name, her eyes break away and land on me. God knows how many men have withered under such sapphire radiance. But my strength stays with me. I stand tall, returning her gaze in equal measure—a tactic she finds neither expected nor comforting. She fusses her fingers nervously over her dress, smoothing away some nonexistent wrinkle. An air of superiority overcomes her. "You may leave those with me," she says, in a tone normally aimed at domestic help or unruly children.

Plucking the shirts from me, her soft skin brushes my bare forearm. She jerks back, foundered by a charge of electricity that rocks us both, only I mask my reaction far better than she. Flustered, and caught without a response befitting her station, she settles on indignation. I see the ire rising—directed at me—fixing to explode from her. She intakes the air for the volley that will befall me, but Boone, of all people, intervenes.

"Harlan, here, is the cause of all this hoopla. Without his bravery, there might not be a hanging day." The words kick her anger off course a bit, causing her to reconsider her line. I was rather looking forward to seeing her scrunch her face up red and try to look ugly, but that will have to wait.

She takes a stare at me top to bottom, lingering a moment too long on my shirt. All at once I forget the comfort of it and see only the frayed cuffs, the odd splatters of coffee and bacon grease from too many hastily consumed breakfasts. The confidence that had kept my head high deserts me faster than rats fleeing a burning barn, leaving in its wake the country bumpkin that I am.

"Yes, I heard about you," she says. "Clearly the outdoors suits you." She gives a little nod and heads back into her room. "Good day to you both."

"Ma'am," I say, to a door that is already shut. Who am I to think I can stand in her gravity? Then again, she makes fools for a living.

Boone puts his hand on my shoulder. "A fine and proper young woman, Miss Bichard. Hence the separate quarters from her companion." He walks with me down the stairs. "I would hate to have folks get the wrong idea. As you saw, her door remained open as we conversed. Even so, best not to let a rumor fester. The town has enough to deal with, what with stages pulling in by the hour. We can let this stay between you and me." He goes on, his voice drifting to some far-off place that my ears ignore. I think only about the two ten-dollar pieces rubbing against one another in my pocket and how quickly I will be rid of them.

We reach the door of the hotel and step out into the street, which has increased its population even in the few minutes since last I negotiated it. Boone says something about having me out for Sunday dinner when all this foolishness has passed, or some such. I mutter a word of gratitude, unbothered by how effortlessly the false sentiment comes out of me. It is easier to lie a second time, just like it is to aim a gun at a living soul after you've already shot your first. *It gets easier.* Foreign voices curse my passage as I sprint through the fray of clacking, dust-churning wagons that clog the thoroughfare. I bound through Hezekiah's door and slap my silver on the counter.

"Let me see them new shirts."

CHAPTER FOURTEEN

She throws her hips into me, arching her back in the gray of the waning daylight. My bed is wet from her, from us. The newness of her scent—rose water, lavender, sweat—charges the familiar air of my room, gracing it, for the first time, with the presence of a young woman.

She reaches her arms behind her, finding my shins for support as she sinks farther onto me. Her motion builds, a soft, yelping cry rising forth from where there was only quickening breath. Her fingers dig in as she lets go, lost in herself, but still connected to me.

She is beautiful, Maria. Her perfect breasts, shuddering in the white-hot throes of her epiphany, point unapologetically skyward. She tightens her grip, challenging the resolve of my kneecap not to pop out of place. I drive into her, spasming at the sight of her tumbled raven hair, which parts, like the rest of her has, to reveal a gentle, conspiratorial smile that she soon brings to my lips. The damp firmness of her body collapses onto mine, spent.

I feel the words forming in my head as sure as I feel her warm breath on my arm. I should tell her. I *need* to tell her. The voice of every person who raised me—Mamma, Sheriff, Mrs. Pardell— thunders in my ears, scolding me that I was brought up better than this. But I am also a man, whether I am ready to be one or not, and men are what she knows. I have seen such knowledge once today already.

"Maria, you ought not be walking out here alone and unannounced like that. It is too far from town. I coulda been out hunting, or off somewhere."

"So I wait for you."

"When I go off, I go days at a stretch. And you shivering out here in the dark? Madam Brandywine would call in the Texas Rangers to track you down. You can bet she would have you scrubbing floors for a year, after she busted a couple broom handles across your backside to get the point across."

"You would not let her." She sees me ponder that, just long enough to know that she is right. I would not allow it.

"That does not mean you would not deserve it." She smiles and punches my shoulder. I roll out of bed and find my britches behind the chair where she'd flung them.

"How about I never go back? I stay here with you."

"And do what?"

"Cook for you . . . give you babies . . . be your wife." Her eyes stay on me, waiting for me to say something. I walk past my balled denims on the floor and open the wardrobe.

"Crazy talk."

"Why? Because I am whore?"

"You know damn well I take no issue with that."

"I wish you would." Her mouth scrunches into a pout that makes her look even younger.

"Whoring made Mamma no less a woman. I said *crazy talk* because you are too young to talk marrying."

"I am seventeen!" I barely look at her before she withers from the lie. "I will be sixteen soon enough."

"You ought to be in school. No sense to a man and wife not one of them able to read." I pour some water in the basin and dip my comb in it. "You save up some money. Pay off your debt to the Madam. Be your own woman, free and clear. Till then . . . you best get dressed. You are not on the floor, ready to work by sundown, there will be hell to pay. As it is, if I do not send you back with twenty dollars, old Scratch Gardner will pay me a visit with the pointed reminder that the girls from Madam Brandywine's do not make house calls."

"They no know I am here."

"I assure you, they do." I work the comb through my hair, finding the natural part like Mrs. Pardell would have me do on Sundays before preaching. It was a boy's face in the mirror then, not the guilty scoundrel staring back today.

I flatten my unruly cowlick with a dab of pomade for a respectable result. But the stubbly shadow across my face and neck negates the procedure. *If I can drop Maria in time, I might still catch Valdez at the barber's before he locks up.* A guilty lump kicks in my stomach, pulling me back to the present. In my hands I find the clean, starched sleeve of my recent purchase—I have absentmindedly unwrapped it from its box by the basin. I catch Maria in the little mirror—she is trying not to cry. When her eyes well up anyway she gives up trying. I am hog-tied clear as day by my own wandering fantasy.

"You wear that for her."

"Town is full up of people. Time I start cleanin' up more proper."

"You wear that for her," she says again, lowering herself onto the chamber pot. I button my new shirt, knowing she is right again.

I ease Storm into the alley behind Madam Brandywine's—for Maria's sake, not mine. She grips tightly to my waist. For all the bustle now saddled upon the Bend, the only people who could notice her secretive entrance through the kitchen are the cook and whatever drunks are relieving themselves in the piss pond behind the Jewel across the alley. A solitary figure contributes to the stream as I help Maria down from the horse. She smiles, adjusting the stiff collar that I am not yet used to.

"You look nice," she says.

"So do you."

"I smell like your bed."

I give her a squeeze and brush the hair from her forehead. "You watch yourself in there tonight. Keep your head about you." She turns to go.

A voice peals from the darkness. "Sweet as pie, that is. Brown kissing brown." Jed Barnes steps into the faint light, bringing the stench of stale and fresh urine with him.

"Go on, Maria." I send her off with a gentle shove that leaves no debate. She slips up the back steps and disappears into the kitchen doorway. Jed Barnes sloshes through the mud toward me, taking his time, relishing the blind luck that left him the only witness to my encounter with Maria.

"You stick to poking squaws, half-breed," he says. "Leave that pretty Mexican cunt for white folk." I snap a straight left jab that connects true and glorious into the gristly meat of his nose. The drunkard staggers back, stumbling in white-hot pain, before splashing ass-first into the puddle of human waste. I close in, spinning the Spencer from my shoulder as I go. "You speak of her like that again, I will do more than that. So help me God, Jed Barnes. You stay the hell away from me."

Jed Barnes howls into his blood-soaked palm. "You broke my nose, ya dirt-worshipin' bastard! I'll have your sorry Injun ass in jail!"

"Never a Pinkerton around when you need one. Too bad for you." I glide back onto Storm and face him toward the road.

"You'll swing for this. No half-blooded heathen strikes a white man and gets away with it."

I show him the gloved fist of my offending left hand. "Was the white half of me hit you, Jed. Injun half woulda kilt you." Storm gives out a snort of agreement before leading us off into the night, and leaving a bloody Jed Barnes to soak in the piss of a hundred strangers.

In a few hours, the stench on his clothes will cost him his scalp.

CHAPTER FIFTEEN

I push through the door of the hotel, my freshly razored chin braced by a soothing shot of after-shave and my left hand ignorant of any pain from the evening's prior encounter. The jab landed that true. I had found Valdez's barber's chair not only available, but still warm from the previous occupant, with a line of customers building behind me as the little man from Juarez worked his magic upon me.

The hotel, I discover, is equally busy. Moving past the reception desk, long since abandoned, no doubt, due to a full complement of lodgers, I pass Cookie on his way out of the kitchen, a tray of silver-domed dishes perched on his fingertips. He lights up when he sees me. "Lawd, Mister Harlan. Ain't you looking sharp?"

"You too, Cookie." His sweated-through bell-man's tunic from earlier has given way to a pressed, black shirt and tie beneath a stiff, white waiter's apron.

"Some these folks want their supper brung up their room. You ever hear such a thing?"

"Sounds like high living."

"White folks sure is good at thinkin' of ways to fritter off money," he says, dabbing his forehead with a linen napkin before limping up the staircase.

At the entrance to the dining room, Brunson Stone plays the role of restaurant man, overseeing a crowd of new and hungry bodies waiting to be seated, some decked in Sunday finery, others looking like they just stepped off their wagons.

Beyond Stone, the dining room swirls with harried serving girls, rotating in and out of a kitchen door that never once comes to a rest. A tinny drone of clacking silverware rises from the tables, all filled to capacity, save for a prime one in the center of the room, clearly reserved for a prominent party of four. Stone's eyes fall upon me, pausing in a brief window of startled recognition, and then drift disapprovingly back down to his ledger.

"May I help you?" he says, not looking up.

"Here for supper," I say. He grimaces, flips a page or two of his little book, and finally forces his gaze square onto mine.

"Yes, well, we are fully committed at present. Perhaps you will find the board at the Jewel more to your liking." I say nothing, letting the man squirm beneath his ill-fitting suit. "Or," he continues, "if you would prefer to wait, something should open up in about half an hour."

"So be it," I say, letting him turn away before I do.

I ease over to the last unoccupied stool and park myself between two visiting drummers: the cigar hawker I passed earlier and another man who, evidenced by the case he has open for the benefit of the woman next to him, earns his keep as a purveyor of ladies' handkerchiefs.

"Three dollars apiece or two for five, madam. The finest silks, direct from Pair-ee!"

The woman's husband reaches over and abruptly slams the case shut. "If my wife's aim was to get picked clean by vultures, we would ride out of town and wait for road agents to set upon us. We need no such attention in here. Come on, Miriam," the man says, pulling his wife toward the exit.

"These hayseed peasants would not know French fashion if it crept up and bit them on their collective ass!" the drummer says to his colleague.

"Ah, now *there* is a real lady," says the cigar man.

She steps down onto the carpet from the bottom stair as gracefully as she descended from the coach yesterday, only this time her dress carries no concern for the utility of travel—its intention now is only to dazzle in a curving dance of tawny silk and shimmering pearl. Escorted by the gentleman gambler, she allows her hand to be held in his as they glide across the room, parting the traffic as if by divine intervention. The dude matches her elegance with a dashing suit of his own—peacock blue with a black, satin cravat.

Men rise in her presence. I am no exception, removing my hat as I do so. For her part, Miss Bichard acknowledges her subjects with a nod unburdened by eye contact.

Reaching my full height, I stand a good four inches over the drummers. The disparity alone must be what earns her passing glance. I care not the reason, only that in that fleeting moment a flicker of recognition, and then, upon reflection, an infusion of surprise and embarrassment flutters across her face . . . which delights me to no end.

Her gloved hand releases that of the dude and she turns to face me. "Why, Mister Two-Trees. You have . . . transformed. Appears there is a gentleman inside you after all."

"Evenin', ma'am." I feel the two drummers wilt away and vanish into the ether. At the same moment, Brunson Stone rushes over and begins his obsequious blathering to Mr. Willis, leaving me, for all intents and purposes, alone with Miss Bichard. "I hope the evening finds you well," I manage to say.

"The hotel is a rustic accommodation, but I hardly hold you responsible for that." There is a sudden softness to her tone that dared not reveal itself during her strident exchange with me this afternoon. Could a shave and a shot of cologne and a clean shirt really carry such sway? Mamma always said white women were the silliest of all. Either way, I plan to buy that little Mexican barber the coldest glass of beer the Jewel can offer.

"I 'spect you are used to much nicer," I say, apologizing for the town, as if it is beneath her standing, which it is. But she picks up on something in my voice that compels her to sweeten her course.

"Oh, but there is a certain charm to it—as with many aspects of the town."

She holds my gaze, unable to fight off a darling, nervous smile until the arrival of the dude breaks the moment.

"Ah, Mister Willis," she says, "May I introduce

Mr. Harlan Two-Trees? He was the one I was telling you about."

She has been talking about me.

The dude turns toward me, taking newfound stock of my presence and pairing it to some mental image he had already conjured of me. "Why, Mister Two-Trees. It is a privilege, sir. Your name is on the tongues of many around the poker table, not to mention the lips of Miss Bichard here."

Her lips. Her perfect, rose-budded lips.

"Lest any man forget," Willis continues, "it is your brave deed that is the root and cause of this hoopla."

"Honor is all mine, sir," I say, grasping the hand extended out in my direction and giving it a proper shake.

"Have you dined?" Willis asks. "My man Stone here is holding a table. You simply must join us. I will not take no for an answer."

"Well," I say, "if the lady does not object."

Willis holds the chair for Miss Bichard as every eye in the dining room falls upon our table. Stone, forced to hold my chair, chews a sour mouthful of fresh crow at the sight of my backside about to sully one of his threadbare seat cushions. I take my time descending into the chair, waiting for Miss Bichard to be firmly situated and the dude, in turn, to take his place, before finally lowering myself down completely. "Your best bottle, Stone," the dude says, dismissing the proprietor with an irrefutable wave.

"Right away, sir." Stone slinks off through the kitchen door.

"It is not every day I get to share a table with a bona fide hero," Willis says, carving into his pot roast between sips of port. "Besides, tonight is just for fun. The real work starts tomorrow. Ain't that right, darling?"

"Why, Mister Willis, I know better than to inquire about your luck at the poker tables."

"Luck has nothing to do with it, my dear. Any gambling man worth his weight can tell you that." I feel Willis watching me as I unfold the linen napkin and set it in my lap, half-ready to hear a scolding from Mrs. Pardell if I absentmindedly stick it into my shirt or—God help me—sneeze into it. "The key to a man's hole cards is not what he's holding. It's in his eyes, the way he reaches for his chips. It's in the way his breath shortens when he's sitting on rolled-up aces, or the pulse in his neck after venturing a bluff. Let's take Mister Two-Trees here, as an example," Willis says, turning toward me. I wipe my mouth, clear my throat. "I deduce that you were well taught by a Christian woman how to comport yourself at table. But it has been a month or more since you were last called upon to do so in the presence of others."

"Cannot say I have missed much," I concede, with a nod to the shriveled, gray piece of meat growing cold on my plate. Miss Bichard's face melts with a naughty schoolgirl's grin.

"No argument there," the gambler says, laughing.

"I would wager the Bend's surrounding chaparral is missing a few coyote carcasses this evening."

"What do you mean, 'the real work starts tomorrow'?" I ask.

"The poker, sir, the true reason for my visitation to your fine town. The day before a hanging's when the serious money starts to roll in. At least I hope so. I have spent the entire day playing dollar stud with the drunks down at the Jewel. Now I admit, I don't mind separating a drinker from his bankroll, but for stakes that low, I could've played Parcheesi at my grandmamma's church social and saved the expense of travel."

"Why, then we would not have had the pleasure of meeting Mister Two-Trees," the woman offers.

"Quite right, Miss Bichard." Willis pushes away his plate, only half-empty, and lights a cigar. "The day was not a total loss, though. I managed to get the Jewel's proprietor to set an agreeable rake for the game."

"Merle," I say.

"Yes, Merle. Not a bad poker player himself. Always good to have a saloonkeeper who's willing to sit in when the game is shorthanded. Yes, we've got a nice little corner set up down there. All we need now is the action."

"I expect you will find no shortage of that after the morning train arrives," Miss Bichard says.

"I expect, my darling, that after the train arrives, you won't be seeing much of old Avery Willis. Enjoy me while you have me." He smiles and blows a mouthful of opaque smoke toward the ceiling. "And if the saloon gets too packed with looky-loos, I've arranged to have the game moved upstairs to our . . . to my room for the duration. By then, word will have gotten 'round that the biggest game is over at the hotel."

"My goodness," she says politely. "Whatever shall I do to amuse myself?" Her eyes catch mine briefly.

"Take in the local color," Willis says, well aware of her gaze.

Behind him, a nervous, elfin man in spectacles approaches our table, removing his bowler at the sight of the woman. I know not what he is selling, but I find myself instantly aware that I do not wish to buy. "Ah, Standish," Willis notices the man, motioning to the empty chair next to me. "Join us for a drink."

The little man bows deferentially and fumbles the chair out for himself. "With pleasure, Mister Willis. Good evening, Miss Bichard." Standish earns himself an indifferent nod from Genevieve.

Yes, Genevieve. Surely that is what Willis calls her when they are alone in their adjoined quarters. And I now shall do the same in my thoughts.

The gambler nods toward me, "And Mister Two-Trees I think you know."

A wispy palm thrusts forth in my direction as the gold-framed eyes bulge eagerly with opportunity. "Mister Two-Trees, of course. We have not been formally introduced. J. Webber Standish," the newspaperman says as he curls into his chair, a pencil stub miraculously appearing in his fingertips along with a scratch of writing paper. "I say, Mister Two-Trees, I have been meaning to follow up with you on your firsthand account of recent events—the abduction of the Snowman, specifically."

"I said it all square in the courtroom. Story is as you heard it."

"Of course, sir," Standish turns his chair perceptibly toward me. "But I assure you our readership eagerly awaits any of the more vibrant details of your harrowing account, perhaps some juicy morsel, no matter how trivial, that would have been too scandalous to introduce during a formal legal proceeding?"

I feel little need to respond. I let the silence fester, building on itself, for a long, lingering moment. Standish licks his lips like a hungry dog. Willis eyes me curiously. And Genevieve, for her part, allows her unguarded, cornflower eyes to bathe over me as I relish the power of the pause. "Seems like what the Snowman done is scandal enough," I finally say.

It is Willis who smiles first. "Well said, Mister Two-Trees."

"Well, should anything come to mind, sir, please look me up here at the hotel. The entire territory, make that the country, hungrily awaits the slightest as-of-yet-unrevealed detail."

All at once, a high, piercing sound assaults my eardrums. The water glass slips from my grasp and shatters on the floor. My fingers jam themselves into my ear canals to relieve the torment. The rest of the patrons, their mouths agape, clearly hear it too. A second later, the sound comes again, closer this time. I recover from the initial shock to my senses and identify the noise as the urgent scream of a Pinkerton whistle.

My head snaps toward the window. Flying from

my chair, I cross to the portal. Through the waving undulations of the cheap glass, I see that the disturbance emanates not from the jail, but from across the street, from Madam Brandywine's. A cold knot of dread blooms in the pit of my stomach. The Madam herself, with blood streaked across her ghost-white skin, points toward her establishment as the Pinkerton man lays into his whistle a third time.

CHAPTER SIXTEEN

One of the whores—Carmelita, judging by the meatiness of her grip—paws at me as I enter the front door. I bust free of her and bound full-steam up the stairs, gobbling them up four, five at a time.

Scratch Gardner slumps against the far wall of the waiting room, putting all his faith in a sopping red bedsheet that holds his belly together. Two blood-splattered white girls tend to the gash in his neck. A man's finger lies in a crimson puddle on the carpet, and a piece of another near that.

I move toward Scratch. Every step sloshes in the stickiness of what was recently inside him. How he still breathes is a mystery. That his one good eye falls on me as I bend down next to him is nothing short of a miracle.

"I tried, Harlan. His razor got the drop on me."
His razor.

The cold knot of dread punches though my gut again—I feel like I am choking down a mouthful of river stones. I turn to Maria's door, or what is left of it. Splintered wood litters the floor inside. The amber glow of her single lamp catches the dark stain where the water from the tub spilled over, soaking the rug. Maria's arm hangs over the copper edge. I run in, bellowing some wordless sound, and pull Maria's body from the water. She still wears her dress. Her raven hair shines black as pitch as it falls heavily from her face, exposing her bare neck and deep, bluing rings where his hands held her under. His vile blood drips from her fingernails. She fought him.

"We heard her screaming," says a woman's voice, laced with tears, from behind me. It is Carmelita. "Jed Barnes come in here, stinking like a sewer. Madam tried to send him away while I run in the kitchen to fetch Scratch." I turn Maria on her side and watch the water pour from her mouth and nose. Her sad, brown eyes stay fixed—wide as saucers—in the same tragic gaze that was her last. I cannot bear the sight.

I close her eyes, wiping away the drops of water from her cold face as if they are her tears. But they are mine.

"Jed musta knocked Madam aside and charged up here," Carmelita continues. "He was hell-bent on Maria, calling, 'Where's that Mexican whore?' Next I hear, Maria's screaming for him to get out. That he stink and she want nothing to do with him. Then it was a scuffle from inside and Scratch come running up and kick the door in to get her. That's when Jed turned on him with that razor."

I pick Maria up and lay her gently on the bed. This poor, sweet creature, the daughter of a Matamoros laundress. All she asked was that her men not stink and if you did she would draw a bath for you and pull off your boots. Jed Barnes took offense at that and gave her a bath instead. But had it not been that, it would have been some other slight, falsely perceived, that incited his murderous ways. He had no intention of bedding her. He came here to kill her, to hurt me through her. I swear by the spirit of my mother, by the one God of the sheriff and the white folks, by the law of nature that guides every man and fills my throat with the boiling lust for vengeance—the drunkard will not see another dawn.

CHAPTER SEVENTEEN

The valley spreads before me like the soaring wings of a condor. The night will get brighter when the little eye rises, fat and amber, from behind the Sangres. But for now it is black. And in this cool, darkest window of night I free my mind from the poison of rage. I cannot dismiss the anger entirely, any more than I could absolve the scoundrel guilty of causing it, but a predator must hunt without emotion. Feelings are the burden of the hunted.

Twenty minutes ago, Jed Barnes ran out the back door of Madam Brandywine's and stole the first horse he came upon, a two-year-old palomino with an alabaster mane tied up outside the Jewel. This was confirmed by Merle, who saw Jed through the window. From there he headed west out of town, where I now find myself.

To track him farther, I must weigh the limited options through his eyes. If I can assume the state of mind of a panicked mule deer or an injured bighorn, no reason I cannot put myself into the head of a drunken murderer atop an unfamiliar mount. Heavendale is too far. To attempt such a journey without water would mean to die by mid-morning. Jed Barnes knows this much, despite his addled brain. The Sangres are out of the question. Jed is no mountain man. And with nothing to trade, the Navajo would sooner kill him for his horse than lead him through their holy wilderness. The empty flask on his hip, no doubt, proves a powerful motivator. He needs whiskey to steady his nerves and people to give him cover.

I angle the stallion slightly to the south and bring him to his quietest canter. I make it quarter past ten as the little eye crests the first peak. Storm demands to know where we are headed at such an hour. "Agua Verde," I whisper. He answers with a grunt, accepting that this will be the last we speak on the matter. *Silent as the snow.*

Only Merle knows I am out here, and he has the tight lips of a saloonkeeper. Well, Jed Barnes knows, but he will not be speaking of me or anything else ever again.

Madam Brandywine has her hands full, what with the girls clinging to one another in the upstairs parlor, too frightened to take on new customers now that their security, Scratch Gardner, lies leaking all over the carpet.

The Pinkertons, for all their bravado, will not be venturing into the night to track down some drunkard for the killing of a Mexican whore, especially if it means abandoning even a single post in the protection of their precious Snowman, who is set to swing in just over twelve hours. This mission falls on my shoulders alone. And that is fine by me.

I hold Storm to his canter, the correct gait to run

down Jed Barnes. If he has that palomino in a gallop, she will burn out in three miles and either collapse and die under his brutal spur, or defy him and break for the creek. Either way, the waxing moonlight will give him away. *Eyes of a hawk.* But if, as I suspect, he cannot maintain the gallop from an untrusting mare, he will have to trot, and thus wither under Storm's punishing speed.

A mile out of town, as the glow from the little eye begins to take hold in earnest, a shift in the wind forces me to reconsider my tactic. I pull back on Storm's reins, bringing the stallion to an uneasy halt. Corrupting the air beneath the sweet scent of sage and creosote lurks the acrid, foul stench of human urine. I can smell him. *Nose of a wolf.*

The breeze comes straight at me from the west, from the Sangres, but this makes no sense. Could Jed Barnes be such a fool? The great mountains boast a thousand ways to kill a man, ways that only matter if he reaches them alive, and no one would bank on that. Between me and the Sangres' nearest foothills lay twenty miles of unforgiving wasteland. Jed Barnes has no supplies, no shelter, and no skills of survival beyond his handiwork with a razor. For him to head into the vast heart of the valley would be sheer suicide. Perhaps his intent is to hide amongst the rocks and hardscrabble shrubs until I pass and then to sneak back into town. If so, he would make the Pinkertons' job easy and would soon find himself sharing a bunk with the Snowman before his own date with the gallows.

I sit there in the saddle, trying to figure the play, when all at once the answer comes singing across my ears. A train whistle blows faintly in the distance. *Ears of a buck.*

Of course. The train. The night run of the Santa Fe–Duke lurches out from Heavendale at ten o'clock and rumbles across the valley to Agua Verde. There, it restocks the coal cars and thunders off again, bringing its bounty of copper and turquoise to points unknown. Jed Barnes means to hop it, the slick bastard, and stow away to freedom.

I bank Storm due west and kick him up to an easy gallop, straight into the wind. The night train moves fast enough to suck a man under, should he try to grab hold while standing still. To jump a steaming locomotive, a body best be running alongside, or better yet, keeping pace atop a horse that does not spook. I cannot figure that a strange palomino would proffer such bravery for the likes of Jed Barnes. The scoundrel needs an alternative stratagem.

I trace the tracks over in my mind. There stands hardly a tree more than waist-high along that line of rail until well near Agua Verde. Yet the rank odor assaulting my nose bears from a heading straight out toward the barrens, where the only hint of elevation is Hatchet Rock.

The whistle cries louder. In no more than five minutes, the Santa Fe–Duke will pass the cleaved chunk of red rock that spikes from the ground like the weapon that bears its name. It will pass close enough to kiss it. An easy, running leap would land Jed Barnes safely into the salvation of an open-top coal car. I coax from Storm everything he can muster. We fly across the desert, letting the building

wail of the churning steam engine hide the stallion's
thundering gallop.

The billow of white vapor coughs from the tracks
in the distance as the train's headlamp glimmers
like a tiny star on the horizon. Hatchet Rock, a
slate-gray slab in the pale moonlight, erupts into
view. I slide the Spencer from my shoulder without
breaking Storm's stride. No sooner do I chamber
a round than I see a figure charging straight at me.
It is the palomino, without her rider. The frightened animal, spooked into retreat by the growling
locomotive, screeches in abject terror at the sight of
Storm—a locomotive in his own right—head down
and frothing at his bit. The palomino breaks left as
Storm holds his line. And then I see him.

Jed Barnes clamors up the side of the rock, his
frame silhouetted by the headlamp. He slithers
over the top edge and finds his legs with the nimble
step of a rapidly sobering man. The train reaches
the rock and jerks sideways, the track demanding its
sharpest corner. Jed Barnes takes a running start
for the far ledge, nearest the track. He throws himself into the air. I aim the Spencer, standing tall in
the saddle, and squeeze off a round that would
earn the approbation of the Snowman.

Jed Barnes grabs his backside mid-flight and
slams awkwardly against the top lip of a passing coal
car. The coal cars whisk past the rock, carrying Jed
with them. A mile of boxcars trails behind.

Beneath the deafening roar of the engine, ampli-
fied by the natural resonating chamber of the
rocks, I swing Storm alongside the train. I lose sight
of Jed. One misstep from Storm, or the slightest

whiff of panic, and the wheels would churn us to butter. But there has never been such a stallion. We pull next to a rail ladder and I have to ease back on the reins to keep Storm from overrunning it. I stow the Spencer and reach out with both hands. The force of the train carries me upward. Storm instinctively slows, letting the train do the work. The stallion grunts for my speedy return before banking off to safety.

Clutching the rungs of the ladder, I scale up the side of the train, humbled by her bone-jangling power. Her deafening roar obscures the sound of my ascent, but would swallow any last-second prayer as well. Steam spews from the blastpipe, choking the air around me and cutting visibility to little more than a step or two.

The boxcar roof lurches and kicks beneath my feet. Every step challenges my usual sure-footedness. The train is a beast. And I am at her mercy. But Jed Barnes must contend with her as well. For that, I take only small comfort. I crouch low, finding a stretch of clear air beneath the thick torrent of steam, and creep forward. The cloud of mist obscures the moonlight entirely and the tender car, three cars ahead, blacks out the weak backwash from the headlamp. The darkness is a blessing, as the pearl-handled Colt jutting from my fist attracts no attention.

The nearest coal car, filled to overflowing with chunky shards of pitch, appears at my feet. I hesitate at the gap, where somewhere down below the hitch clatters menacingly, begging for an ill-placed bootstep to shred my flesh across the tracks. I leap onto the coal, sinking more than I expect. It is my

first time atop a mound of coal, and my first time
on a train. I move across the car. At each stride, the
ground gives way beneath me like iced-over snow.

The breach between this and the next car, a four-
foot maw of blackness, will require momentum to
traverse. I build as much speed as I can and throw
myself into the air. Something shoots upward from
the breach—a coal shovel—and catches my leg
above the knee. Sharp pain spikes through my
body, tilting me off my line. I brace for impact
against the coal. The jagged chunks give hardly at
all now, feeling more like razor-sharp teeth, as I
slam into them.

The Colt bounces from my hand across the
pitch. I paw for the second Colt as I roll over onto
my back. Jed Barnes climbs from the breach with
one hand, gripping the coal shovel in the other. He
stands upon the lip of the car, about to stomp down
on me. I fire at his middle, rolling left as he falls
toward me. The ugly clank of lead against steel cuts
the air as my shot hits the only thing I did not want
to hit—the damn coal shovel. The blade of it snags
my hip. I hear a voice that must be my own cry out
in pain. I roll to my feet and pray my hip goes with
me. My own weight, pressing down on my pelvis,
sends a current of agony deep into my bones.

Jed Barnes rises from the coal, opting to continue with the newfound shovel instead of the trusty
razor that got him this far. The folly of that decision
drives me forward. He swings the shovel, club-like,
unaccustomed to the awkward distribution of its
mass. I backpedal as it misses me completely. I hurl
a hooking left fist that finds the meat of his neck.
My knee follows, burying itself squarely in his rib

cage. Jed Barnes doubles over. I kick him in the face. He staggers to the side and falls down onto the coal. I turn back in search of the Colts, both of which lie somewhere among the obsidian snow.

The nickel barrel catches a glint of moonlight before the blastpipe belches another cumulous yawn into the night. I snatch up the pistol and pivot back, raising the gun as I do so. Jed Barnes emerges from the fog, charging me at full bore. The shovel sits poised above his right shoulder like a woodsman's ax about to be unleashed upon unsuspecting timber.

Jed Barnes lets fly a haymaker blow. I parry to the side. He brushes past me. The momentum of his ungainly swing yanks him toward the edge of the car. I follow right behind with a mighty shove into his spine. A sound, something between a startled gasp and a child's truculent whine, tells me the fight is over. Jed Barnes sails off the edge of the car, lands like a sack of flour on the desert floor, and rolls pell-mell to a broken-bodied halt.

I move with purpose. A brief window of idleness from the blastpipe sends me scampering for my belongings. I holster the first Colt. The train hits a turn, kicking up a gust of air that sends my hat rolling toward me across the coal. I pluck it up and press it firmly onto my skull. I hurt in more places than I can count and am not done putting myself at pain's doorstep. The second Colt rattles not far from where I dropped it—another blessing. I am halfway down the side ladder, the unfriendly ground speeding by, before the true understanding of what is about to happen sets in. I am going to jump from the most powerful machine man has ever created into the most treacherous landscape in God's design, and the only thing breaking my fall will be prickly pear, and rocks, and an unshakable desire to see Jed Barnes dead. I pray for the little eye to protect me as I spring outward from the bottom rung. The night is cool. There is a brief whiff of sage. And then blackness.

I open my eyes to a sky bursting with stars. The little eye is small. Night has set in. The Santa Fe–Duke whistles harmlessly in the distance. I sit up. Pain explodes from a hundred places, and somehow is so prevalent in my body that the sum of it keeps me from fussing too particular about any one spot. On the horizon, the blastpipe spews another mouthful of smoke. I was out for maybe a minute. Two legs. Two arms. Ten fingers. One aching right hip. All parts accounted for.

Two guns. One hat. I stand up.

Thank God for the tracks. They will lead me to him. My eyes, my ears, my nose can stand down. I do not know how long I walk. The throbbing in my skull pulses a steady, dull reminder of my landing. I hope I rolled when I hit. I meant to. I do not remember. I remember her face, though—sad and scared, even in death.

She had a smile, Maria, a sweet little girl grin that would show itself in fleeting moments like the sun peeking through storm clouds. That girl had loved me. And I had bedded her, deposited her at her place of death, and gone off to get a shave to impress another man's woman. A budding sickness in my stomach cripples me more than any of my injuries. The shirt I bought today on a vain and foolish lark clings sweaty and tattered and blood-stained to my guilty flesh. I did not love her as she wanted, for that I cannot apologize. But her death, in which I will forever be implicated, will haunt me.

"Sorry, Maria," I whisper into the night.

I see it. It moves along the ground—there at the base of the rocks—slow and useless, like a lizard with a busted spine. The trail of blood and trampled sage starts at the tracks and drags along about fifty yards to the thing that used to be Jed Barnes. I walk up on this creature with no regard for the sound I make. I want him to hear me. He is on his belly, pulling himself along with one arm. He cackles as I approach and stops crawling.

"Let me have a drink, boy."

"If you need a drink, you are going to hell still needing it."

"Well, I never was the Pearly Gates type."

"She was a sweet girl."

"Was she? I would not know." He fixes his eyes on me best he can. His neck wrenches back to see me. "Come on, boy. I know you got a flask on you. Just give me one shot. All I ask is one shot."

"Sure." I draw the Colt and fire point-blank into the back of his thigh. His scream is more surprise than pain, until the pain sets in.

"Don't do this, boy. You're better than this."

I holster the Colt and drop down, driving my knee into the fresh wound as I land on top of him. Now he screams like a girl. I holster the Colt and draw my knife. I keep a plenty sharp blade, but it is

no razor. I *could* use his razor. It would be fitting.
But I think better of it. A little dullness never hurt
anybody. Unless you are Jed Barnes.

"No, I am not," I say into his ear. "And when I see
you in hell I will do it again." His hair is foul and
wet—I grab a thick, greasy handful of it. I feel,
for the first time in hours, nothing. I am at peace. I
am Navajo.

CHAPTER EIGHTEEN

The desert floor passes beneath me, washed pale gray by a moon that holds small and bright in the sky. I follow the railroad tracks. My vision is clear again, the pain in my head nearly gone. The stiffness in my back and arms slows me a little, but the burning in my hip, where the shovel caught me, turns my walk more into a limp with every stride.

I call again for Storm and am answered back only by the cool breeze rolling down from the Sangres. Far to my left, a gray pulse of movement draws my eye. I spin toward it and see nothing but rocks and fat fingers of cacti. Then from behind me a high-pitched *Yaaooo* punctures the night. A signal. When I look forward again, the flicker where a shadow had been is now a young man, seated atop a piebald mare. He cannot be more than thirty yards from where I stand.

All at once I know three things:

1. The tracker in me has been out-tracked.
2. If there is one in front of me, so conspicuous,

then I can bet my silver that there are plenty more lurking in the dark.

3. They will probably kill me.

The scout's hair, parted in the middle and blacker than the coal smeared across my shirt, hangs down to his elbows in two ropey braids. He sits bareback. True Navajo. Saddlery is the fussy business of white men. Cradled in his arm I make out a Kentucky Longrifle—ancient, from before the war—aimed casually, but unequivocally, in the vicinity of my heart. I continue toward him at an easy, unthreatening pace.

A rifle shot cracks the air behind me and kicks up the dust at my feet, close enough for a pebble to skitter against my boot. It is either an effective warning or a dismal kill shot. Whichever it is, I stop.

Horses canter up from the rear. I do not turn around. A chestnut gelding passes close enough to touch. That is the intent, I gather, when the moccasin of its rider jabs me in the shoulder. This second scout's face comes into view, set firmly in a sneer. He already does not care for me. He steers the gelding with his knees, his hands occupied with more pressing business. From his left, a rope drapes behind him to the bridle of an unmounted horse. It is the palomino. And behind it, gnawing unsuccessfully at the rope and thoroughly dissatisfied with the current state of affairs, is Storm. The scout's right hand holds my own Spencer rifle and I find myself staring down the barrel of it.

"Gaagii," he calls to the other without taking his eyes off me.

The younger one, maybe nineteen, same as I, edges the piebald over and takes the rope. A rusty lock opens in my brain. Words, forgotten sounds from a lifetime ago, stretch from their slumber. *Gaagii.* Raven. The younger one is called Raven.

"*O'o, anaai,*" Raven says, taking the rope. *O'o.* Yes. *Anaai.* Brother. No. More than brother. *Older* brother.

The elder scout hurls words at me I do not understand. I know none of them are kind. He wears his hair tied back, practical, ready for battle. He doubles back on the gelding and shoves me again—more of an inspection than a blow, like a kid poking a lifeless dog with a stick to see if it is really dead. I react only enough to catch my balance. Something about that bothers him. He spins the Spencer around and slams the butt against my head. I go down. He flies off his horse and meets me on the ground. The cold edge of a tomahawk, dulled by the bones of a hundred cavalry soldiers, finds the skin of my cheek. He holds it there while the steady stream of invectives continues to pour out of him.

"Ahiga." A new voice, graveled with age and soft with authority, freezes my tormentor. He rises off me, slightly, enough to let me see the ghost. A pale gray pony—the exact color of the moonlight— stands before us. Seated atop him, draped in white buckskin, is a silver-haired man with a face as cragged as the great Western Canyons. He raises a single, quieting finger. I know at once that he is the scouts' father. And when a subtle wave of that finger backs his son off me completely, I know he is also their chief.

The pair of Colts riding my hips pops into my head. I could fell one brave for sure, maybe even

the chief, but then the other one would see to it
that I died slowly—burned at the stake is my guess,
as the wailing squaws feasted on my skin. I glance
over at the young scout, Raven, with that well-oiled
Longrifle. If his weapon of choice predates the
Union I reckon he is mighty confident in its accuracy. So even killing one scout would be a stretch.
As I consider the Colts, the chief seems to hear my
thought and does the same. You do not get to his
age in the Bloods without taking a few precautions.
"Ahiga," the chief says again.

The warrior son comes back to me and grabs at
my waist. The holster unbuckles and drops to the
ground. He shoves me away. *Ahiga*. The word falls
into my head. Fighter. The chief named his son
Fighter and the son has made good on its meaning.
He argues a hard case to his father that my scalp
would look better tied to his belt than sitting intact
in its present location.

Two men discuss my fate while I stand by with my
arms up. I feel the tide turning in the wrong direction. Words that I have not heard or uttered since
I was a boy bounce inside my skull, but I have no
trust in my command of them. English troubles me
enough. The Dineh tongue wields its biting force
with a serpent's power.

"Dineh," I say, using their word for Navajo. I
touch my chest and say it again. The silver-hair
levels a withering, hawklike gaze upon me, appraising me with fresh eyes. Raven perks up noticeably,
his aim now bereft of its earlier lassitude. The butt
of the Spencer slams into my gut. I double over. But
the pain never comes. I have been beaten so much
today that even the pain is wore out.

"*Bilagáana!*" Ahiga hovers over me, spitting out the Dineh word for White Man and a few others unsuitable for church.

Somehow I start breathing again and find the strength to look up. "*Ama,*" I say. *Mother.* "*Ama* was Dineh too." The silver-hair brings his pony closer, curious now. If he deems me a liar—or worse, that my intent is mockery—he will slay me himself. But I speak true.

"What name, mother?" the chief asks. And something about his drift into English makes me feel Death's icy fingers dance across my neck.

I answer him. "Yanaha. Yanaha Begay." I could leave it at that, but for some reason I keep talking. "But white folks called her Rosie."

I swear that in the moonlight I see a flicker of a smile dash across his lips before he can quash it. It is a smile I have seen before, on the faces of men of a certain age, when I mention Mamma. But then the chief grows reflective, as if a forgotten, wretched soul had called out to him from the Spirit Realm.

The chief raises his eyes skyward, beseeching the heavens to guide him. His voice carries a lilting prayer high into the night. My fate rests on a warm breeze that nudges gently at my back and then shifts abruptly to sweep across my chest.

The chief's brown eyes pop open, startled, and fall on me with genuine surprise. "You puzzle the Spirits. You speak words of the Dineh, but are clothed in garments of the trouser-wearers."

Ahiga blurts out that all I am is a trouser-wearer

and that that alone should warrant the spilling of my blood upon the desert floor.

"No, my son," the silver-hair says, using English for my benefit. "This man *hok'ee.* Abandoned. His spirit cannot rest. Two worlds tear at him. Dineh and *bilagáana.*"

The warrior son wants to hear none of it. He steps in front of his father, gets in my face with that ax, itching to split my skull open. He says something about all trouser-wearers being the same and how I would use the White Man's guns to slaughter the Dineh if the White Man asked me to. I see the silver-head mulling the prospect and again I feel myself compelled to speak.

"Tell me how white I am." I bring my arm down slowly, giving Ahiga all the excuse he needs to raise that ax up over my head. A supplicating gesture— my open palms—earns me the slightest currency to continue. My fingers descend into my coat pocket and wrap themselves around the sopping, hairy mass I have stored there. Blood squeezes from it like a sponge. "You come for the scalp of a white man. You have it." I place what I have ripped from Jed Barnes's head into the outstretched hand of the stunned Navaho warrior. I close my fist around his and let the blood bind us. It seeps through our fingers, down our forearms, forever uniting us in the spirit under which we were both born. "You follow them tracks, you will find the rest of him."

His trophy secured, Ahiga retreats to his horse and I turn my attention to the chief. "The palomino there, he will serve the Great Leader well. But the stallion, I will not trouble you with him. Best let me ride him off." The silver-hair turns toward the horses. Storm picks that exact moment to let every chiseled sinew of muscle flex with perfection as if he were the star of the auction block. His coat shimmers in the moonlight.

"Good horse," chief says. "Will honor me with strong ride."

"Got a devil's spirit, that one," I say, not giving myself a chance to think about it. "Mean as a badger. Thickheaded, to boot."

The chief shrugs. "Then we eat him."

"I swear, even his flesh is deviled. One bite of his poison blood and you drop where you stand." The chief eyes me suspect. I do not budge. Sweat drips down my back. Talk may not be my strong suit, but let's see that slippery cigar drummer back at the hotel try to hoodwink a wily Indian chief—a hairsbreadth away from killing him—out of a perfectly good stallion. Every ounce of moisture drains from my mouth.

"I see no devil in him," the chief says.

"Storm!" I yell. All at once, the stallion rears up on his hind legs and lets out a heinous cry that no rider would ever want to hear again. The force against the rope jerks the head of the hapless palomino and nearly topples Raven from his mount. Ahiga runs to the rescue, but Storm's fate is already sealed.

"He has the spirit of your mother," the chief says, before addressing his sons in Dineh. "Cut the stallion loose. We will leave these two tortured brothers to the winds' mercy."

Raven defers to his obedience and begrudgingly

slices the rope. Storm dances back from him. My Spencer hangs from Ahiga's broad shoulder as he parades the palomino in front of me.

"That Spencer is a tricky bitch too," I offer.

Ahiga climbs atop his horse and spits out a grin. "Don't push your luck, half-breed."

CHAPTER NINETEEN

The smell of coffee swirls up from the bar where Merle refills my cup from a fresh pot. "You get any sleep?" he asks with a probing eye.

"'Bout two hours," I offer.

"That's two more than me," he says. Early morning light splays mutedly through the greasy sweat and splatters of whiskey that coat the panes of the Jewel's front window. Merle has not yet gotten there with his rag, but I know he will have the place spit-shined by opening. "Noon can't come fast enough. Get that bastard hanged and in the ground so I can get some goddamn shut-eye." Merle looks at me, grimaces, then looks away. "You hear about Scratch Gardner?"

"Not more than what I saw."

"Dead before he got to Doc's. Died on the wagon." Merle pauses at a white gob stuck to the bar. He picks at it with his finger. "Goddamn chewing gum! You believe this bullshit? I don't care how good the till is running, this ain't a fucking schoolhouse."

The door to the street clangs open and a weary

traveler, dusty from the road, steps into the saloon. "We're closed!" Merle barks. "Come back at nine."

The little man looks at Merle, dumbfounded, then digs out his pocket watch. "Why, it's twelve minutes to," he says.

"Then piss off and come back in twelve minutes." Merle snaps his rag on the bar for good measure. The man slumps and shuffles back out the way he came.

I grip my mug with both hands, letting the warmth seep through my aching fingers. The blood from last night washed off easily enough, but the coal dust required an extra going-over with lye soap—making for one hell of a cold bath in the pre-dawn darkness beneath the water pump behind the barn. Then it was two hours of thin, restless sleep before I pulled on the last of my new shirts and headed down to the Jewel. I felt compelled to check in with Merle, my lone conspirator—he apparently felt the same. With Jed now feeding the crows, the Jewel need no longer be a place to avoid.

"That head Pinkerton and the mayor come in here last night looking for you."

"What they want?"

"Did not say. But I told them, 'If Harlan is the object of your search, well, El Dorado would be easier to find.'"

"I 'spect that set well."

"You assume correct. But since I knew you wouldn't mind my saying, I told the gentlemen that if you were not at home, an unscheduled hunting excursion beneath the full moon was the most likely culprit." Merle leans in and pitches his voice to a whisper, concealing his words from the ears of the two other souls in the room. "And on that point, I doubt I was wrong."

"Much obliged," I say.

Merle reaches beneath the bar and comes back with a bottle and two shot glasses. He pours generously. "To long nights." We clink our glasses.

The liquor slides down and I know that this is the last we will ever speak of it. Still, I am uneasy that Mulgrew and the mayor would take time to search me out. The business with Maria seems hardly a matter to concern themselves with, but I figure avoiding them sends the wrong message and reason I might ought to amble over to the jail after my coffee.

"Dude looks like he found himself a game."

"And then some," Merle says. In the far corner, Avery Willis plucks a few poker chips from his stack and tosses them into the center of the table. A sandy-haired stranger sits across from him. "Fourteen hours and counting. Everybody else bust out, except them two." The stranger sports a chocolate brown suit that has seen better days, but his crisp white shirt looks fresh out of the box. Only the untied scarlet bowtie dangling from his collar hints at the duration of the game.

The stranger thinks for a moment before pushing in his chips. "I call ya," he says, and then picks up the deck to deal. "You ain't hit your flush yet."

"Gave his name as Jessup," Merle whispers to me. "Out of Kansas, I think. Throwing the dude all he can handle. Then again, the dude is the one with the horse."

"What horse?"

Merle motions to the window. A giant brown

figure, obscured by the gauzy film of the glass, bobs gently at the tie-pole out front. "A fine, dappled filly. Some half-witted sot put her up in the stud game. Turns over a pair to the dude's straight and dude has got himself a two-hundred-dollar racer."

"He can tie it to the back of his coach, I guess."

"I better keep them lubricated," Merle says, drifting toward the table, coffeepot in hand.

"More coffee, gentlemen?" Merle's cheeriness is lethal. "Or perhaps you're ready for a more substantial eye-opener?"

The front door clangs open, followed by the shuffle of eager footsteps. "We're fucking closed!" Merle barks. Then he smiles. "Oh, it's you two."

Big Jack bounds in from the street, followed closely by Elbert. "Morning, Merle," Big Jack says before noticing me. "Harlan! Hell, you been outside? Folks is gatherin' up for the hangin' even now."

"Ten-deep in some places," Elbert adds. "And every type of drummer right there to shill 'em something. Heck, I oughta set up outside with a bottle of rye. Five cents a pull!"

"Elbert, you so much as hawk a glass of lemonade to my would-be customers, I'll cut your hands off."

"Shit, Merle, I was just supposing."

"Good. Coffee, boys?" Merle asks.

"Sure thing," Big Jack says. Merle pours them each a cup. "I hear they're predicting a thousand."

"A thousand? Shit," Merle says. "I better tell Rico to shovel some more lye over the piss trough. Where the hell is Rico anyway?"

"Your boy is outside, tending to my new horse," Willis says from the table, without taking his eyes off his opponent. "Thanks for the use of him. Please charge my tab accordingly."

"No trouble at all, sir," Merle says.

"Two pair," he then announces, turning over his hole cards.

The one called Jessup shakes his head with a little embarrassed snort. "You had me till Seventh Street, but I fell ass-backwards into a boat." The Kansan flips up the three aces that complete his full house and starts raking the mountain of chips toward his side.

Avery Willis watches coolly as half of his stack changes ownership. "Merle, I shall take that whiskey now."

"Coming right up, sir."

Elbert glares over at Willis in disbelief—not at the dude's misfortune, but at the inconceivable notion that he would choose to spend the entire night in a musty saloon rather than at the hotel . . . with her.

The woman. I had shut her out of my mind like a door against the howling wind. But all at once her face comes back to me, the brush of her gloved hand as she descended the stairs at the hotel. A pang of guilt kicks angrily inside me. I do my best to push it away.

"Seems a crime, do it not?" Elbert begins, careful to keep his words from reaching the dude's ears. "Leaving a woman like that all alone? Lord mercy, I could think of 'bout a hundred things I could do with that fine piece of ass and ain't one of them involve a deck of cards."

"It is 'cause you are not married, Elbert," Merle says. "I don't care how comely a woman is. Some fella, somewhere, has grown bored of her dewiest charms."

"Might I point out, them two ain't married neither," Big Jack says. "What do you think of it, Harlan?"

I down the last of my coffee. "I think the lot of you gabble like a pack of hens."

"The aces seem to love you today, sir," Willis says as the Kansan riffles the deck to deal.

"I make no claim to explain the fickle variance of cards, Mister Willis. Their love can turn to ice as quickly as the wind shifts." Jessup splits the cards and flutters them back upon themselves.

"But I cannot help noticing that the aces favor you considerably more kindly on your own deal then they do on mine." The dude's tone makes Jessup freeze. All at once, Avery Willis flies up from his chair and slams a vise grip down on the wrist of the unsuspecting Kansan.

"What the hell?" Jessup cries as Willis rips open the man's shirt cuff.

"You black cheater!" howls Willis as he pulls the fabric back, exposing the clover of the ace of clubs tethered to the Kansan's forearm. "I'll cave your blasted head in!"

Jessup counters with a lightning-quick draw of his forty, which holds steady and unwavering in his left hand, the barrel locked on the dude's head. Jessup steps back from the table, only then shifting slightly to bring the four of us at the bar into his view. He keeps the gun trained on Willis. "Now listen here," the Kansan says firmly. "Ain't no man here need to be a hero or jump into that what ain't his concern."

Each steadfast, backward step carries the card-sharp closer to the door, until his free, groping hand finds the knob. I think about the Colts weighing on my hip. The twelve-gauge Merle keeps behind the bar would be the second option. But the Kansas cheater has not aimed his gun at me. Cheating might be wrong from the pulpit, but I feel none compelled—not after Jed Barnes—to catch even a grazing whisper of a poorly aimed slug. It is not my money and not my fight. Willis would be in his rights to draw on Jessup. He might get himself killed. If the gambler were dead . . . I do not even let myself think about it. I push the woman's face out of my brain as quickly as it rose up there.

"Leave that derringer in your pocket, Willis," Jessup says as he swings the barroom door open with his leg. The sounds of the street rush in— shouts and laughter and clattering wagons. "You take them chips as your own and we'll call it square."

"Like hell we will," Willis sneers.

The Kansan turns and bolts out into the crowd. I am on my feet and moving, Willis and the others a step behind me.

I catch sight of the fleeing man as he bobs through the crowd and across the road. "There he is!" I point to the Kansan as he unhitches his pony at lightning speed.

"Stop that man!" Willis shouts. Merle's Mexican bar boy, Rico, looks up at us from the tie-pole where he brushes the dude's handsome new acquisition.

Jessup hops in his saddle, kicking the pony out of

his nap. They disappear into the far alley, no doubt set on the open desert. Merle unleashes a sharp whistle that draws the eye of the Pinkerton sniper on the roof of the Dry Goods.

"Thief," Merle yells, "on the pony!" The sniper looks back, confused. Merle's words get swallowed up by the din of the street, leaving the Pinkerton man straining to interpret a charade of points and gestures—to no avail.

"He's getting away, dammit," Willis cranes his neck and sees a second Pinkerton man directly over the Jewel, watching over us with some curiosity. "Sir, I have been swindled by that blasted man on the pony!"

"There's a hanging today," says the Pinkerton.

"I know there's a fucking hanging. We still have laws against thievery!"

"Can't spare a man, sir. We hold our ground. We have our orders."

"Useless, these Pinkerton oafs!" Willis stomps the ground in disgust.

"Now don't you worry about the money," Merle interjects. "He took no cash off the table and all the chips go to you."

"I will not be cheated!" Willis barks. "It is reputation at stake. Word gets out, every two-bit river gypsy from here to Atlanta will think they can shark Avery Willis!"

"Not one of us will ever speak of it. You have my word," Merle says.

"Mine too," offers Elbert.

"And mine," says Big Jack.

But I see the gambler's eyes narrow with stony resolve. He pulls from his waistcoat a silver-plated forty-four, considerably larger than any derringer. The gun could take a man down at a hundred paces. He shifts it to his front waistband for a speedier draw.

"Lock up my chips, Merle." Before anyone can counter, Avery Willis charges past me. "Untie her, boy!" Rico, wide-eyed with fear, paws at the lashing and flicks the horse free. Willis leaps off the porch and lands squarely in the saddle of the unsuspecting filly. A precise heel to her flank, timed with a confident pull on the reins, dissolves any unfamiliarity between mount and rider. The filly flares up and pivots around at the gambler's command. "Yaah!" Willis cries as the powerful animal sprints forth into the street.

Startled spectators scatter like mice—save for a lone, wretched woman who nearly trips over her own gown. Already at full gallop, Willis orders an elegant sidestep around the woman with an imperceptible tug of the reins, a maneuver that further flaunts the indisputable expertise of a talented horseman.

Merle is the first to find the words that voice our collective sentiment. "Lord, have mercy! That dude can *ride*."

CHAPTER TWENTY

The Pinkertons aim to transport the Snowman from jail to the gallows in the bed of a two-mule wagon, standing upright, by the look of it. The crank gun sits in the back of the wagon, its rotary of barrels pointed out the rear as a formidable deterrent to any ill-advised rescue attempt.

Delmer, the Pinkerton gunner, fusses an oiled rag lovingly over the swiveled base while his grizzled and burly associate, Casey, fastens a heavy iron bracket to a wooden pole that extends skyward behind the driver's bench. That is where they intend to secure their prisoner, amply guarded, but still in plain view during the entirety of the proceedings.

Casey eyes me with suspicion as I stride past him toward the jail door where Bix, the number-two Pinkerton, stands sentinel. He holds his ten-gauge at the ready and keeps a Remington rifle on his back for good measure. The sight of it reminds me how naked I feel without my Spencer.

"Stop right there," Bix says, raising a halting palm at me. The two men in the wagon pause from their chores long enough to let me know they are watching.

"Your captain asked for me."

"What's your name?"

"Two-Trees."

"Wait here." Bix backs away and disappears through the door into the jailhouse. The interior buzzes with activity and voices—that awful, familiar cackle rising above it all. The door slams and I hear Bix announce my name, followed by Mulgrew's grumbling baritone. The two Pinkertons behind me glare their hateful daggers into my backside as I stare blankly at the door. A second later it opens and Bix summons me through with a discourteous nod.

The Snowman stands at the near end of the cell, eagerly gripping the bars as he tries to participate in—or disrupt—the conversation transpiring before him. He lights up when he sees me. "How many's out there, son? Is it a thousand?"

"Quiet!" Captain Mulgrew lurches up from the sheriff's desk and whacks the bars with his truncheon, narrowly missing the Snowman's retreating fingers. "Next time I don't miss."

"Harlan, have a seat." I turn to see Mayor Boone pacing near the boarded-up window. He motions to the only other chair in the room, the chair I used to claim as my own. I ease into it, set my hat down on the edge of the desk.

"Messy business last night," Mulgrew says.

"I hear it was."

"What I hear, is that you lit out after that drunkard what drowned himself a whore. My men say he ain't come back yet."

"Would you come back?"

The captain glowers at me, his nostrils flaring, a powder keg of indignation. He is not a man accustomed to questions thrown back his way, especially from someone he would rather use as cannon fodder. "You got a lip on you," he says through gritted teeth.

"Oh, who gives a damn about that?" Boone says anxiously. The mayor steps into the light and I see how worked up he is. He looks tired. Hell, we are all tired. Even the Snowman appears a casualty of sleepless nights thanks to this sordid ordeal of his own creation. "Harlan, I need another favor."

Boone comes around the front of the desk and leans against it. An engraved, ivory-handled thirty-two sits snug in a pristine leather holster on the mayor's hip. I cannot recall ever seeing him armed. The hysteria of an impending, violent attack has claimed the mayor as well. "We need someone to cut the condemned from the rope and get him in the box. We'll have to prop him up for the picture first—that newspaperman has a camera in position—but right after that, you will want to box him up as quick as you can."

"Why not one a' them Mexicans what built up the gallows?"

"Would you believe it?" Boone says with obvious frustration. "One of those blasted fools spotted the likeness of the Blessed Virgin Mary in a goddamn pine knot! Took it as a sign. The lot of them run off for the border, clutching that wood plank like it was a holy relic." His words hang there a moment and then the whole room busts up laughing, myself included. The Snowman finds special delight in the story and falls about himself, cackling.

"That's enough out of you," Mulgrew bellows.

"Why me?" I ask.

"Well, frankly, Harlan, it is not for the faint of heart. I figured with your vested interest in the matter—"

"Don't worry, boy," shouts the Snowman. "Ain't no way I'm gonna swing. My gang'll bust me outta here long 'fore you have to mess with any of that."

Captain Mulgrew bolts from his chair, his club rising. "So help me God, you will shut your mouth or I will knock you stone out!"

"It's all a bunch of wasted talk and supposin'," the Snowman cries, backing away from the bars. His fiendish smile taunts the captain, but there's a strident, uncertain tenor to his voice, as though the confidence in his impending escape has diminished with every passing minute. The wall clock makes it half past nine.

"That's it! Gag this cocksucker," Mulgrew motions to the guard by the front door. The Pinkerton goes to the cell and opens it, producing along the way the cloth strap that will soon find the yellowed bite of the Snowman. "And get him changed out of them rags. He'll die in that goddamn suit if I have to nail it to his body."

"Go on, gag me up. My boys know where to find me."

"And get the barber in here. We'll cut his hair while we're at it."

"You ain't touching my hair!"

Mulgrew drives his club into the Snowman's

belly, doubling him over as the guard wrenches the gag tightly into his mouth.

"I hate to even ask this of you, Harlan," Boone says. "But with our being shorthanded, Pinkerton-wise . . ."

"Will you quit sayin' that?" Mulgrew grumbles. "You got you the finest shots in the valley out there, nearly every badge in the territory."

"As much as I hate to say this in front of him, Captain, you underestimate the Snowman."

"And you underestimate my men! Every direction is covered. His gang gets within a hundred yards of this town, the Pinkerton guns will shred every last one to ribbons."

"Who's to say they are not already here?" Boone waits for an answer that does not come, so he continues. "Folks been streaming into town for nearly a week now. Hell, I don't know hardly any of them. His men could have been trickling in, one by one. Maybe they are simply waiting for us to bring him out in the open before they unleash their fury. What are your snipers going to do then, Captain? Shoot into a crowd where the bandits stand shoulder-to-shoulder with honest, God-fearing citizens? It will be a right bloodbath."

"My agents have not reported anything to support that theory."

"A girl was killed last night!"

"An isolated incident," Mulgrew counters. His eye brushes over me. "And one I shall investigate thoroughly as soon as I pull the lever on this sumbitch, here."

"Maybe it was, maybe it wasn't," Boone says. "But I tell you this, Captain. We got almost a thousand people out there. Might be twice that by high noon. If I were you, I'd scrape up every last Pinkerton I could find and have them dispersed throughout that crowd."

"Every agent within a hundred miles is here in the Bend, Boone. All but a skeleton detail at the banks in Heavendale and Agua Verde."

"Lord sakes, man," pleads Boone. "There's nobody *left* in Heavendale or Agua Verde! They're all standing out in my thoroughfare, waiting for the show."

"Thank you, Boone, but this is not the first lever I've thrown. I will marshal my agents as I see fit and won't be told otherwise, not from you or anyone else!"

"Very well, Captain. But God help us all if you are wrong."

"The bastard kicked me!" the guard tending to the Snowman cries out. Mulgrew charges into the cage, unleashing a beating on the half-dressed prisoner.

Boone comes over to me, exhausted. He wanted this hanging in the first place and now bears the weight of a hundred bad decisions. For once, I feel something close to pity for him. He looks a decade older than he did two weeks ago and that bastard writhing on the floor in his own piss is the cause of it. The cost of the Snowman's destruction will exact its toll on the people of the Bend for years to come. I am no different. The sheriff. Maria. Taken from me.

"Will you help us, son?" the mayor asks with all that is left of his strength.

"Be glad to."

The sounds of voices and shuffling feet rise from outside. The door bursts open. Bix jams his head through. "Captain, you better come quick."

"What is it?"

"Indians."

Two horses approach from the west in steady, deliberate trot. I know before their faces come into view that the lead rider is Ahiga and behind him, atop the stolen palomino, is Raven. Navajo raiders rage at full gallop when they want blood, and are tougher to hit than swarming mosquitoes. But the brothers employ no such tactic today. Their pace is stoic, even solemn. Guns cock behind me and from the rooftops. "Hold fast, men!" Mulgrew's breath lands hotly across my neck.

"It's no war party," I say. "Ain't but two of 'em."

Mulgrew ignores me as he barks his orders. "No man fires without my signal!"

In the light of day, the brothers' pitch-coal braids seem even blacker, their skin red and weathered. I spot the Spencer across Ahiga's back, barrel down to show a lack of aggression . . . which I am sure is hard for him.

Their arrival at the sleepiest corner of the Bend spares them the full attention of the raucous throng that mobs the center of town. But a small contingent of spectators gathered outside the jail, no doubt in hopes of an early glimpse of the star attraction, catches sight of the maneuvering Pinkertons. Townsfolk fall in behind the line of black-coated gunmen, adding to the edginess of the confrontation. The riders stop thirty yards out, well aware of the two dozen rifles and one crank gun aimed at them.

Ahiga breaks from his younger brother and draws closer. He makes no attempt at English but begins to address the crowd in Dineh. The wind swallows most of his words and the ignorant ears of those in attendance discard the rest. I hear him, though. Enough to understand.

"What's he saying?" Mulgrew demands.

"A warning," I say. "The desert belongs to them."

Raven holds a woven sack down by his side. He starts to swing it, building momentum.

"What's he got there?" a voice shouts. Raven lets the sack fly. It arcs through the air and lands, skidding and heavy, at the feet of a Pinkerton. The agent toes it with his boot. Something rolls beneath the coarse fabric. He picks up the sack by its corner and out spills a blood-covered stone the size of a melon. It has ears and a nose and what used to be hair.

And then someone screams, "It's a head! It's a human head!" The Pinkerton staggers back into Jasper Goodhope as a collective gasp of disgust escapes from the crowd.

Jasper pushes around the black-coat and bends down, horrified. He announces what I already know. "It's Jed! It's Jed Barnes!"

A tremendous boom explodes over my shoulder. The air fills with a choking plume of ashen smoke. Women shriek. The gun is close enough that the shock wave pushes against my back. I instinctively step left, keeping my eyes forward. Raven slumps and begins to slide off the palomino. Ahiga springs from his horse to catch his brother, but is too late. Raven is dead before he hits the ground.

I turn to see, right behind me, the smoking muzzle of the engraved, commemorative thirty-two. Boone holds it in his right hand.

"Boone! You bleeding idiot!" Mulgrew storms past me, enraged. The mayor wears an expression of profound confusion. "What in God's name are you thinking?"

"Those savages . . . don't get to do that," Boone says, unsure of himself.

Ahiga howls a deep, pained cry as he glowers in our direction. He sees the shooter clear as day and me next to him. He sails back up atop his mount, hoisting his brother's body up with him and letting loose a haunting wail. The warrior in him has returned. He kicks up the horse and thunders off.

"You just started a war with the blasted Navajo," Mulgrew spits. The captain grabs Bix by the shoulder, but keeps Boone in his eye as he shouts his order. "Get to the telegraph office. Pull every man we got. Agua Verde *and* Heavendale. I want them in the Bend within the hour!"

"But what about the banks?" Bix stutters.

"Tell them they're fucking closed!"

CHAPTER TWENTY-ONE

The Snowman's final journey through the heart of Caliche Bend happens much like his first—as a prisoner on parade. The transfer happens quickly. From his exiting of the jail cell, shackled by wrist and ankle, to the clank of the iron lock that secures him to the wagon, no more than ten seconds elapse. The Pinkertons keep a tight schedule. And Mulgrew's truncheon, pressed firmly against the Snowman's spine, leaves little room for procrastination.

I hear that during the war, the captain hunted down Union deserters. I can only imagine how many frightened boys he strung up in the prison courtyard without trial or mercy. The Snowman reminds me of one of them now.

I had expected the noise from the crowd to be deafening, with pent-up nerves and drunken revelry crescendoing to an orgiastic peak as the trapdoor opens, but there is none of that. The mob's God-fearing, Christian souls will not allow it, despite their best efforts to the contrary. Instead, solemnity reigns, ensured by the skittish trigger finger behind the crank gun and the quartet of Pinkerton men, all with double-barrel twelves, flanking the rickety wagon along its procession.

The smattering of grim-faced black-coats interspersed among the spectators provides a second layer of deterrence. And beyond them, dotting the rooftops like thin, black spires, stand the eagle-eyed sharpshooters, equally prepared for an imminent assault on the town or a surprise insurgency from within.

Nearly two thousand restless townspeople and strangers, crammed like sardines beneath a withering midday sun, stare in schoolroom silence as the two mules strain down the ravaged thoroughfare toward the gallows.

Mulgrew had been clear in his instructions to me that I leave the pine casket open at the bottom of the stairs. Let the Snowman see the box that will hold his rotting bones as he mounts the scaffold. I pull off the casket lid and lay it down on the dirt. The smell of fresh pine rises from the sanded wood. It is a well-made coffin, far finer that it needs to be, considering the itinerary of its future occupant.

The newspaperman bustles up to me. "Now, we will not have much time, Mister Two-Trees, but my equipment shall require at least a five-count of complete stillness in order to ensure proper focus. Perhaps you could lean the casket up against the scaffold for better visibility of the subject?"

"I doubt he will complain."

"No, of course not. Remember, it's for posterity's sake. Our readers would like to see."

I lift the casket up and lean it against the frame,

right next to the shiny new hammer and box of copper nails that Jasper has pulled from his stockroom for the occasion, along with a carton of lead for the Colts.

My new job as undertaker pays two dollars. For that fee, I am expected to perform a second, but perhaps more important task—keeping my eyes peeled for anyone or anything suspicious. I have seen more faces of the Snowman's gang than any man alive, a fact that they are as keenly aware of as I am.

I reload the Colts with fresh bullets and check the chambers. An open assault from the desert would deteriorate quickly into a bloody free-for-all. And if there is a sneak attack, I would be the first target. Either way, the pistols get hot.

A crow caws from the church tower. The horses tied up behind the crowd nicker against the buzzing flies. Every snort from the mules brings the wagon closer. It seems only humans hold much reverence for the silence.

I step lightly up the side stairs of the scaffold, careful to avoid even the slightest creak. No one notices me. I stop halfway up. All heads stay fixed in the other direction. Bix steers the wagon through the parting crowd. Mulgrew sits beside him, constantly appraising the threat and prepared to defend any frontal assault with the sawed-off ten across his knee.

Faces turn as the wagon passes. I scan the crowd. Every living soul I know is out there, and many more I don't. I skip over the familiar faces and focus on the strange ones. Mulgrew motions to his right and Bix corrects the wagon toward the stairs.

The change of direction forces the multitude to push back on itself, only there is nowhere to go.

"Stop shoving!" a voice cries. The sniper above me steps toward the edge of the roof. The spectators closest to the front backpedal onto the toes of those behind them. The folks farther back steady themselves against their neighbors. The disturbance ripples like a wave through the multitude. Delmer perks up behind the crank gun. His left hand joins his right on the handle, inciting an instinctive retreat from anyone within a stone's throw of the muzzle. The captain stands in his seat, bringing the shotgun up with him. The move has an instant, mollifying effect on the crowd and order quickly restores itself.

All at once, I see her. Her simple, forest green dress cuts through the sea of dusty, drab garments that surround her, betraying her attempt to escape attention—as if Miss Bichard could ever do such a thing.

Jostled by the crowd, she regains her footing, and when she looks up the fear has not yet vacated her eyes. I bound down the stairs and charge into the throng. I stay fixed on her position even though I lose sight of her. How tiny she is among these booted cowpokes in their oversized Stetsons. Something about the way I move through the crowd inspires people to give me a wide berth. I weave through a pair of burly ranch hands and there she is. Her eyes dance with surprise at the sight of me, but there is a tinge of relief beneath it.

"Mister Two-Trees."

"Ma'am, you ought not be out here by yourself."

"Yes, I am starting to see that. Mister Willis was supposed to join me."

"He lit out after a gambler what cheated him."

"Yes, and he has returned, thanks be to God. About an hour ago."

"He track that fella down?"

"Heavens, no." She rolls her eyes at the thought of it. "And I am not sure what he would have done if he had. Running off like that. Hmm. A night of whiskey and no sleep clouded his judgment, that much is for certain."

"Glad he is all right."

"More embarrassed, than anything, I should think. You will understand if he is back at the hotel sleeping it off. I will admit," she says, indicating the tempest surrounding us, "that this was more than I expected."

"You stand over here with me." I touch Genevieve's far shoulder and she does the rest, carrying the gentle scent of rose water with her as she comes to a stop right in front of me.

We cast our eyes upward together. Garrison LaForge, the dreaded Snowman, the most feared outlaw in all of the Southwest, huffs beneath the cloth strap that gags him. The wagon clatters to a stop by the stairs. From this close, I see puddled tears in the eyes that comb the horizon with limitless expectation. The beads of sweat on his brow glisten his raven hair in the high noon sun.

Mulgrew turns and wastes no time unlocking the shackles. He guides his prisoner around the crank gun and into the arms of Bix, who leads him down the stepladder to the ground. Delmer stays glued to the Gatling. Two thousand heartbeats quicken as the Snowman touches the bottom step.

"Go to hell, Snowman!" The voice could belong to any of a dozen men, and speaks the sentiment of the entire congregation. She pushes back in to me ever so slightly. The crushed velvet of her frock brushes against my chest, igniting a charge of electricity which courses straight through to my bones. Neither of us pulls away. We stay there, bound to one another in furtive contact amidst a sea of unsuspecting eyeballs. I have never been more grateful for a crowd, and never more unbothered by a violation of my personal space. Staring off in the same direction, instead of at each other, we somehow give ourselves permission to touch, as if the orientation of our gaze makes the act less wrong. And yet it feels so right.

Mayor Boone and the padre appear at the base of the stairs and follow the Pinkertons up. I do not want to leave her, but I cannot entirely neglect my duties. I can see by the efficiency of the captain's movement that he intends to cut off any possibility of rescue by making speedy work of this. Scanning the crowd to my immediate left, I spy a familiar face.

"Jack," I call to him. Big Jack nods and comes over. People move out of his way even faster than they had for me.

"Hey, Harlan," he says, feeling compelled to whisper. I place both hands on her shoulders and turn Genevieve toward me. My eyes meet hers, tunneling through them, and make a vow to never let go.

"I have a job to do. You stay here with Jack. Anything happens, you do what he tell you.

Everything will be okay." I give her a little squeeze. She nods, understanding. "You good with that, Jack?" Big Jack's expansive chest broadens even further.

"Ain't nobody muss a hair on her head, Harlan. You got my word on that." Jack tips his hat to the woman. "Ma'am."

"Thank you, sir," she says, breathless.

I break from them and make my way to the scaffold. Captain Mulgrew stands with the Snowman on the top deck. The only thing above them is a crossbeam that anchors the rope. Boone and the padre confer quietly on the side before the mayor nods and steps to the edge of the platform. He raises a palm no higher than his waist, quieting the already hushed crowd to utter silence.

"We gather here today by the grace of God and justice." The man loves oratory in any fashion. With two thousand rapt bodies within earshot, his voice competes only with a trifling breeze. "No measure of vengeance can bring back those who have died from the heinous events at this man's hand, nor return to us what he has pilfered."

"Let's get this done, Boone," the captain says, in a stiff, straight-faced whisper. "Enough grand-standin'."

I descend over the back stairs and start down toward the back side of the scaffold. From here I can witness the proceedings and still have easy access to the interior, where the Snowman's twitching body will soon come to an abrupt stop, obscured from the spectators' view by a solid, pine partition. Captain and the Snowman stand above me, their backs facing my way. I see there, below the iron wrist-cuffs, what no one else can see—the trembling fingers of a man staring into the abyss of death.

The mayor carries on with his speech, despite Mulgrew's professed opposition. "A lawful jury has found the accused guilty and a judge has passed the ultimate sentence. And now, by the power vested in me by the Territory of New Mexico in these United States, the sentence shall be carried out in accordance with the law." He turns toward the Snowman. "Does the condemned have any last words?"

Grudgingly, Mulgrew snaps down the Snowman's gag.

"Well f-first . . ." LaForge sputters, "I ought be given my last rites, as is proper under God!"

"The padre done that already," the captain informs the audience, lest anyone agree with the Snowman. "Now say your bit and be done with it." He pushes his prisoner forward. With every step, the Snowman's legs look near to crumpling.

The Pinkerton snipers catch my eye. From my unique vantage, their formation aligns into a black-dotted V-shape extending along the rooftops and down to the vanishing point of the church steeple. Every odd man stands peering out into the desert while his counterpart casts his gaze straight down into the crowd. All deputies look one of those two places. All except one. The black-coat atop the nearest building, at my eleven o'clock, fixes out a point behind me, due north. Something has his attention, but not yet his worry.

I look behind me. The big eye beats her mighty rays down upon the desert floor, whiting the parched caliche like a river. The glare is overwhelming. I climb up a rung, look back, and still see nothing.

"Y'all know what I been accused of, unjustly," the Snowman begins. "A lot of hearsay and conjecture, most of it. Maybe I am no saint, but things being what they are, I am not so much guiltier than a lot other folks what done considerable worse . . ."

Boone edges over to Mulgrew and whispers loud enough for me to hear. "I said final words, not a dissertation."

"Stall tactic. I seen this trick before," Mulgrew growls. "Wrap it up, LaForge." He punctuates his order with a jab to the prisoner's kidneys.

The Snowman grimaces, desperation creeping ever deeper across his face. "Now this here is the last words of a dying man! On your head be it, to cut me off." He turns to the audience again. "To any of my brothers out there, let us not cut the hair too thin. No sense in being dramatic about it." He inches forward, entreating any conspirators among the stony-faced citizenry out there, telling them that now is the time. "How 'bout it, huh?"

The black-coat sniper steps toward the edge of the roof, his eyes unwavering from some far-off object. I find footing on the upper beam and pull myself up. Now at a higher vantage, I pivot back toward the north.

A dust cloud churns across the desert, moving toward town at a thunderous pace. I watch the Pinkerton man reach into his pocket, expecting him to produce the whistle to alarm. Instead he comes out with a small mirror, like what a lady carries in her handbag. He finds the sun and angles the mirror down. The white patch of reflected sunlight crawls along the top deck of the scaffold and up the captain's leg to the side of his face, where it registers in his periphery. The captain turns. His eyes move upward, following the signal to its place of origin on the rooftop. Their silent communication is brief and to the point. *Horses.*

All at once, the captain snaps his head and glowers at the Snowman, who shows no sign of winding down his oration. He grabs the prisoner by the collar and yanks him back.

"No, I am still talking! Come on, boys, now is the time!"

"Get the rope on him!" Mulgrew shouts. Bix unhooks the noose from its concealment. A collective gasp issues from the crowd, as the long-imagined endgame becomes real. The Snowman's boots drag across the platform. He flails violently, freeing his neck momentarily from the captain's headlock and causing his executioner to stumble to the ground. Mulgrew finds his rage quickly, not from the desperate outburst of a cornered animal—he has seen that countless times—but from the betrayal of his own sixty-year-old frame. "Get it on him, dammit!"

Bix, all one hundred and fifty pounds of him, moves in with the rope. LaForge lets fly a rangy side-kick. The Pinkerton man half parries it, avoiding the brunt of the blow, but catching enough of it to slow him down.

Instinct propels me forward. I swing over the guardrail and swoop in behind the Snowman. Time slows to a crawl. My eyes lock only on him. Somewhere far off—it sounds like another world— a cascade of clicks reaches my ear as a dozen snipers swing their Longrifles in my direction. The platform shakes with churning footsteps. A huddle of black-clad men ascend the stairs. Indiscriminate voices erupt from the nervous masses. My arms shoot out and clamp onto the Snowman's ribs. "I got him," I say.

"No, no! Wait, I am begging you!" He catches me in his periphery. "Harlan! Please!"

The captain finds his legs and strides across the platform toward the lever. Bix, black bag in hand, swoops in from behind me. LaForge bucks beneath my grip. With one hand I help Bix crown the cloth sack onto his head. Something slips greasily against my palm, but I hold him there, locked in a vise grip that hell or high water will not break. The Snowman howls his final words as the bag comes down over his face. "No, no! You done got the wrong—*gggrmph*!" Lost in the blackness, his body softens just enough to let Bix apply the rope. There is no time to double-check it for tightness. Mulgrew is a man undeterred. He reaches the lever, and with no regard for my safety or that of his second-in-command, kicks it like a bad dog. I grab Bix by his collar and dive backward. The ground beneath us disappears as the trapdoor bangs open. Bix and I land heavily against the un-forgiving planks. A moment later we hear the sharp crack of a man's neck bones giving out.

Women's voices gasp in true, audible horror. I roll over, staring up at a pale sky sliced down the middle by a taut, groaning rope.

It is done.

* * *

A hand finds my shoulder. Bix lies on the other end of it. "Thanks," he says. My mind returns and I remember the horses. We might at last be free of the Snowman, but the charging marauders from the north do not know that. And I hardly suspect such a revelation would avert them now. I try to get up. An oily wetness coats my hands and forearms. I look down, prepared for blood, and instead discover streaks of shiny, midnight black across my skin and shirt.

"Ready all barrels!" Mulgrew shouts, raising his fist to give the order. The gathered throng begins to understand. Near panic sets in as they realize they have nowhere to go.

"Let us all be calm." I recognize Boone's most authoritative tone. "Everyone just stay where you are. We'll not have a riot."

The cloud of dust rumbles from the desert, down into the small depression where the judge's wagon had upturned several days earlier. I climb up to the top of the rail and await the riders' reemergence over the berm. Every last Pinkerton waits with me, taking dead aim at the fixed point just on the edge of town.

The bobbing head of a horse rises first over the mound. Seated behind it is a small human figure. I squint into the glaring sun, not wanting to believe my own eyes.

"Take aim!" Muglrew commands. I leap off the railing and throw myself in front of the captain.

"It is a child," I say. I make sure my words sink into his brain before repeating. "A child, Captain."

"Hell you say? All that dust?"

"One rider, Captain. A boy. And he is in a hurry."

Boone jumps in, confirming what is more obvious with every passing second. "Captain, wait. I see only one horse."

"Hold the line! Do not fire until my signal!" Mulgrew seems visibly annoyed by his own order.

"He has someone with him," I say, "across the back of the saddle."

A hundred yards out, the boy sees the guns pointed at him and pulls back, but only slightly, slowing his tawny thoroughbred to a canter before stopping her completely. The horse cries out, as though she could not take one more step. She starts to falter, legs wobbling, utterly exhausted. A splintered faction of spectators and armed Pinkertons appear at the rear of the scaffold to intercept them. I race for the back stairs, Mulgrew and Bix following, and somewhere behind them, the mayor.

The boy looks about twelve, his tender skin chapped and sunburned by the blistering ride. His eyes are red from crying and, where tears have been, crusted rivers stream down his face. He jumps off the horse, brave as can be, and starts to pull at the man laid facedown over the haunches. He slides the body toward him and it would surely crush him if Bix and Jasper Goodhope did not intervene. "My pa. The blast got him."

Boone pushes to the front. "What blast?"

"The bank, in Agua Verde," the boy says. "Pa was standing behind it when . . . it just blew up!" A fresh round of sobbing overcomes him. They set the boy's father down on the ground and stretch him out on his back. And then we see it.

"Oh my God," Boone mutters. The man clings to life by the grace of angels. His entire front side—arms, torso and head—lays charred in a ghostly white powder. A raspy, dry cough sputters out of him, misting the air with fine chalky dust. Deep in my stomach a dull, sickening knot tries to kick itself free. Boone's mouth hangs open. "When . . . did this happen, son?"

"'Bout an hour ago. And the doc weren't around. Everybody's here. I run him straight over."

"This happened in *Agua Verde*?" the mayor asks.

"Yes, sir. You gotta save him, please. Please!"

"I'll fetch the doc," Jasper says, sprinting off.

"And someone tend to that horse," Merle says, appearing behind me. I turn to meet his eyes, and find in them the same disbelief that mine must show. I look to Mulgrew and finally to Boone, whose stunned face confirms the impossible.

"It cannot be. It cannot *be*," Boone says. He looks back at the body hanging inert below the scaffold. I remember my hands. The black liquid mixes with my own sweat and runs down my forearm into my shirt. The faint odor of alcohol and spirits reaches my nose. I bring my hands up and take a sniff, all at once recognizing what it is.

"If the Snowman is still out there, then who the hell did we just hang?" Boone asks.

"An impostor," I say, extending my blackened palms for all to see. "Shoe polish. He was dyeing his hair with it."

"That's why he kept askin' for it." Bix interjects. "Son of a bitch!"

"But . . . why?" Boone implores. "Why would a man let himself get hanged?"

"Hold on just a minute," the captain barks. "Who says we hanged the wrong man? We don't know that. Just 'cause of some boot polish? We are not jumping to any conclusions. We don't know what happened in Agua Verde."

"For God's sake, Captain. Look at the man," Boone says, pointing to the boy's dying father. "White as a bedsheet. It's his trademark."

"Could be copycats."

"You know it's not," Boone counters. "No one can rig a bomb like the Snowman. Even his own men cannot do it."

"Enough!" Mulgrew shouts. "I'll not hear another word of this until I get confirmation. Now you, half-breed, you get in there and cut that sumbitch down!"

I reach into to my pocket, searching for that two dollars to throw in his face, when a voice rises from the crowd behind us. "Make a hole! Coming though! Western Union, coming through." All eyes turn to see Bertram Merriman bound down the steps of the post office and into the throng. The crowd parts for him and he comes running over, deeply troubled, the ribbon of telegraph paper whipping from his hand like a streamer. "Captain Mulgrew! Telegram for the captain," Bertram says, panting.

"What is it?" Mulgrew grumbles.

"Urgent news, Captain. There's been a robbery. At the bank."

"We know that, Bertram," Boone says, annoyed. "In Agua Verde. A boy rode that news in faster than your machine could deliver it."

"No," Bertram says. "Not Agua Verde. This comes from Heavendale."

"Heavendale?!" the captain growls. "When?"

"About five minutes ago." Bertram gazes down at dots and dashes and reads aloud. "Heavendale Trust robbed. Two clerks dead. Massive explosion. Snowman."

I turn and stare out at the desert. A sultry haze bakes on the horizon. Somewhere to the west, a band of riders, laden with the riches of the entire valley, is charging full bore for the hills. I recall a tall man in blue and have no doubt he leads the way. There will be a party in the Sangres tonight. And a black-haired outlaw named Garrison LaForge will pour the first drink.

PART III
SNOWFALL

CHAPTER TWENTY-TWO

Until this morning, Silas Townes was the wealthiest man in Agua Verde. Now he sweats through his waistcoat in the Bend's meetinghouse and laments the violent departure of the bulk of his fortune. "Dammit, Boone! The entire valley's bankrupted and it happened on your watch. Incompetence, top to bottom."

The rest of his words get swallowed up in the roar of shouts and insults that has consumed the proceedings for the better part of an hour. I lean against the back wall where an open window offers small relief from the close, dank air that accompanies broken dreams and finger-pointing.

"Now hang on," Bennett Whitlock interjects, coming to the mayor's defense. "You cannot lay this all on Walter. We all thought we had the Snowman. There was a trial."

"Conducted by Boone and his ill-prepared nephew," Townes says, seething.

"And a federal judge out of Heavendale. Don't forget that," says Captain Mulgrew, one of the few men lucky enough to occupy a chair in the cramped room. "The judge was sent under authority of the governor himself."

"Yes, I have been in contact with the governor, Captain. We cabled one another not thirty minutes ago. Let me assure you that Santa Fe is most distraught and embarrassed by this catastrophe."

"He said all that by cable?" Boone asks.

"The governor and I are fast friends, Boone. Such is the respect one gets when you're the mayor of a real town and not some dusty hamlet that just sunk the territory."

"Monsignor," someone cries. "What news of the boy?" All eyes fall upon a gaunt figure whose black robe darkens the doorway, obscuring the moonlit sky.

"The doctor is doing his best," says the monsignor. "It is in God's hands now." Heavendale is a godly town. Within its borders there is no doubt some rich businessman like Boone or Townes who calls himself mayor, but the real power in Heavendale lies with the church. And its ranking official just walked into the room, followed dutifully by our own padre.

The monsignor moves toward the table where Bennett Whitlock finds himself rising to surrender his chair. The clergyman descends into the seat with a slight nod to Townes and then lets his eyes come to a scornful stop upon Mayor Boone.

"Now, about our money . . ."

The leaders of three towns—three chiefs in a sweat lodge—have been brought together under the banner of a single calamity for which no one appears eager to claim responsibility.

"Easy to sit in judgment, gentlemen," Boone begins. "But I'll not let any man here claim that he would have done anything different had the situation been reversed. This patsy of a fellow was *in* the bank! He was positively identified. He claimed to be LaForge, steadfastly, up until the moment he stood at death's door, and in that moment a man will say anything to spare his neck."

"Except it was the truth," Townes says.

"Do you not see the brilliance of the ruse, Silas?" the mayor says with a dose of incredulous admiration. "The real Snowman was clearly one of the other bandits who got away. This mysterious man in blue seems the most likely candidate. That poor sap in the gallows genuinely thought he was to be rescued. He was as duped as we were, tricked into his own death by some false promise. So let us add betrayal and manipulation to the already extensive list of the Snowman's sinister abilities."

"Perhaps had you not been so greedy in your salesmanship of this hanging spectacle," the monsignor announces, "the bank in Heavendale, where the church, I will tell you, had extensive savings, would not have been left so vulnerable. Nor the bank in Agua Verde."

"Hear, hear!" cries a voice that is quickly seconded.

I take a look at the faces around the room and determine that the citizenry of Caliche Bend is represented only by a third of those in attendance. The rest are strangers—angry, bitter folks from the far corners of the valley smarting from the newness of being robbed.

It's your fault, Boone!" shouts a red-faced woman.

"No, it's the Pinkertons who bear the blame! We pay you good money to safeguard our own, not to leave it unattended."

"You check that tone, sir," growls Mulgrew. "We were acting on an order from the governor to protect that man until his hanging and that is what we done."

"While neglecting your other duties!"

"The Pinkertons are still on the job, sir! We'll find the money and string up the men what stole it."

"I suggest you do just that, Captain," Silas Townes says, "because the governor also made it clear that he is halting payment to the Pinkerton Company, pending further investigation."

"He can't do that. We had a signed contract with the territory."

"The territory, by all rights, could sue you in court for negligence."

"Hell, you say."

"You want to avoid a lawsuit, Captain? Get out there and find our money."

The captain explodes and jabs his meaty finger in my direction. "I'll remind you that it weren't the Pinkertons who brung in the wrong man!"

All at once the air drains from the room. I feel the threatening pricks of a hundred daggers just waiting to pierce my flesh as most eyes turn toward me.

"It's true. Harlan Two-Trees brought this misery upon us." I turn to see Polly McPhee, her voice quavering with rage. "He brought that patsy right into our town."

"Hear, hear!"

"I'll wager he's in on it," Silas Townes adds. "I hear he lost nary a nickel when the Loan and Trust got hit."

Then the voices bark from all direction, some achingly familiar, others tinged with the barb of anonymity. "You can't trust the heathens!"

"And a whore-lovin' one at that."

"Hold on now, folks," Boone says. "Harlan showed great courage . . . despite . . . perhaps . . . some overzealous judgment."

"He could have grabbed the loot, though! He was right *there.*"

"You cannot expect this miscegenated orphan to know the proper course. He is of . . ." Boone's voice trails off.

"Of what?" I ask.

"Of limited faculties. Forgive me, son. I urged you not to go up there alone. I did."

I push forward off the wall, the hairs on my neck standing at full attention. I want no one behind me, no one I cannot see coming. The sound drops from the room again as I start to speak. "I asked all who was willing to ride out there with me. Not a soul spoke up. Do I misremember? Polly, your boarding-house been full up for a week and I did not hear you complaining about that. Still, if you all want to lay it on me 'cause of my skin, or what mamma did, or 'cause I am a bastard, so be it. But if you think I am one of them who shot down the sheriff who loved me, who raised me as his own? Let any man here say as much to my face."

A boot scrapes across the floor. Two black shadows rise in my periphery. Pinkertons. I cannot remember resting my palm on the handle of the Colt, but I feel it there now, sure as day. A click comes from behind me and I know the captain has drawn his gun.

"Go home, Harlan." It is a voice I know well, but it rings void of its usual friendship. "Just go on." I pivot my head to see Big Jack. He looks like he has aged ten years since this morning and somewhere along the way learned how to be mean. I hold him in my gaze until he breaks away. There is a loneliness that overtakes a man after two or three days in the desert by himself, but it is nothing compared to what weighs on my heart as I stride toward the door of the meetinghouse.

"May the Lord have mercy on your soul, my son." I stop and glance back at the monsignor, who has not bothered to stand.

"Your Lord got nothing to do with it." I step outside without closing the door.

CHAPTER TWENTY-THREE

Weather shifts on a dime in the high desert. The seasons sneak up without warning. Just past sundown the cold moved in, not too long before the stares of the townspeople—who had viewed me kindly or at least with smug indifference until now—turned icy.

Storm takes it easy on me as we make our way behind the Dry Goods out toward the fire road that leads back to Sheriff's. But as the church clock strikes up midnight, the stallion finds the excuse to get ornery and makes sure I know that it is long past his bedtime. I tell him to quit his fussin', that it has been a long day for me too.

Save for those bodies clogging up the meetinghouse, and the two dozen or so more working through the whiskey down at Merle's place, the Bend has mostly emptied out. The exodus was quick, leaving streets littered and ravaged as people scattered like roaches back to their homes in the wake of the day's stunning revelations. The cleanup—a disheartening prospect—looms as tomorrow's problem.

I welcome the quiet and the return of the familiar sounds of night. The wilderness calls to me, pulling at my blood. I think about how things could be different. That first night in the Sangres, I could have just kept going, not tangling with the Snowman at all. The mountains have claimed better men than I. Or maybe I could have stayed up there, with a beard as thick as bramble, surviving on what the hard land provided and nothing more. But to steer that course would not have done right by the sheriff, not for all the good and care he and Missus bestowed upon me.

My mind reels. Maybe the blame for this sorry affair lies at my feet after all. Had my Injun nose not been so eager to key on a single whiff of quick match, the sheriff never would have gotten down to the bank in time to catch a round from the Snowman's barrel. The Bend would still have its lawman instead of being poisoned by Pinkertons. Boone's unchecked hubris and boundless greed—without Sheriff's calming presence to temper them—managed to sink the town in barely a week. If I had kept my mouth shut, as I had most of my life, this blackness would have never found purchase.

It was pure vengeance that drove me up into the hills and a thirst for glory that brought me back down again to march through the center of town with that cursed impostor trussed up behind me. It was attaining that glory that drew Maria's eye. And it was my vanity and lust for another woman that cost Maria her life.

Jed Barnes hated me for the color of my skin, but it was my refusal to carry myself as anything other than a godless, hooting savage that truly enraged him. Now I trudge home with a heavy, sickening understanding that what the rest of the town thinks about me is hardly any different than what Jed Barnes thought.

The morning will bring clearer heads, I know. The hysteria of blame will blow over and this melancholy that now grips me shall pass with no more disruption than a bout of indigestion. By the twelfth clang of the bell, I feel almost myself again.

As we pass the public stables behind the hotel, I hear a horse bray. The low, coaxing voice of a man trying to soothe it follows. The baritone utterance hardly coincides with that of the squeaky-voiced stable boy—Otis Chandler's eldest—who would normally be the one shoveling out manure at this hour. Either that or dozing on his bench. A quick scan of the perimeter shows no sign of the freckled lad. The weak glow of a lantern flickers far inside the rear door among the stalls.

My mind goes quickly to the prospect of horse thieves. I drop down off Storm and silently order him to stay put. The ground appears and vanishes beneath my toes as I glide toward the edge of the barn. Easing my thumb down onto the hammer of the Colt, I slip in through the wide-open door and train my eye on the darkness, waiting for the first hint of movement.

"Easy, girl." His voice, pitched barely above a whisper, carries such soporific mellifluence that it could surely return even the most colicky baby to the depths of slumber. *The gentle horse rustler.* I close the distance between us, bring up the gun, and step into the lantern's paltry throw.

"Hold it there—," I say. But the words have only just left my mouth when I recognize the familiar line of his sideburns and angular slope of his cheekbones and nose.

He turns, startled at the sight of the gun, but then slides seamlessly into a comfortable disposition of kinship. "Ah, Mister Two-Trees," says the gambler.

"Mister Willis."

"I see your reputation as a near-phantom is not ill-placed. You took me for a horse thief, I gather."

"That I did," I say, holstering the Colt.

"Well, you certainly had the drop on me. Well done, sir."

"We're all good at something."

"She's beautiful, is she not?"

"Come again?"

Avery Willis turns from me and runs his hand along the muscular, chestnut neck of the filly, his spoil from the poker game. "Her name's Athena. The goddess of beauty."

"A fine horse."

"One of the best I've seen."

"I know you've seen many."

Willis turns, serious now. "What do you mean by that?"

"The way you steeple-chased her out of here today after that Kansan—a horse you never rode? A man like that is no stranger to the saddle."

The gambler casts his eyes downward, almost embarrassed, and lets his grimace fade into a smile.

"Guilty as charged. Tennessee is horse country. My people start riding almost before we learn to walk."

"No shame in handling a horse."

"No, none at all. But I have found myself to fare better at the poker table affecting the manner of the citified gentry. Seems to inspire the gulls to push in their chips when they think they'll take down a tony fop who's never laid ass in a saddle. That blasted Kansan made me show my cards, if you'll pardon the pun."

I nod and let the matter drift. Willis produces a few slices of apple and offers them, one at a time, to the filly, who plucks them hungrily from the gambler's flattened palm. When he is finished, Willis wipes his hands on his dungarees and stuffs them into the pockets of a plain brown jacket. Without his fanciful suits, the gambler looks more like a ranch hand than a prominent riverboat gambler. His cheeks have filled in with a shadowy stubble and I think how laborious his grooming must be when preparing to step out in the company of Miss Bichard. Such would be the effort required to keep pace with her elegance. He appears tonight, by any account, like a man who slipped out alone for a private errand and did not envision encountering *anyone*.

He picks up our conversation again, of his own accord. "I could've run him down, you know. The Kansan."

"I have no doubt."

"The scoundrel lit straight for the mountains, you see, but this filly here, she had not been properly cared for by that turnip who lost her to me and she started to cramp from lack of water. I eased up

on her and decided to let the Sangres take care of
the scoundrel. I feel certain the Bloods kept their
end of the bargain."

"So you come down to check on her?"

"Indeed. I have grown fond of her. And with last
night's marathon game and today's—I don't yet
know what we're calling today—I could not sleep.
Something about a stable has always given me peace."

"What happened to the stable boy? Little red-
headed fella?"

"I sent him for fresh hay. I would not stuff a
coffin mattress with the moldy chaff they serve in
here." Willis cranks up the wick on the lantern,
stretching the pale glow a little deeper into the
recesses of the barn. In the brightening light, the
chocolate leather of his jacket bears the ashen
desert dust of a man entirely unconcerned with
form or fashion. The transformation is wholly
remarkable.

"Say, hold the bridle, will you? I want to put a
blanket on her," he says, leading the filly a step
down the stall, in my direction. I take the bridle in
my hand. Willis picks up a fresh blanket from a
stack in the corner. He unfolds it as he walks,
sidestepping a faded gray satchel on the floor.
"Cold is moving in," he says.

"Winter be here 'fore you know it." I reach out
with my other hand and pet the filly's neck. The
steam from her sweat rises into the night.

CHAPTER TWENTY-FOUR

The sharp odor of autumn coaxes me from a dead, dreamless sleep. My limbs feel like lead. Every stiff, sore muscle groans for more rest. From far out in the barn I hear Storm announce his objection to some irritation or another. I blink my eyes to the graying dawn, but cannot keep them open in the stinging, acrid air. My lungs fill with morning and cough it out again.

Smoke.

Smoke!

The thought rams its way to the front of my brain. I roll out of bed onto the floor, pawing blindly for my trousers. I stuff my legs into them and stumble for my boots. Fiery motes of snowflaked ash dance in the thickening haze above my head. I crawl for the door and barrel through the choked air out onto the porch, where I buckle, hacking a hoarse, dry cough from the pit of my guts. Heaving on all fours, my hand falls upon a patch of tacky wetness. I bring my fingers up to my face and try to make sense of it through the burning water that wrecks my vision. It is paint. White paint. Drops of it spread across the floor of the porch back toward the door. I do not know many words by sight, but this one, scrawled across the front siding in bold, hastily slapped brushstrokes, is all too familiar:

HALFBREED

The letters barely have time to register when I force my mind back to the fire. The torches—branches of cured oak wrapped in oily rags—stick out from the crawl space at each corner of the house. I kick them free, one by one, and fling them out into the open, barren yard, but the flames have taken hold in places. I pivot and sprint for the pump behind the barn. I manage three paces before Storm's frightened wail cracks the air, freezing me in my tracks.

The barn is completely ablaze. Its clapboard roof pulsates from the heat in the waning seconds before the imminent collapse. I find my legs and churn them toward the sweeping flames that scratch their way between the slats in the barred swing-door. As I close the distance, the heifer's insistent lowing reverberates beneath the panicked, fluttering cries from the henhouse. I hear nothing from the goats or mules, and that is bad, but Storm's voice sounds strong and full of fight.

I throw open the door and am swallowed by a hungry, billowing wall of smoke. Pounding erupts from the stalls followed by the crunch of splintering wood—a caged animal kicking free of its confinement. I think about crawling through the hay and manure across the floor but figure my getting trampled would be the most likely outcome. So I crouch down, pull my undershirt over my nose and mouth, and scurry in, feeling my way from memory in the blinding blackness.

I trip over something and go down hard. My face smacks against a flank of meaty horsehide. It is Buster, the gelding, already felled by the smoke. I can do nothing for him. He runs with the Spirits now.

Wood splinters again to my right and I find my way to the nearest stall, not certain which one it is. I throw the crossbar and fling open the door. Strawberry, the mule, sits with her legs splayed out on the ground, wide-eyed with urgency. The two other mules lay dead behind her.

"Come on, girl!" I grab her brindled mane and yank her to her feet. She tries to resist but I tell her if she is smart enough to hide from the smoke, then she is smart enough to live. Grudgingly she rights herself and blows past me toward the square of daylight at the open door. I fumble my way down the stalls, throwing every gate I pass, knowing Storm is in the last one. The lowing from the heifer peters down to a faint, guttural buzz and then cuts out completely. I come upon the final stall as the stallion's mighty hoof thunders against the wood. The bolts of the hinges teeter precipitously from their screw-holes, drawn farther from their purchase with every blow.

"Easy boy, do not kick me!" The gate falls open at my touch. Storm is already off and running—I follow his darting tail through the smoke. Charred rafters crash to the ground about me. We leap out into the fresh air as the roof gives way entirely.

Storm bucks and kicks across the dirt, smoke shooting from his nostrils like a dragon in a fairy tale. On my way to the ground, I catch a glimpse of the mule laying flat on her side. All her strength went into getting out, and now she will not get up. I roll over, away from the seething inferno, and land my eyes on Sheriff's house—my house—where along the walls and roofline, the flames have gone to work in earnest.

CHAPTER TWENTY-FIVE

I ring the little bell at the front desk and it shatters the quiet of the lobby. Brunson Stone appears from the inner office, his mouth pursing disapprovingly as he lays eyes upon me. My hat, overcoat, and the pearl-handle Colts are all that I was able to salvage from the fire. I wear the coat over my undershirt and have not yet had the chance to wash the char and smoke from my clothes or skin.

"Can I help you?"

"A room, please."

"Yes, we are at full occupancy at the present. Very sorry."

"We both know you got rooms. Folks been leaving in droves since yesterday. I have money."

"Perhaps you would have better luck at the brothel," he says pointedly.

"Is there a problem here?" A firm voice barks from the stairs. I turn to see Willis, returned to his former glory—impeccable suit, pristine fingernails and trimmed beard—marching toward us. Having discovered him so at ease in his denim and leather the night before, it is the elegant finery that now strikes me as the costume. His face, upon seeing the blackened version of me, swells with grievous concern, but there is a hint of relief behind it, as if my walking around at all is reason to celebrate.

"No problem whatsoever, Mister Willis. Nothing to concern yourself with."

The gambler silences Stone with a halting finger and puts his hand warmly on my shoulder. "Mister Two-Trees, thank God you're all right. I heard what happened. Damn barbaric. This will not stand. How fare you, man?"

"I am alive."

"And what of your livestock?"

"Stallion made it out. Lost the rest."

"Bleeding cowards. Of course you need a room. Stone here will attend to you."

"Well, unfortunately, sir . . . as I was telling the gentleman, we are full-up at the moment."

"Nonsense, Stone. Can't you see this man requires accommodation? Be quick about it."

"Well, it's just that . . ." Stone's voice trails off, as if sharing a secret with his most distinguished customer. "Well, we have a certain reputation to uphold."

Avery Willis places both hands gently on the desk in front of Stone. His brow furrows. "Are you saying that you will not rent to this man?" Willis cocks his ear slightly, negating any chance of mishearing.

"It would," Stone begins, far less confident than he was a few seconds ago, "upset our other guests."

"You mean the white guests," Willis says, dusting a gloved finger across the lip of the inkwell.

"Why, of course, sir."

"I see." The gambler turns as if to leave, his face a sudden rictus of disgust. Then he rushes back to the desk, his left arm flying up and catching Stone's throat in a white-knuckled throttle. He yanks the hotelkeeper down, the side of his face slamming hard against the open ledger on the desk. A tornado of rage bursts forth from Willis, consuming him as he pounds an overhand right fist into the older man's nose—then a second time, and a third, the gambler's face reddening with every blow.

Stone's nose erupts in an explosion of blood. Holding him by the neck, Willis plucks up the inkwell and dumps its oozing contents all over the innkeeper's face, into his sputtering mouth, down the flaming, swollen nostrils of his busted beak.

"Who's the white man now, cocksucker?!" Stone can only wail a shrieking, wordless cry by way of response. But the cyclone of rage from Willis is not yet complete. "You're gonna get this man whatever he needs or so help me God I will cut your scrawny head off. Do you understand?" Stone manages a quivering nod from down on the desk. "Now give him his goddamn key!"

His head still pressed against the ledger, Stone flails an arm back and comes up with the first key he can find. Willis lets go. The hotel man slinks straight to the floor in a whimpering, gruesome heap. The gambler turns to face me, almost embarrassed. He straightens his tie. "I apologize, Mister Two-Trees. I did not mean to imply that you cannot handle your own affairs. Please forgive the step-in. I meant no offense."

"None taken."

Avery Willis nods. His ability to surprise me seems to have no end. "You must join us for supper." And with that he walks off, disappearing up the stairs, past a trembling Cookie, who can do nothing but watch his employer sully further his threadbare carpet. I grab the key off the desk and look down at Stone.

"Send over the tailor," I say, turning for the stairs. "Need some clothes."

I ease back in the tub and let the water work its way up my neck to the base of my skull. It feels good to close my eyes, giving the warmth a chance to venture deep down to my aching muscles. The gray, sooty water reminds me of my last proper bath.

I open my eyes again and stare up at the white-washed ceiling, stained yellow from the cigar smoke of countless wayward travelers. It is hardly a different view than the one from the tub over at Madam Brandywine's, only there the boiling kettle got poured with a smile from Maria and not from Cookie, who complained the whole time how the handle was burning his fingers.

A knock comes weakly at the door. The tailor, I reckon. "Who is it?"

"It's Miss Bichard."

"Just a minute," I say, glancing down at the undeniable nakedness of my situation. I stand and reach for the towel, sloshing the water loudly.

Her voice tightens at the sound. "Oh, I am disturbing you! You are indisposed, please pardon the intrusion."

"Just stay there," I say, scanning the room. My

denims are beyond repair. I step damp-legged into my union suit and open the door with my overcoat draped over my bare chest. Genevieve startles back at the sight.

"Mister . . . Two-Trees. I should go, you are not decent." She stays put. I step back from the door and motion her to enter.

"Please, come in."

"I had heard you were here at the hotel. I am terribly sorry about the circumstances that have brought you here." She has chosen, for her visit, a cornflower dress, one that matches her eyes, which, right now, look red from crying. "It's awful, everything that's happened. I could hardly sleep last night worrying about that poor child who rode all that way from Heavendale, bless his little heart. And then to awaken to the news of your misfortune. I tell you, Mister Two-Trees, it's enough to make me lose faith in humanity."

I peek over at the sideboard where two dusty shot glasses cry out for a bottle. "Sorry I, I have nothing to offer you. I can holler down for something."

"No, I don't want to be any trouble. I've come here out of concern. We are now neighbors, as it were."

"So we are. For a day, anyway."

"What? Why only a day?"

"Tomorrow I ride for Santa Fe. Close out my accounts. Find an agent to sell off Sheriff's place. Nothing for me here anymore."

"That's hardly true." She rubs her hands nervously. In my daily recollections of her, I have credited her a few inches of stature. She is, in fact, a tiny creature, now made smaller by her sense of intrusion into my space. The top clasp of her collar hangs unfastened, providing the slightest glance of lace camisole.

"Where is Willis?" I ask.

"Playing cards. Where else?"

I turn to the door, which yet stands agape.

"Please leave the door open," she says.

I close the door. Her breath quickens. She angles her gaze toward the window. "The child is improving, thank heavens."

"Is that what you came to tell me?" I move toward her, close, until her eyes have no choice but to look up at me in surrender.

"I thought . . . you would . . . like to know."

I kiss her. Our lips melt in a dizzying, electrified embrace. Her hands slide under my coat and up my bare back as I pull her tight against me, every curve of her figure a searing discovery beneath my touch. The overpowering sweetness of her taste—I could devour her. We hold there, an entanglement of desire and raging blood—until the salty river of tears trickles from her delicate cheek to my tongue. She breaks from me.

"We cannot . . . not yet, not here." She settles on the chair and assembles her gown where she has come undone. "Not while I am in the possession of one Avery Willis."

"You are no man's property."

"Avery has funny ideas about that. I have no intention of marrying him. He has asked me and I have avoided answering for as long as I can. Soon he will demand a response. My reputation will be ruined, if it's not already, but I don't care. I simply won't be with him. I can't. I would rather kill myself!" She breaks down, sobbing softly into her fist. I kneel next to her and brush the hair from her face.

"Why would you say something like that?"

"He is not always kind to me. Oh, Mister Two-Trees, he has a violent streak in him, a vicious temper."

"I have seen it."

"Then you know! I fear for my safety, for my very life."

"Has he hurt you?"

"No, but it's only a matter of time. Once I am his wife he can do what he wants to me."

"Then you have to end it."

"I am afraid to. He might kill me on the spot. Or he might be slick about it—murder me on the way home and dump me somewhere out in the desert."

"You say he might go that far, maybe he would. He has a temper—I will give you that. Not a day goes by, Willis don't show me a new color. Hothead-edness aside, though, a man does not get to where Willis is without knowing how to be reasonable. You tell him he does not have your heart, he will not like it, but he just might accept it. He might even leave you here."

"I'm afraid you don't know him like I do, Mister Two-Trees."

"Now on, you call me Harlan."

"Harlan," she says tenderly. A current of un-guarded affection flutters across her face. "It is a nice name."

"Belonged to my father. At least that's what he told Mamma."

"It was his Christian name?"

"Only name he give her." I lean back against the bed. Beyond the windows, the Sangres glow golden brown in the light of the waning day. The sound of chopping and splintering wood echoes from the street below, where a fresh batch of laborers lays siege to the gallows.

She picks up my hand and looks into my eyes. "There is another option."

"What is that?"

"Take me with you."

"What?"

"Take me with you to Santa Fe. We can be together! There is no need to formally break it off with Avery. We'll just light out, the both of us. We'll leave this place and never come back. Who's to stop us?"

"Folks not too happy with me right now. I would hate to mix you up in that. Might be best I move alone."

"Is it that you do not want me?"

"I want you more than I have ever wanted anything in my life."

"I do not fear for my well-being in your protection. In fact, just the opposite."

"I would keep you safe, and you would never starve. On those counts I can give my word. But short of that, I cannot promise you much in the way of high living, at least until I get things sorted."

"You think I care about any of that?"

"Women don't much like going backwards."

"Love is always backwards. That's half the fun." She earns a smile out of me on that one and I give her hand a little squeeze. But then I break and cross to the window. I do not want to get used to her face, not until I know it will greet me with the dawn every morning until I die.

"You would give up your life, and your people, for a fella what cannot even read?"

Her eyes go serious. A stern finger rises to reprimand me. "Now listen here, Harlan. You may have the town fooled that you are some kind of simpleton, but not me. I see right through you. I look into your eyes and I see a man powerful intelligent. Why you or anyone else would ever believe anything to the contrary is beyond me."

I stand before her, called on the carpet like a schoolboy, and I know that this is the way it will be between us, our deepest secrets laid bare.

"I mix my letters up, is all. And my numbers. Always have. Makes reading damn near impossible. Nothing wrong with my vision, though. I got the eyes of a hawk."

"That you do. And lovely ones at that." She turns away, unable to conceal a little smile.

"Are you making fun of me?"

"Heavens, no. I only . . . well, your shyness about your affliction in endearing. I am confident, Harlan, that the only burden with which you are truly afflicted is the curse of being raised in this unenlightened, hayseed town. My own cousin suffered as a child from the very condition you have just described. His parents were at wit's end over what to do. Then word came about a doctor, in San Francisco, no less, who had some bold new treatment. My young cousin was carted off to see him.

He returned home a year later, his nose buried in a book. And do you know what became of him?"

"What?"

"He is a professor of literature at Harvard University."

"No foolin'?"

"Honest injun." And with that, we both bust up laughing. She puts her arm around me, letting her head fall against my shoulder.

"You make me smile, girl."

"Please forgive me for what I am about to say . . . but I feel it was . . . divine providence that brought us here together."

"God did not burn my place down. Men did."

"I do not believe in coincidence. If there is a silver lining to be found in your tragic loss it is that I have been given the chance to make my true feelings known. As have you, yes?"

"Yes."

"Then we are decided. Mister Willis has sent for the coach the morning after next. We have until that time to make our escape. First to Santa Fe to handle your business and then off to San Francisco."

"Slow down now. We cannot just hop on the train together, you and me. Can you ride?"

"Well, I won't fall off, if that's what you mean."

"I'll need to make provisions. We ride at night. That will take some planning, finding you the right horse and whatnot. Leave that to me. You do not talk to anyone until I come find you. We clear on that?"

"As a bell, Mister Two-Trees." And then her mouth finds mine again.

CHAPTER TWENTY-SIX

"The game broke an hour ago," Merle says, sliding a warm beer across the bar to me. "I reckon the gambler's back at the hotel, licking his wounds. It wasn't his night."

"You hear anybody lookin' to unload a pony?" I ask.

"Not offhand, no. But tough times tend to put folks in a selling frame of mind."

"Lost the mule in the fire. Need something that don't spook."

"I'll keep an ear out." Merle picks up his chamois and goes back to his polishing.

The Jewel has settled back into its usual rhythm—a handful of regulars getting a jump on the night's drinking before the sun has even set. The door bangs open and closed again. I feel a sturdy figure move up behind me. I turn to see Big Jack. He removes his hat and nods to me.

"Harlan. I owe you an apology, speaking to you like I did last night. I feel just awful about it. Them folks what is blaming you for any of this are dang fools and I don't care who knows it."

"All right."

Jack spies the empty stool next to me and lays his big doe eyes on me. "Mind if I sit?"

I slide over a hair and Jack plops himself down, relieved. Merle sets up the three shot glasses and uncorks the whiskey.

"Everybody's friends again," Merle says. The door bangs once more and purposeful footsteps click across the floor toward the bar, right for me. It is Bix, the Pinkerton second.

"Afternoon," he says stiffly.

"To you too, sir," Merle counters. "What can I get you?"

"It's him I want," Bix says, nodding at me. I look over from my stool without turning. "We're putting a team together, governor's orders. We're going to hunt down LaForge, bring back the money before they have time to spend it. Dead or alive, his reign of terror's over."

"Tall order," I say.

"Pinkertons doing this job on their own?" Merle asks.

"We got a need for one or two more, someone who knows them hills. Maybe could intercede if the Indians get squirrelly."

"Captain send you in here with that?" I ask.

"Tell you the truth, he's not crazy about it. So don't make me beg."

"You don't have to. I wish you all the luck."

"Look, this was my idea. I figured what better way for a man to clear his name of any involvement than to be part of the team what sets things right."

"So, you come in here for *my* benefit?"

"Not entirely. Truth is . . ." Bix trails off, aware of listening ears. He bends down and barely whispers, "Without you, I don't think we'll ever find them."

"Thank you all the same, but my days of charity are over. Sorry."

Bix straightens again and clears his throat. "Job pays a hundred a day, plus a share of the reward on the Snowman and his gang, plus a percentage of the recovered loot."

Her face comes to me, a flower in the soft morning light. We will need money.

"A share?" I ask.

"That's the deal."

"Where is the captain now?"

Bix steps aside and motions toward the door. I rise and follow him out, Merle and Big Jack tailing behind us.

Outside the Jewel awaits the full complement of armed Pinkerton men, nearly two dozen strong. In the middle, seated atop his horse and eyeing me suspect, is the captain.

"He's in," Bix says.

"He can tend the horses. We leave in an hour." He starts his horse toward the jail and I stop him.

"Captain," I say, allowing my voice to find its full weight. "If I ride it's for an *equal* share. Same as any other man."

The captain glances over his shoulder, but only far enough to catch Bix's eye, not mine. The nod is barely perceptible. Bix spits in his hand and extends it my way. I slap my palm into his.

"Witnessed!" Merle adds, from the steps of the Jewel. But it is the captain who has the last word. He calls over his shoulder as he rides away.

"You defy my orders, I'll shoot you myself."

Casey comes around the corner of the jail, a stack of folded blankets under his arm. "Two per man," he says, doling out a pair to each of the men in the staging area. A cold wind whistles down from the Sangres.

"What about for the horses?" I ask, taking the bundle from him.

"Well, you can always share."

I cinch the blankets behind the saddle pack and pull the rope taut. Storm hates the cold, and likes plunging his hoof into a snowdrift even less. But the slate gray sky to the east tells me the first frost is still a day or two away. So we have our window.

I take stock of the Pinkerton men as they load up with extra socks and enough ammunition to stop a train. Despite their surly grumblings, they retain the aura of professional lawmen, capable, as anyone can be, of the mission at hand. I put our odds at even money, which, short of enlisting the aid of the U.S. Cavalry, is as good as anyone could expect going up against the Snowman's gang.

But the scale of advantage tips in LaForge's favor when I do an honest headcount. With the captain and me, we are twenty, a large enough force to match nearly man for man with the outlaws' numbers, but not so small that we will catch them by surprise. No matter what we do, the Snowman will see us coming. And so will the Dineh.

"Five minutes!" Bix cries, checking his watch against that of the captain as they make their way down the steps of the jail. I climb up on Storm and lead him over to the trough for a final drink. A small, pale figure steps out from the alley to my left, long enough for me to see her, and then retreats hastily to the safety of the shadows. It is Genevieve. I slip down from the saddle and disappear, undetected, into the alley.

"You should not be here," I say.

"You were going to leave without saying good-bye."

"I left word with Cookie. He'd have found you."

"What about us?"

"Our plan has not changed. I have to do this first."

"You speak like it is an errand to the Dry Goods. You most likely will get killed."

"It is good money. We need it. And it is the right thing to do."

"Is there anything I can say to make you stay?" Her eyes puddle with tears.

"This should not take more than two days, one way or the other. Can you stall Willis that long?"

"I'll find a way. I will wait for you."

"There is a chance . . . I will not come back."

"I'll just have to pray that you do." She turns and walks quickly down the alley. I vow here beneath the Spirits and the White Man's God that she will see me again.

* * *

Four minutes later, the team thunders through the center of town toward the west, dead-on into the sights of the big eye as it retreats behind the cragged peaks of the Sangres.

Our departure is void of pageantry. The curious glances of a few scattershot observers seem to convey a sense of irritation at the noise more than any aspirations that this solemn band of lawmen, of which I find myself a part, represents any hope of vengeance or restitution. That would require optimism—of which the bankrupted souls of the Bend are fresh out.

But there is one spectator who surveys our exodus with fitting reverence, as if he alone comprehends the gravity and complexity of our mission. Avery Willis.

He stands at the open window of his suite in his shirtsleeves, a cigar perched gently between his fingers. My eye catches his and he offers a gracious tip of his head. I return the salutation and resume my place in formation.

How small the town seems now. The buildings fly by until all that lies between the team and the chalky wasteland of open desert is Otis Chandler's house. As we ride toward its fence, the front door bursts open and Chandler himself charges out, wailing with grief. In his arms he carries the rag doll body of a boy, maybe all of fifteen, dead.

"Whoa!" The captain shouts, shooting up his arm in an L-shaped position that stops the team on a dime.

"Look what they did to my boy!" As Chandler lumbers down the paving stones toward us, I see the mortal results of the child's injuries. His head is sticky with dried blood where hair used to be and his face and neck bear the deep, plum-purple of violently ruptured veins. "Savages killed my boy!"

"What happened to him?" the captain demands.

"He never came home from the stables. I went looking, found him out by the hay yard. Oh, his poor mother. Forgive me, son. Dear Jesus, forgive me!"

Bix weaves his bay up next to me. "Who is that?" he asks.

"Stable boy."

"Looks like they strangled him 'fore they took his scalp. See them dark bruises across his neck?"

"Yeah."

Chandler crumples to his knees, choking out tears. A woman howls from inside the house, her unfettered grief drowning out the gentler sobs of small, frightened children.

"Your kind did this!" Chandler jabs a finger at me, spitting out the words. "Damn you all, damn every last red-faced one of you!"

CHAPTER TWENTY-SEVEN

Caliche Bend fades from view like a distant, dying star. We cross the desert toward Heavendale, hoping to pick up the Snowman's trail before sundown. The tight formation of horses slackens on the open tundra. I spot Delmer, the crank-gunner, struggling to keep up. The labored breath of his charcoal mare steams in the chilling air.

"She's overloaded," I say, pulling alongside.

"No shit," he says. "The stand alone weighs thirty pounds, the barrels another fifty. Then I got a good six cases of munitions. This old nag didn't bargain for that."

"Headed uphill. Going to get a lot steeper too," I warn him.

"You travel light," he says, noticing my spartan load.

"I do not own much."

"Say, take the tripod, will ya?" He starts to pick at the rope that holds the folding iron stand.

"I will not carry anything you point at Indians."

Delmer sighs, his wiry shoulders slumping. "How

'bout the saddlebags then? Nothing but coffee and hardtack."

"Give 'em here." His thin arms begin to hoist the leather bags and I reach over and do the rest.

"Much obliged."

Up ahead, Bix blows into his fist to keep warm. "Any sign, Captain?"

"We'll pick it up," Mulgrew says without turning. "Every man leaves a trace. I used to ferret out deserters on nothing more than a piss stain."

The open desert gives a man time to think. Every passing mile groans from the weight of all that has transpired—a swirl of fire and screaming livestock and the ugly voices of a town betrayed. Even the beauty of her face as I remember it in the hotel light grows leaden with the thought of how I will care for her. I puzzle over each thought until I have whittled it down to the bone. And after a while there is nothing but the desert. But that's when the new thoughts have time to peek out from their darkness. Sometimes the hardest puzzle to solve is the one you did not even know was there.

I fall in next to Bix. "Something sits wrong with me, Lieutenant."

"What's that?" he says.

"Snowman's gang hit the bank in Agua Verde at eleven-thirty in the morning."

"So?"

"What time they hit Heavendale?"

"Ten after twelve."

"That's forty minutes."

"What's your point?"

"Story is, Snowman does all the blasting himself, that right?"

"Well, any fella can hurl a stick of dynamite, rig up a booby trap and whatnot, but when it comes time for the precise stuff, it's true, all reports say that LaForge handles the vaults directly."

"Agua Verde to Heavendale is about fifteen miles as the crow flies. That's a lot of ground to cover in forty minutes."

"Hmm. Nearly impossible. Even at a full gallop he'd just make it."

"And ain't no horse gallop forty minutes."

"Captain," Bix says, trotting forward, "we need to stop."

Bix draws an X in the sand. "This is Agua Verde," he says. Then he scratches another X about a yard away. "Heavendale's here."

"How many men hit the first bank?" I ask.

"The boy counted six," Mulgrew says, unsure where this is going and more than a little annoyed. The rank-and-file Pinkertons look on with modest interest, using the break to smoke or take some water for the horses.

"But by the time they got to Heavendale," Bix says, "their numbers were three times that."

"Makes sense," the captain says. "Heavendale's a bigger town with a bigger bank. You'd need men stationed outside, plus the ones in with the vault."

"So where'd the other fellas come from, the extra twelve?" Bix asks.

"Could've been hiding out in Heavendale, waiting for LaForge to get there."

"Could be," Bix says. "But that still don't explain how LaForge covered that ground. And the time-line don't fit with the train schedule, so that's out."

"Look," says the captain, growing frustrated, "he can tell us how he pulled off his magic trick when he's standing on the gallows. All this speculation is wasting daylight. The move is to go the last place we know the Snowman was and pick up his scent there. That's Heavendale."

"Excuse me, Captain," I say.

"What is it?"

"That display we witnessed around the jail last week, Snowman's gang riding in circles like that, getting everybody riled up. How many riders you count?"

"Twenty souls exactly."

"And how many hit the bank in Heavendale?"

"Seventeen, maybe eighteen, we're getting con-flicting reports."

"Point is, less than twenty."

"What are you getting at, Two-Trees?"

"There's two, three men unaccounted for. I'm saying six men ride out from Agua Verde, full gallop. LaForge is one of them. Somewhere along the way, they stop. Change onto fresh horses. LaForge and those six carry on to Heavendale. Meanwhile, the two or three who are waiting lead the spent horses up into the Sangres to the meeting place."

"Could two men corral six horses?" the captain asks.

"If they know what they're doing, easy."

"LaForge's gang are all solid horsemen," Bix says. "I have no doubt they could do it."

Captain Mulgrew lets out a dissatisfied grunt more suited to a bull than a man. "You don't just stand around with a half dozen horses and no one notice, even in the open desert. The train conductors would've seen something on the morning run. There's hardly a tree trunk in this infernal wasteland, much less a hiding place smack in the middle that's big enough for six goddamn horses."

I know the midpoint well. It is where I killed Jed Barnes. I take the stick from the lieutenant and jab it down on the line, halfway between the Xs. "Hatchet Rock," I say. "You could hide an army regiment behind it, no one see a thing."

The captain grunts again and Bix pulls him aside. I overhear their conversation. "We're still an hour from Heavendale, Captain. But we can be at Hatchet Rock in ten minutes. If we find something, we might could get the jump on them."

"And if we're wrong we lose a day."

"They had to change horses, Captain. No way around it."

The captain gnashes down on what's left of his cigar and hurls the stub into the dust. He grinds it beneath his boot heel. And then, glowering over at me, he says, "You better be right about this, Injun."

In the gray half-light of the waning day, Hatchet Rock juts from the desert floor like a slab of tombstone granite. The thread of railroad track winnows off to the horizon, a far cry from the pounding lifeblood that still echoes in my recent memory.

Storm remembers too. The stallion opens up his stride as we cross the rails.

"Champing at the bit," Delmer says.

"He knows this place. We hunt out here."

Circling around the back side of the rock, we fall in behind the captain, forming a single line to minimize our tracks. Reaching the jagged end of the far western corner, we dismount entirely and proceed on foot.

"Bix, you and the Injun follow me," the captain says. "Rest of you stay put, keep the horses out of it." My eyes stay with the ground as we tread lightly toward the rock. I know what to look for. Animals leave their marks, same as men do. But a tracker needs soft eyes. The signs have to come to you, not the other way around. Presumption is nothing but ego, and it will steer you right off a cliff, or leave you standing in the wind with your pecker in your hand.

"Nothing but windswept caliche," the captain says.

"Horseshit."

The captain's chest expands as he sucks in the air to unload on me. "What the hell did you just say?"

"Horseshit. I smell it." I follow the scent to the base of the rock, where drifts of sand have settled. Clumps, like buried stones, rise above the surface, a quarter-inch at most. But a quarter-inch is enough. I poke at the mound with my boot and it gives way, betraying a soft, spongy presence beneath the sand. I drag my toe back toward me, smearing a greenish-brown stain across the white surface—dried manure, caked with hay. "They tried to bury it."

"Captain, look at this," Bix says, running his finger along a crack in the rock. "Somebody wedged a knot of rope down into the crevice." Mulgrew walks over to inspect it. "Looks like they cut it in a hurry."

"I think we found ourselves a corral," the captain says. "Now let's figure out where they went." The three of us step backwards from where we stand, clearing the area like we had stumbled upon a sleeping bear.

"Wind's been too heavy," Bix says.

I take a knee and still cannot see it so I drop to my belly and gaze out across the desert floor. The ground is trying to tell me what it knows, but my brain will not let it in. And then, for all my faults and trespasses, the Spirits grant me a fond, unexpected memory—the bighorn. That day out in the foothills, so many years ago, Sheriff and I had stood twenty yards from the herd and been ignorant of their proximity. It was only upon gaining some distance that I was able to detect a subtle flash of movement from the blessed creature whose stuffed head hung on Sheriff's wall until yesterday.

"Hold on." I get up and stride toward the massive boulder. "Gimme a hand here," I say, finding a narrow toehold. Bix appears behind me and throws his weight into mine as I propel myself upward along the rock face. The cold stone, a stark, sobering reminder of the approaching winter, passes beneath my fingers. I grapple my way to the top and will myself over the upper ledge into a cool, rippling autumn breeze that crackles with life from the farthest reaches of the valley. Her song sings to me, honing my senses to razor sharpness. I peer over the edge and am slapped in the face with the glaring signature of the hunted. The gentle, undulating imperfections scream out to me from beneath a dusty blanket of sand, like the faint ruts from a wagon after an hour of snow.

The churned hoofprints swirl at the captain's feet and proceed north, finding focus as the horses built speed, before branching off into two streams. One fires straight toward Heavendale. But the other, lighter of step—evidence of free-running horses—shoots off toward the mountains.

Rising from my knees, I follow the river of ruffled sand with my finger as it winds north, across the valley, up past the foothills and into the Sangres, until it kisses the sky at a point where the mighty range shows the faintest glitch in her armor. Two peaks rip from each other, leaving a steep scar of a ravine between them.

"There," I say. "That's where they will try to cross."

Bix breaks away from his private meeting with the captain and comes over to address the rest of us where we stand, huddled by the horses. "Here's what's we're going to do—divide up into two squads. Casey, Two-Trees, and the Frey brothers, y'all are with me. Rest of you ride with the captain into Heavendale and pick up the tracks from there."

"We split up, we weaken our numbers," I say. "Why even mess with Heavendale?"

"Triangulation," the captain says sternly as he walks over. "One team follows one trail, the other picks up the second: We should meet in the same place."

"Which team are we?" Casey asks as the men begin to splinter off into their respective details.

"We go straight into the hills," Bix says. "In the dark."

CHAPTER TWENTY-EIGHT

My dearest Caroline,
   *I write this by the first light of dawn near a
little stream somewhere in the Sangre Mountains.
We slept but an hour and will push off again as
soon as the men finish their coffee. Once again,
Captain Mulgrew has proved a worthy tracker.
He picked up the Snowman's trail outside of
Heavendale on nothing more than a cigarillo butt
stubbed out on a rock. Then, every two hundred
yards or so, sure enough, we'd find a horse patty
or a stain of tobacco juice and that was enough to
bring us to where we are now. I don't know when
I will be able to write again. We are hot on the
heels of the Snowman's gang and moving like the
wind. But don't you worry about me. We have
reinforcements waiting for us farther up in the
mountains. And with the firepower we're carrying,
these outlaws won't know what hit them. Give little
Toby a kiss for me.*

      Yours always,
      Delmer.

CHAPTER TWENTY-NINE

Bix pulls the spyglass down from his eye and offers it to me. "You want to take a look?"

"No, I see them." The captain's team skirts the canyon along a thread of cut trail about a mile down the ridge from where we sit. They ride single file, painfully slow.

"I did not expect them till after noon," Bix says. "They must've gone hell-bent through the night. Don't know why they're creeping along now."

"Sangres will do that to you. One misstep and that's all she wrote." Between our position and that of the captain, the canyon forms a bottleneck where two sheer granite walls leave little more than a horse-width of wiggle room through which to pass. They should hit it in about five minutes, and then they will wind upward through the ravine to the clearing just below us.

"That's a narrow bitch of a squeeze they're heading for," Bix says. "Glad we came up the back side. Your jittery stallion would've bucked you into that wall."

"Only if your face spooked him."

Bix snorts and hands me his flask. I take a nip. The whiskey, warm and sweet, spreads through my belly. "Much obliged," I say.

We have been here for an hour, hiding out among the boulders on a steep, narrow slope, well protected by overgrowth. Casey dozes on a flat patch behind me and I cannot say I mind having a break from his prickly temperament. The Frey brothers, a Germanic, towheaded trio of rooftop snipers, seem to be in a contest of who can spit the most and say the least, but their quiet is conducive to the greater good of our purpose. We have still not caught sight of the bandits or their horses, but the droppings are fresher, a few hours at most. And unless the Snowmen have abandoned their mounts for billy goats, their only course is surely deeper up the pass.

"Where's the scout?" he asks.

"Just below that ridge on the left." I spotted the Navajo scout just after dawn, guiding his pony along the tree line. And he made sure we knew that he saw us too. Since then, he has kept mostly out of sight, but he is still up there, watching with a cautious eye, ready to dash off and report our numbers to the chief and his bloodthirsty son.

"How old you make him?"

"Sixteen, seventeen at most."

"Stalking us all by his lonesome? He best not get any closer."

"Oh, he can't kill us. But he could run off and fetch the ones who could."

"You let me know if he moves. I best signal the captain." Bix produces a small mirror like was used on the rooftop and angles it into the sun. He flicks his wrist three times, sending the beam in the captain's direction, but Mulgrew turns at that exact moment, distracted by a disturbance to his rear. Delmer's horse balks at the tapering gap in the rocks and pushes back. The wiry Pinkerton wrestles the reins and tries to force the nag through.

"Fucking Delmer. That old stepper belongs in the glue factory instead of under his scrawny ass. I'll fire off a shot, let 'em know we're here."

The lieutenant draws his pistol, pointing it sky-ward, when I dive up and snatch it. "No!"

"What the hell, Harlan?"

"Something's wrong."

"What? What is it?"

Through the shifting breeze, a thin trace of an odor arouses my senses. It is familiar, a strong and pungent burst that I cannot put a name to. "You smell that?"

"I don't smell anything."

And then, all at once, I connect it in my mind. "Oh my God."

"What?"

"Quick match." The words barely cross my lips before the explosion obliterates the air. A pile of rocks belches from the front end of the crevice, laying waste to everything in its path. The captain simply vanishes before my eyes, vaporized in a puff of pink mist. He is the lucky one.

The captain's retinue bears the brunt of the shock wave, a violent torrent laden with stones the size of cannonballs that leaves a trail of carnage in its wake.

Through the choking, black storm of airborne earth I see a headless horse stagger sideways, drunkenly trying to right itself. An ash-covered human torso slides off its saddle, leaving a pair of twitching legs in the stirrups. Dirt and debris rain from the sky, crashing like hail against the hard ground of the canyon.

The overwhelming stench of cordite poisons every breath—mining-grade TNT. A pitiful, wailing chorus begins to issue from the fog—the sound of old men commiserating in slow, agonized death. But these are not old men. They are strong, vital soldiers cut down in their prime by a mad, ruthless genius who lured them straight into his web.

And then the second blast comes. The *far* end of the crevice erupts in a hellfire of fragmented boulders, thrusting the decimated ranks forward into the smoldering crater of the first explosion. The shock wave ripples up the side of the canyon, this time in our direction, knocking me backward into the reeling brothers. Chunks of charred horseflesh fall from the sky along with dismembered human limbs wrapped in singed, black wool.

Bix lies across my chest, Casey entwined somewhere at my feet. The six of us—a snarled knot of boot leather and sweated flannel—begin to kick free, pawing over each other to untangle ourselves. I get to my knees and scramble to the nearest boulder. Bix joins me and we peer over the edge, down into the aftermath of the massacre.

"A trap. A goddamn trap!" he hisses.

And what a trap it was—a perfect killing machine. With no open space to siphon off its power, the force of the detonation multiplied against the sheer, immobile sides of the rock face in the cleaved, shoulder-width gorge. The forward ranks of the pursuing posse walked headlong into the first blast, while the second charge at the backside annihilated the retreating survivors.

Bix stares down at the wreckage, shaking his head in stunned disbelief. "And there, but for the grace of God, go I."

The youngest of the Frey boys, praying softly in German behind me, punctuates the lieutenant's sentiment. "Bust out that spyglass," I say. "Maybe somebody made it."

"Be a bloody, sorry stump if he did," Casey says.

Bix yanks the spyglass to full extension and scans the smoke for the living. A flicker of movement draws my eye along the slope to our left. It is the scout, meeting my gaze with a face of uncomprehending horror. He was probably a baby when the mines were last in use and has never heard a boom louder than thunder. But now, in the course of half a minute, he has learned the full extent of the White Man's technical powers and the callous depravity with which he is wont to unleash it.

The boy seems to find some small comfort in my face—and understanding of common blood—but is left clueless as to how I could align myself with the trouser-wearers. Then his face grows awash with a new, sudden terror. He points toward the canyon.

"Holy shit, we got some live ones," Bix announces. "I see Baker, he's moving. And there's Joe! He's hurt bad, but he ain't dead."

I cannot bring my eyes away from the Dineh boy. His pointing continues as he backpedals and finally ducks behind the rocks and over the nearest ridge. I follow the line of his finger and realize that the cause of his fresh horror was not the bloodshed at the bottom of the gorge, but the approaching danger at the canyon's upper edge. Across the ridge, a line of men nearly twenty strong and toting rifles comes over the top and takes aim at the survivors. Fish in a barrel.

"That's them," I say. "That's the gang."

"Good God," Bix says. "They're lookin' to finish 'em."

"Like hell," Casey growls, slinging his rifle off his shoulder. A volley of gunfire kabooms from across the canyon as the Snowman's henchmen unleash their weapons down into the gorge.

The Frey brothers need no prodding to do what they were put on this earth to do—shoot guns. Three rifles crack from behind me, Bix and Casey joining in with their thirty-aughts.

I drop behind the boulder and come back up, pistol blazing. The bandits produce such a racket with their own guns that they do not, at first, pick up on ours, until one of them drops, then another. And then the faces look out across the canyon— faces and outfits I recognize from the bank, from the campsite, from that taunting, circular exhibition around the jail. Their confusion is short-lived. Their weapons soon turn in our direction.

"Fan out, goddammit!" Bix shouts. The brothers scurry off to the right and take up positions along a fallen tree. I dive left, bullets zinging past me close enough to hear before ricocheting off the rocks. The entire canyon descends into an unholy cacophony of thunder, every shot echoing a hundredfold down the length of the giant, stone coffin. Pinned where I lay, I can see down to the canyon floor.

A figure springs forth from a shadowy crack in

the rock face. He holds a double twelve and cranes his neck upward to bark a command at his associates. "Don't shoot me by accident, you idjits!" A bandage around his head protects an injured right ear. *Percy, the one I winged up at the campsite. Of course. The fuse man.* Someone close to the charge had to light the quick match. He has probably been down there for two days, waiting. And now, methodically, one by one, he walks up to each dying Pinkerton, ready to put a slug through his chest. Boom. Boom. He works his way down the trail of wounded men. The ones already dead get a slug for good measure.

The bandits use the emergence of their compadre below to concentrate their efforts on us. Bullets careen off the boulders, eager for soft flesh. My only view is down at the swath of blood and body parts. Combing my eyes to the tail end of the line, I see a crowbait nag slumped against the rock, her front legs blown clean off, tongue lolling almost comically to the side. A pair of human hands appear underneath her—just a flash of ghostly white, bony fingers—and then vanish again into the dark recess beneath the animal's carcass. The crank gun and its assorted pieces lay scattered nearby.

"Delmer's alive." I say. "He's hiding under that dead nag."

"We gotta get him out," Bix says.

"I will go," I say. "But you need to make a right mighty stink with them rifles or I won't get ten feet."

"We got you covered, Two-Trees." Bix rolls on his back and shouts toward the others. "On my go, we are up and blastin'. Be precise. Pick your man and put him down!"

"Got that right," Casey says.

"Yah," agrees the eldest Frey, echoing the sentiment of his nodding brothers.

A volley of gunfire cracks from across the canyon, skidding off the boulders behind us in all directions. We press flat against the dirt where we lay and wait for a lull in the onslaught. A break comes, and with it the sounds of men shouting commands and chambering fresh ammunition.

"Get ready to run like the wind, Two-Trees," Bix says, jamming every bullet he can into his rifle until it will take no more. I let out a breath. I am the Spirits' to guide. "Now!" he shouts.

The four of them spring up, surrendering their positions in an all-or-nothing gamble for the lives of a skinny crank-gunner and the half-blood Navajo who is fool enough to go after him.

I leap from the rocks and throw myself down the slope. The ground sails beneath me. I focus on nothing but the next footstep and where it will land, willing myself not to stumble.

More shouting rings out from the Snowmen, this time laced with urgency, as they scramble from the open cliff to the protection of the rocks along the ridge. A man screams, then a blur of color whizzes past the corner of my vision. A second later comes the thud of the bandit's body slamming onto the canyon floor. Percy pauses from his execution duty to look behind him at his fallen cohort.

The ground beneath me starts to level as he turns and I bring up the pistol. His eyes narrow, the door of recognition pounding open, his memory aflame.

"Son of a bitch!" he howls, raising the shotgun.

In one fluid motion I stiffen to a sudden stop, take dead aim, and squeeze the trigger. A small red dot appears on his forehead as the back of his skull explodes in soupy ropes of blood. His legs take a moment to get the message and then give out.

I sprint past him and slide to my knees beside the fallen nag. "Delmer! Come on." I reach under the horse and find what feels like a woman's ankle. Delmer flails at the touch, kicking and panicked like a cornered badger.

"No! No!" His legs churn in the dust as he tries to crawl away. I get a good grip on his belt and yank him back toward me. He rolls over, his stunned, terrified eyes meeting mine.

"Two-Trees!" he yells. "I can't hear nothin'. I'm deaf." I grab him by the shirt and pull him up to me. His whole body trembles.

"Can you run?" I say, slow and deliberate.

"Run. I can run."

"Stay close." I get him to his feet and turn back toward the hill. A fog of rifle smoke pools among the boulders where the Pinkertons lay down the covering fire that keeps us alive. When I glance back at Delmer, I find him cradling the gleaming rotary of barrels from the Gatling.

"Forget the crank gun," I say. Delmer kicks the crank's stand in my direction and throws me a box of munitions. I know he cannot hear me, but when he levels those cold eyes at me I know he understands what I am saying.

Delmer shakes his head. "You want to live or not?" he says.

CHAPTER THIRTY

I load what munitions I can carry and turn back from the fallen nag. A thunderstorm of gunfire bellows from the top of the ridge, but it is not meant for me or Delmer. The bandits have regained the upper hand, flushing the threadbare Pinkerton squad from the boulders and sending them into retreat. Bix sprints down the canyon slope in our direction followed closely by Casey, firing his rifle one-handed at the advancing gang who venture from the safety of the ridge, smelling blood.

Last to abandon the boulders are the Frey brothers. The heavyset middle boy charges from the rocks, only to catch a scatter gun in the ribs and lose his footing. He falls hard to the ground. The brazen youngest wails in horror at the sight of his injured kin and bursts forth to help him, stepping headfirst into a swarm of flying lead. The boy's skull snaps violently sideways, his eyes rolling white in their sockets. He drops dead where he stands.

I let my armload fall to the ground and draw

both pistols. Darting out into the open, I move left, unloading both cylinders into the pack of marauding outlaws. I disrupt their offensive long enough for Jacob, the oldest of the siblings, to spring from his purchase and scoop up his wounded brother, who dazedly finds the strength to keep his legs churning. The youngest boy is too far gone to consider.

Delmer skids to his knees behind me and starts to assemble the crank barrel into its swivel. Bix barely slows as he passes me, grabbing Delmer by the collar and yanking him up.

"Run, Delmer! Run!" Casey hustles past me after Bix and I snatch up a Winchester rifle from the dirt—it looks like the one the captain carried. Thick, acrid smoke plumes from the barrel as I work the lever, pumping rounds into the loose cluster of outlaws. They know better than to hug too close. I aim for the middle and keep firing until the group splinters and I am looking at their backs.

The brothers stumble down the slope, the heavier one wheezing, his skin white as a bedsheet. He is losing blood. I duck my shoulder beneath his arm and lift the left side. The three of us scamper along the trail, Bix and the others bobbing ahead. Voices rise behind us as the shooting trickles to sporadic, ineffectual spurts. We are out of range. The shattering silence of the aftermath provides the outlaws an opportunity to regroup and affords our meager numbers the chance to do the same. The peace will be short-lived, I fear.

As we trudge forth, the steep, barren cliffs of the canyon give way to the pine-covered hills that roll back southward toward Heavendale. We find Bix and Casey hunkered down behind a knotted trunk just inside the canopy.

Delmer collapses on all fours behind them, sucking in huge gulps of air. "I'm deaf! I'm deaf!" he cries.

Jacob speaks softly to his brother in German, but the brother's steps have slackened and we are mostly dragging him when he slides off my shoulder into the soft pine needles next to Delmer.

"Hans. Hans!" Jacob falls to his knees, cradling his brother's head in his hands. Hans gurgles a weak bubbling breath and then his eyes gloss over. His breathing stops. Casey aims his rifle back into the canyon, scanning the far slope for movement, but the bandits have withdrawn from view.

"I'm sorry, Jacob," Bix says, removing his hat. I remove mine as well. "We'll get your brother's body out of that canyon too. Just can't do it now." Jacob says something else to his brother, his voice cracking. Tears cascade down his cheeks, forging a clean path through the dust and smoky grime from the firefight.

Bix pulls at my shoulder and we drift toward the tree, letting the brothers have their private moment. We replace our hats and crouch down behind the trunk, where Casey keeps sentry over the mouth of the canyon.

"I did not see him. Did you?" I ask.

"Who?" Bix says.

"LaForge."

"Can't say I would know him by sight."

"Stands about six foot, maybe an inch over. Black hair. Fancies the color blue."

"I saw no such cocksucker," Casey says.

"Me neither," says Bix. "Not among them what came at us."

"Then he must be over the ridge, with the horses," I say.

"And the loot," Bix says. "I reckon the Snowman cares more for protectin' them saddlebags than he do his own men."

"What about *our* horses?" Casey says. "Them sumbitches likely to steal 'em, eat 'em, or both."

"You just keep that rifle pointed up at them boulders," Bix says. "Anyone crosses the ridge toward our stock, you cut 'em where they stand. And if they come this way, you do the same."

"Aye, Lieutenant."

"They come this way, we are in trouble," Bix says, confiding in me as he turns.

"They will come," I say. "Too few of us left not to finish off."

A hand tugs at my trouser leg. Delmer sits there on his haunches, looking up at me, scared. "Say something, Two-Trees. I hear a ringin'." He shouts his words, unable to regulate his speech.

I pull him to his feet to hush him up. "You will get your hearin' back, Delmer. You are gun-deaf, is all."

His eyes light up as I speak. "I hear you!" he says. "I think it's coming back. Say something else."

The canopy of trees shifts in the swaying breeze. Sunlight streams through the branches and dances across the fallen pine needles where Jacob Frey closes his brother's eyes with a final brush of his palm.

"Are we out of danger, Two-Trees?" Delmer asks. Something in the wind, a wisp of sound, sends the hair on the back of my neck to full attention. A patch of sunlight blooms over the chest of the fallen brother, only to be invaded by the shadow of a human figure. I turn and find myself staring into the muzzle of my old Spencer rifle.

"No," I say.

Jacob sees the shadow too and, drawing his pistol, spins toward the trees behind us. A flash of brown sizzles the air. Jacob gasps and slumps forward, run clean through by the Dineh arrow. Three brothers dead in five minutes.

"Easy," I say. Bix and Casey pivot. Ahiga stands in full view, unguarded by trees. For protection he has with him two dozen armed Dineh, their faces painted for death—a war party. They filter through the trees, revealing their numbers slowly. I raise my arms in surrender. Bix and Casey do the same and by then Delmer has figured it out as well.

Ahiga keeps the Spencer trained at my head. The young scout who spotted us earlier now kisses the string of his bow tight against his lips, his arrow itching to fling forth into Casey's belly.

Letting the Colts drop to the dirt, I step away from the holster, careful to keep my movements slow and deliberate. The thud of guns hitting the ground follows in short order. Only when we are completely removed from our weapons does Ahiga step to the side, letting the chief clomp forward on his pony.

The old silver-hair looks us over and then sighs, disappointed. The irritation he feels at our not possessing whatever it is he is searching for will hardly be salved by our imminent slaughter. He raises a hand, instructing his warriors to take aim.

A chorus of bowstrings groans to within its final ounce of tension. It is cold comfort that when that hand falls again I will be one of the lucky ones to take it from a rifle.

"Wait," I say. And that is when I step forward to talk to the chief.

The thing about an old silver-hair, his face will tell you less what he is thinking than the snakiest riverboat gambler who ever bluffed his way down the Mississippi. I do not know how long I stand there, watching his inscrutable eyes mull over my offer, only that the burning in my triceps means my arms have been up long enough. I put them down.

Ahiga, the third man in our conference, spits and looks to his father, unconvinced. But the chief nods his head and turns back to his pony. Mounting with the agility of a rider half his age, he throws up a palm, the exact gesture as before, only now it inexplicably carries a different meaning. All at once, the warriors lower their weapons and retrace their paths back into the forest, leaving only Ahiga. He shakes his head and pulls his face close to mine. "If you are wrong about this, brother, I will slit you open and feed your insides to the wolves while you watch." With that he turns and sprints off after the rest of his party.

"What the hell did you just do?" Bix says with astonishment as I return to him and the others at the fallen tree.

"Gave him what he wanted," I say.

CHAPTER THIRTY-ONE

We drag Jacob and his brother up against the fallen tree and cover them best we can with branches, no defense against the coyotes, true, but maybe it buys us an hour or two before the vultures get wind of a tasty dinner.

The bodies of our dead, some just fragments of flesh and bone, are the furthest things from my mind, but they will have to be dealt with eventually. Not now, though. There is no time. I pick up the heavy cylinder from the crank gun and turn toward Delmer. He sits on the tree trunk, rolling a cigarette between thin, trembling fingers. "Delmer, what exactly can you do with this?"

Delmer looks at me and strikes a match. The paper flares orangey-red as he sucks the smoke into his lungs and expels it into the air. A wave of calmness befalls him, underpinned by a confidence I have thus far not seen in the diminutive Pinkerton. "Shit, son. I'm not on this team for my muscle."

"What's the best range for it?"

"The Bulldog Repeater is most effective between ten and fifty yards," Delmer says.

"Where you thinking?" Bix says.

"That boulder there," I say, pointing to an out-cropping of rock inside the canyon about a hundred yards from where we stand.

"That'll work," Delmer says.

"Best get that thing primed and ready, Delmer," Bix says.

"Oh, she'll be ready."

"How much time you think we'll have, once it starts?" Bix asks.

"I reckon thirty seconds or so," I say.

Bix clucks his tongue and lets out a sigh. He does not care for the odds. I cannot say I blame him. "Sure would be nice to have a full minute."

"That it would."

"Forget the tripod, Delmer." Bix says. "You can put her on the short sticks. One less thing to carry."

"You read my mind, Lieutenant."

Bix looks over at Casey. "How 'bout it, Case? You ready to run?" Casey dumps a carton of bullets into his coat pocket and slides the bayonet over the tip of his rifle. He snaps it into place.

"Good a day as any to die."

"Well," Bix says, checking the rounds in his pistol and rifle before slinging a heavy case of Gatling magazines over his shoulder. "Better to get shot than scalped." I suspect the lieutenant is right about that, but death spends the same no matter how you sell it. "We go on your say-so, Harlan."

Up above, the cold, lifeless sun retreats behind the wintering sky, taking my shadow with it. A thick, gray blanket covers both earth and heavens. The vanishing division between the two beckons by way of a screeching condor's call. I close my eyes and go to work with my ears.

The woman stands before me in some unfamiliar doorway, holding our dark child to her breast. I push the thought of her out of my head. If I survive the next hour, I suspect I will see her one more time at most, and then never again. Such is the clarity that comes in the stillness before the slaughter.

A hollow, rasping wind holds steady. The only other sound is the pounding blood in my ears. I focus my hearing on the ridge, demanding all of my senses to detect the slightest corruption of the silence. And then it comes, whirling at first, concealing its source as the sound waves ricochet about the canyon walls. But then I realize that the noise—a haunting, high-pitched yelp—emanates not from one direction, but from two. The Navajo have split, surrounding their quarry and approaching from opposite corners of the range. The faint *pop-pop-pop* of a rifle echoes from over the ridge, followed by the distant boom of a twelve-gauge. Indeterminate men's voices fill the spaces between gunfire, all of it against the swelling, repetitive din of the Dineh war cry. Bix utters an opinion shared by all of us, and by anyone who has ever heard that terrifying sound. "Good God, it's awful."

The crescendo of noise on the backside of the ridge, out of our view, builds to a fever pitch. The tide of thunderous gunfire finally drowns out the warriors' bloodthirsty howls, only to succumb to the piercing screams of grown men as they endure the horrors of their own flesh being ripped from their bodies.

"Hold," I say. "Not yet." I squint toward the ridge, awaiting the final visual confirmation before signaling the start of our maneuver. All at once, like a rising phoenix, the mass of white gun smoke fills the air, drifting upward, lipping over the ridge toward the sky.

"Now!" I say.

We spring from behind the tree and, burdened with the weight of all the crank gun munitions we can carry, sprint for the outcropping of boulder. The cacophony explodes as we enter the canyon proper, lending cover for the jangling of our bullets and bones that accompanies our mad dash for position. I see only the rock. It bounces larger in my vision as I run until I am able to dive for the base of it. A body lands on top of me, iron magazines digging into my back.

We huddle in an uncertain mass for a moment and then I hear Bix's voice through the noise. "Delmer?"

"Here."

"Me too," Casey adds. I squirm free and meet Bix's eye. All present and accounted for. Clutching the Winchester, I peer around the edge of the rock. Smoke consumes the top of the ridge, but the fighters—neither white man nor native—have yet to crest the summit. Delmer, now sure of his range, makes his final adjustments to the Gatling, turning the sight screws with precise clicks.

"We ought to spread out," Bix says. "Casey, you and Harlan make for them rocks yonder."

"Who's gonna load the crank?" I say.

"Ain't my first time as gunner's mate. I need you two laying down cover."

"We'll do more than lay it down," Casey says, trundling past me and scampering behind a tall obelisk of sandstone a few yards ahead.

"We are blind here, Harlan. We need your eyes as well. They got numbers on us, no sense in letting them have time to adjust."

"All right, then. I will call out when to throw it. Oh, and Delmer," I say, almost as an afterthought, "if you cut down any of them Dineh, even by accident, them what is left will kill us for sure . . . . Okay, then."

I am about to roll back to the row of stones behind us when Delmer stops me. "You got a smoke rolled up? I'm all out."

"The smoke will give you away."

"I won't light it. I shoot better with something to chaw on."

"It's true. He does," Bix says. I find my last cigarette and hand it to Delmer.

"Much obliged," Delmer nods. I squeeze his shoulder.

Bix whacks my arm. "Go on now. See you on the other side."

I crawl back quick across the dirt and tuck up behind a tawny slab of siltstone. Casey crouches with his rifle to my right. Bix and Delmer are between us and the Snowmen, poised to hoist the crank. We are spaced enough apart so that a bad miss from the charging outlaws will not take out one of us by mistake. In a perfect world, we should be at different elevations, further confusing the enemy, but this formation will have to do. We are out of time.

Pistol shots ring out from the top of the ridge. The raw clarity of the tone—free of the distorted echo found in distant gunfire—tells me the bandits have crested the nearest ridge. It also means they have depleted their rifles and switched to sidearms.

The wall of indistinct shouting soon takes on real, decipherable words. Men bark orders, curse the heavens, and cry in pain as the retreating, backward steps of boots and trousers descend from the smoke cloud. I close my eyes, bring the rifle to my lips, and kiss it. I open my eye to a handful of escaping white men—the most feared outlaws in the West, so accustomed to being the hunters—wide-eyed with fear and firing haphazardly over their shoulders into a fog of gun smoke as the legs and moccasins of Dineh warriors churn toward them.

The bulk of the Snowman's gang tries to hold its ground, engaging the enemy in the type of bloody, close-quarter battle that claimed most lives in the War. Guns give way to knives, then fists, then, in close, teeth. This is a brawl on Dineh terms—a swarming, tenacious tide of blades and stones and bullets that neuters the superior firepower of the outlaws.

Ahiga leads the charge, thrashing his ax with his right arm, my Spencer thundering from his left—a big noisemaker, mostly. The ax does the bulk of the damage.

We keep ourselves hidden as the stream of Snowmen rolls down the hill, straight into the maw of the awaiting crank. I watch the bandits and Bix watches me, both his arms resting beneath the cylinder, ready to hurl it onto the rock. Delmer, with the calmness of a man unafraid, cradles the trigger end. The cigarette, steady as stone, dangles from his lips.

The bandits draw closer, thirty yards, twenty, ten. I pick out a straggler, a gray-bearded bastard in a flat, black Stetson, and bringing the gun up, set my sights square on his chest. I squeeze the trigger, my eyes already leaping to the next target. I see, from the corner of my vision, the gray-beard lurch backward, stricken.

In a fluid, synchronized motion, Delmer and Bix swing the crank gun over the edge of the rock. The stubby legs of the bipod tap once against the stone, then scrape slightly as Delmer makes the smallest correction. Bix drops down immediately, readying the next magazine while Delmer, cool as morning frost, shows all in attendance how he earns his keep for the Pinkertons.

The nearest bandit lets out an audible gasp, a wide-eyed inhalation of understanding as the killing machine screeches to life. A sound like no other—a terrifying cross between a sputtering steam engine and a child's whirling pinwheel— overwhelms the canyon as a seamless rope of lead shreds one outlaw after another.

Casey rises from his cover, working the lever action of his rifle with unprecedented efficiency. I lay into the Winchester, the two of us picking off those that break from the pack with surgical, unyielding precision.

Snowmen fall so quickly that their riddled corpses pile up in a grisly heap in front of the boulders. Within seconds the crank gun cuts their numbers, and bodies, in half. The stunning display of power freezes, for a brief moment, the Dineh warriors, even those in the throes of brutal, hand-to-face combat. And even their enemy—some mere seconds from death—take pause in the desperate struggle for survival.

Thick knots of smoke belch from the Gatling's barrels as steam ripples upward from the immense heat. The first magazine clicks empty. Delmer rips it from its socket—Bix is right there with the replacement, already chambered before Delmer can shift the cigarette from one side of his mouth to the other. But in that brief buckle of time, the remaining Snowmen scatter like roaches. Fresh pistols appear from boots and inner pockets and then, sensing the tiniest window of opportunity, the outlaws commence a swarming assault on the Gatling's position.

Unfazed, Delmer pivots the gun a few degrees and with a short, lethal burst, cuts down the nearest attacker. He swivels the gun left and fires another burst. I expose myself from the outcropping of rock and, with new urgency, defend the left flank despite the Winchester's tendency to pull low and to the right—an annoying irritation that I overcome, finding the rifle's sweet spot.

Savage torrents of lead pulse from the crank, dropping the bandits where they stand and, in a staggering testament to Delmer's artistry, leaving the Dineh unscathed.

To the besieged outlaws, the Navajo warriors are a secondary threat. Neutralizing the relentless crank gun becomes their all-consuming focus.

Their survival depends upon it. The desperados instinctively attack in a flurry of movement, never staying idle for a second out of fear for the dreaded Gatling finding a bead on any fragment of their flesh.

How many of the bandits remain, I cannot say for certain—maybe half a dozen. Ten or twelve braves are left to chastise them from the rear while the four of us unload from the front.

The arena of battle, once an entire canyon, is now decidedly more intimate. Bix, compelled to intervene, draws his revolver and empties six rounds into a pair of encroaching invaders, but a third man reaches the bunker and hurls himself over the boulder. Bix springs upward with his knife, spearing the attacker beneath the rib cage and falling backward to the dirt. Their momentum carries them back away from the Gatling, leaving Delmer to fend for himself on the reloads, which he does, albeit a whisker slower. And a whisker is all the Snowmen need.

As Bix and his assailant wrestle for the knife, a figure rises from the ground, bloodied but not dead. I recognize his shape—the one called Finn, his silhouette burned into my brain from that night at the campsite. He wears a long, chestnut overcoat, from which he unsheathes a short-barreled four-ten. Delmer swings the crank toward him, bullets ripping the air, but the man dives the other way, causing Delmer to jerk the handle. The abrupt motion throws off his aim. Two Dineh warriors, crouching beyond where Finn had stood, crumble, their chests blown apart.

The four-ten booms over the top of the boulder.

Delmer winces, grazed by a passing fleck of buckshot, but then he steadies himself behind the trigger. I run to help him, firing off a round into the belly of an advancing outlaw—a young one, no more than twenty years. Grabbing the closest magazine, I reach up and touch the bolt of the crank gun. The searing heat blisters my fingers as I slam the cartridge into place.

"Mother-scratching bastard!" Delmer barks, snapping the bolt closed with authority.

"Watch left!" I shout. Delmer pivots the gun and snaps off a steady burst into the chest and skull of a bearded bandit. I come up blasting. Ahiga swings his ax into a man's back and yanks it out again, just in time to parry the blow of a second, stronger adversary. Finn fires the shotgun point-blank into the face of a howling Dineh. The warrior's skull vanishes.

I hear Bix and the other man scuffling behind me. Turning, I watch as Bix buries his blade into the man's chest. Bix collapses on top of him, utterly spent.

The steady crack of Casey's rifle turns to an ominous click. Undeterred, he leaps out from behind his rock and charges forth, his bayonet leading the way. A grizzled, hatchet-wielding outlaw is there to greet him. Casey slides left as the hatchet slices nothing but air. He spins back, clocking the butt of the rifle against the outlaw's spine. The man grunts, winded. He tries to straighten up, but instead finds the red tip of Casey's bayonet protruding through his vest. He sighs again and then slumps. Casey shucks him off his blade and turns back toward me, a thin, satisfied, smile spreading across his face. Then a quick flash of light blooms from up the hill, followed by a sudden, crisp *pop*. Casey's head snaps to the side, a spray of pink mist erupting from his skull. He falls dead.

"Sniper!" The cigarette flies from Delmer's lips as he yells out the warning. I dive for safety behind the sandstone obelisk, the sniper's bullets pinging off the rocks above me. I roll onto my belly and peer out around the edge. Far up the hill, a hundred yards at least, two granite slabs lean against each other, forming a natural stone shelter that serves the sniper as an elevated fortress from which to rain down his lethal fire. I take aim at the sliver of dead space between the two stones and squeeze off a round. The wind takes it right, judging by the wisp of dust that puffs off the granite.

Delmer spits a volley from the Gatling but quickly cuts it short. "He's out of range," he says, shaking his head.

Two of the Snowman's men appear out of nowhere, sprung from their hiding places by the ray of hope shining off the barrel of their sharp-shooting kinsman. The captain's Winchester rifle, with its stubby barrel meant for close-up work, chokes empty, confirming its uselessness.

The first man rushes Ahiga, who finds himself out in the open, a juicy target for the sniper. The unseen rifle pops again, narrowly missing Ahiga as he crouches to accept the impact of the charging desperado. The Navajo locks the man's arm behind his back and, spinning him around, presents him toward the slope as the rifleman unleashes a round meant for Ahiga himself. The bullet catches the bandit square in the chest. Ahiga tosses the dead outlaw aside and reaches out to grab the second man as he passes. The bandit slips through his arms and runs straight for Delmer.

Swiveling the gun hurriedly, Delmer sprays a hail of bullets into the air, but the man drops low, beneath the lip of the boulder, and then springs up and over the barrier. Delmer lifts the gun, wielding it like a shotgun—a last and desperate measure for any crank man. The attacker flies feetfirst at him, kicking the growling crank gun from Delmer's grasp. It skitters across the ground, abruptly silenced. The kick sends Delmer onto his back. He fumbles for his knife, but the outlaw is quicker to draw his own. Delmer throws both his arms onto the man's wrist, straining to slow a blade that works gainfully toward his heart. His muscles will give out before his grit. He does not have long.

"I need a rifle," I say, calling behind me. Bix squats behind a scrubby thatch of bramble that would not stop a sunbeam, much less a pulverizing slug from a bolt-action thirty.

"I'll come to you," Bix says, racing toward me. He holds two rifles, one his own, the other newly acquired from his kill. He closes the distance, the relief visible on his face as he nears to within ten yards. Another pop rings out and his elation shatters. He collapses into me, clutching his side. The blood puddles through his fingers. I pull him behind the sandstone and his eyes start to glaze. "Shit, Harlan," he says, the vigor fading from his voice. "I thought we had this one."

"Stay with me, Lieutenant." But then his eyes take on the death stare and he slackens.

"Harlan! *Harlan*!" Delmer lies on his back, the attacker straddling his chest. The man plunges the knife down, hacking his way through Delmer's flailing, blood-streaked arms. I draw the Colt and aim at the man's head. Delmer finds a fistful of sand and hurls it into his eyes. The bandit rolls off him, blinded. I fire into the rocks, nearly killing Delmer as he bolts upright. Delmer flips over and tries to stand. His assailant wipes the sand from his eyes and turns, with vengeful urgency, toward Delmer, the red-stained bowie knife jutting from his cocked arm. *Pop!* The bullet zings past my ear and I duck back behind the sandstone.

"Shoot him. Shoot him!" cries Delmer, scampering on all fours away from the attack. The man lunges for him, bringing the knife down just as Delmer takes an evasive dive. But the blade connects, awkwardly—an unclean blow. Delmer howls. "Please, God. No!" He kicks at his killer, slowing the man for a brief moment. Then the outlaw raises the knife for the decisive thrust. I take aim, but once again Delmer springs into my line of fire.

"Move, Delmer!" I shout. In his confusion, my words go unheeded, as if, in that moment, Delmer has chosen to stop fighting. But then, in a blur of motion, salvation comes to him from a most unlikely source. Ahiga. The great warrior hurdles the barrier, ax held high. With a single, devastating blow, the Navajo swings the heavy, steel blade into the neck of Delmer's tormentor with such force that the head separates from the torso and careens into the rocks with a squishy thud. I can only watch, awestruck.

"Thank you," Delmer mutters, clutching the lower part of his rib cage. "Oh, God. Thank you." Ahiga looks toward him, then to the crank gun smoldering in the dirt, then back to the dying Pinkerton. A fresh rage overtakes him. He brings up the ax and takes a menacing step in Delmer's direction.

"You kill my brothers with your fire-gun! You die!"

"No!" Delmer says, raising a futile arm in defense. Ahiga hefts the blade high. I spring from my perch, ignoring the sniper.

"Stop!" I shout. I think I hear the rifle pop, I cannot say for certain, but I land on my knees at the feet of Ahiga. For the third time Ahiga holds my fate in his hands. "It was an accident. I swear to it." He considers me for a long moment and then lets his arms drop. The ax bounces harmlessly to the ground. "Get your head down!"

Pop! Ahiga snaps into a crouch, startled. The sniper shoots again. Pop! The bullet dings off the rocks behind us and ricochets into the dirt next to Delmer, close enough to hear the whiz of lead.

"Shit," Delmer cries, slithering tighter against the rock, "he's homing in." Ahiga closes tight against the boulder and then rises up, firing the Spencer four times. I listen for the impact on the other end and when it does not come I know he is wasting precious bullets while the sniper rapidly solves the puzzle of our stony fortress. *Pop—ching!*

A gasp escapes from the ground below me, followed by a sizzling inhalation of air through teeth. I look down and see Delmer pawing at his neck. Blood squirts from beneath his hand, steaming in the cold air. A pool of scarlet liquid turns black against the dusty ground.

I spin toward Ahiga, brimming with anger. "Give me my goddamn Spencer!"

The Dineh hesitates but tosses me the rifle. I flop straight to my belly and slide silently around the far end of the boulder, the Spencer cocked and poised for a quick release. Half a breath finds its way out of my lungs as the sights come into focus. Beyond the little metal tabs, the stone shelter is a muddled blur, but in the center of it, I come to rest on a dark streak of dead space. The trigger folds at my touch, followed by a familiar, explosive *snap!* Something flutters behind the stone slabs, then falls from view. "I got him."

I turn back to the others and see Delmer flat on his back, sucking in slow, shallow breaths that puff, gray and steaming, against the first flakes of a gentle snow. His left hand stays pressed up to his neck, coated with sticky redness, but in his right—tucked between his trembling, blood-stained fingers—is a folded bit of yellow paper. "Get this . . . to my wife." Kneeling down to him, I take the letter and put it in my pocket. There is nothing else I can do for him.

"I will."

"Bet you never thought old Delmer'd be the last white man standing," he says, allowing a smile to come to his lips.

"You are right about that," I say.

Delmer blinks a few times, staring straight through me, and then he stops fighting. The life goes out of him quick. Ahiga falls in next to me, eyeing Delmer with some curiosity. "Little man. Big gun."

"Yeah."

We pause a moment, Ahiga and I, and then, without another word, walk around the boulder and survey the carnage. Bodies lie strewn about the canyon in every imaginable state of contortion and dismemberment. A handful of Dineh pick through the remains, jabbing the occasional spear into the heart of a trouser-wearer for good measure. But all the white men—Pinkerton and outlaw—are dead.

Ahiga moves out ahead of me, pacing himself, as if the business of collecting scalps is more chore than trophy. I methodically check the faces, my mind pulling from memory those eyes that stared down at me over a peacock-blue mascada in that orbiting pageant outside the jail.

Before long I am halfway up the slope. I see the chief, atop his pony, cresting the lip of the ridge. The young scout is with him. Something about that boy's presence eases the weight of what has happened today. The chief held him back and I am glad for it. The chief gazes skyward, his thin reedy voice choked with grief, his arms outstretched in supplication, and offers a lilting prayer to the Spirits. A good dozen of his men lie dead in the canyon.

I feel Ahiga beside me. "He is not here," I say. "The Snowman."

"Bandit chief, no." Ahiga says.

Flipping the Spencer around, butt first, I extend the weapon toward Ahiga. I cannot say the Dineh have much need for the White Man's laws of ownership. Ahiga is no different. What he steals is his. But he dismisses the offering with a wave of his hands.

"Gun, part of you," he says. Then he holds up his weathered ax. "This, part of me."

I nod in gratitude and find my thoughts settling back onto the chief and the Snowman. Both men sent their soldiers forth to fight for them by proxy. It is not cowardice. It is survival of the species.

Ahiga taps my arm and grunts—his preferred way of addressing me. Down below us, a figure crawls, belly-down, across the canyon floor. Making slow, labored progress, he leaves in his wake a blood-streaked trail from the stone shelter to the rocky berm where he now finds himself. The sniper. He wears a dark brown suit that I recognize. Not two days ago, I sat across from it at the Jewel. As we approach, he gives up on his escape and rolls over, sizing up both of us with a glazy stare.

"Which one of you shot me?" he asks.

"I did."

"Hell of a shot."

I step up to him and push his hat back off his face with the tip of the Spencer.

"Your name is Jessup," I say. "The Kansan."

He tries to laugh, but in his weakened state there is no sand to his breath. "I've gone by a lot of names in my day. I guess that would be one of them." He is dying quick and I do not have much time.

"Where is LaForge?"

"Wish I knew. Can't help you."

I drive the rifle's muzzle into the lower part of his

abdomen where the bullet caught him. A scream bleats from him—he sounds like a castrated lamb. "Listen to me," I say, gesturing to Ahiga, who lowers the ax from his shoulder. "This fella here is going to cut your tongue out and feed it to you." The Kansan's face, already ashen from loss of blood, goes ghostly white, even against the ground where the snow has started to take hold.

"Don't let him do that. Please, we're not savages, are we?"

"Tell me where the meet-up is and he will kill you quick."

The Kansan's eyes flip from me to Ahiga and back to me again. A lone tear leaks down his cheek and into the thin blanket of fresh powder. "The salt flats. Hour after sundown. If he finds out I told you, he'll hunt down my wife and young 'uns. Don't tell him it was me . . . tell him . . . tell him it was one of the old-timers."

"All right," I say. I turn to Ahiga and nod him forward. "Keep his suit clean."

CHAPTER THIRTY-TWO

The Snowmen had hidden their horses, nearly twenty in all, far down in the adjoining ravine, guarded by a single, broad-shouldered bandit with a ten-gauge shotgun and a Union carbine rifle. The Dineh chief shot him from the top of the ridge as the battle raged in the canyon. He was the silver-hair's lone kill today.

The horses, save for a pair of sturdy pack mules, became the prize of the Dineh. But the saddlebags that hung on them, brimming with the coin and bullion of the legendary three-town spree—all the loot itself, every penny of it—rides with me. All in all, it is a fair divvy, as the Navajo, even at their most mercantile, would rather barter in livestock than the White Man's silly trading-paper and precious metals.

As an added bonus, I granted the chief and his men the bulk of *our* horses, which had weathered the thundering skirmish from a concealed bluff just below the canyon's uppermost ridge. The chief, in return, left me with enough sackcloth to wrap up what bodies and body parts could be salvaged from the killing grounds. He even had his men fashion me a travois to transport them back to town. I am glad that Delmer and Bix and the brothers will get proper burials. The kin of the others will have to be content with closed caskets and memorials.

The sled drags heavily down the mountains—twice I have to dismount and lift it over some hindrance or another. Storm, still reeling from the echoes of war, squawks more mightily than the mules that carry the load. I rub his neck and remind him of the warm blanket and fresh hay that await him when this is over, but the stallion still makes sure his displeasure is noted.

We reach the salt flats some time after four, although the hour proves tough to discern. The sky and earth meld seamlessly in a wash of sunless gray that obscures the horizon behind a squall of thickening snow. It will cover our tracks, and that is good.

The Kansan's woolly brown suit scratches at my skin, showing its cards—it is a costume unsuitable for everyday riding. But at least it is warm and fights off the biting cold that sneaks through my topcoat.

Stretching for miles, the barren sweep of basalt and sand offers little in the way of cover. Many bighorn, disoriented or wounded from imperfect rifle shots, have stumbled their way down the mountains and into this nothingness. With nowhere to go, those summer hunts ended quick.

For all its featureless expanse, I knew precisely where the Kansan meant when he confessed the name of the place. At the north end of the salt flats, a strange circle of sandstone formations juts improbably from the ground. The effect, when standing inside the structure, is like being in a sort of amphitheater, the desert zephyrs' whistling through the stone towers serving as applause. It is a perfect meeting spot, obfuscated from passing horse or rail rider and remote enough to engender the curiosity of only the most determined tracker.

Daylight drips hurriedly through winter's bony fingers. If I work fast, I have just enough time to settle the animals and scrounge up fuel for a fire, but the labor is a blessing—anything to take my mind off the day's carnage and the searing, leaden pull of a shattered heart.

CHAPTER THIRTY-THREE

I rub my hands in the warmth of the meager flame, my back to the westward approach. The orange light cuts the darkness, dancing off the rocks and the crystals of the fallen snow. A horse whinnies in the distance, drawing closer, no doubt excited by the smell of burning sagebrush and the humanity it intimates. Without taking my eyes from the flame, I detect a second rider a few yards behind the first.

An exasperated male voice barks at me before the speaker has bothered to dismount. "I said no fires." I hear the man swing down from his saddle and hastily tie off his horse. "Ain't they teach you no brains in Topeka?"

I snap-pivot from my seat and bring up the Spencer, leveling the barrel at his chest. His arms go up instinctively, but there is an amused aspect to his silhouette, an attitude befitting a man wholly accustomed to staring down the business end of a weapon.

"Keep 'em up," I say. "And walk over to me, real

slow." The Snowman, the dreaded marauder of the West, complies. He steps toward me, into the light.

There in the flickering fire, his face exposed, I see what Sheriff must have seen just before the killer's slug ripped through him—how perfectly the outlaw's blue mascada, knotted around his neck with an elegant four-in-hand, matches his murderous eyes. But the final confirmation comes not from the sight of the peacock bandana, but from the absence, in his voice, of the slightest Dixie twang. "Evening, Two-Trees," he says.

"Evening, Willis." The mere utterance of the phony name causes a pearly-toothed grin to bloom across his face. I pluck the pistol from his holster— the same silver-plated forty-four he unveiled at the Jewel—and, pawing about his waist, discover a snub-nose backup, which I also liberate from his reach.

"Can I assume that the previous owner of the suit you're wearing will no longer need it?"

"It ain't my blood stained across it." I push back from him as a woman's voice chirps from the other side of the rocks.

She strides around the corner, steaming the air with her breath. The tone out of her mouth is put-upon, coarse, even bitchy. "Where the hell is everybod—" Her tiny, delicate frame, swaddled beneath a thick, woolen blanket, startles upright. The whites of her eyes spread wide as saucers.

"Harlan!" she says, dumbfounded at the sight of me. But then, without hesitation, she bursts into tears and runs toward me, her voice softening. "Oh, Harlan! He has kidnapped me. Thank God you're all right."

I keep the gun trained on the dude. She touches my arm, but the mind-sucking electricity is gone, replaced by a hollow, algid emptiness.

"Get off me," I say, nudging her away. "Go sit by the fire." She blinks at me, wounded, her mouth hanging open.

"I swear to you, I don't know what's going on. He dragged me here—"

"Ain't you spun enough lies, sweetheart?" I say. Genevieve moves numbly to the fire and sinks down onto a dry stone.

"Clever work, slipping into his suit like that," the dude says, though there is not much duded up about him tonight. The well-worn leathers, the splattered boots—every inch of him is accessorized for a hard night's ride. Soft gloves protect his precious, bomb-making hands—his bread and butter—with the forethought of a surgeon. He has even let his beard go—smart, another layer from the cold. The silk bandana is the only hint of flair.

"I reckon we are both guilty of playin' dress-up. 'Cept you got to be a right more fancy in your costumes."

"Let's talk about this reasonable."

"What was his name?" I ask.

"Who, Jessup?"

"No, the poor sap you let hang in your stead."

"This is crazy," Genevieve says, jumping up from her perch. "Do you mean to suggest that Avery is the blasted *Snowman*? Harlan, put that gun down. You're not in your right mind."

"Nothing to suggest. He told me himself. Do not make me tell you again to sit down." She plops back down, a scolded child in the corner. "See, there have been all sorts of little dribs of things that did not quite fit in all this. Like how come a famous river-boat gambler no one ever heard of comes to a little Podunk town like the Bend and proves himself to be, by all accounts, a pretty piss-poor gambler? Be honest, what with all that has been happening I cannot say I ever would have had cause to put two and two together. But as it is, the only fella I ever seen you beat at a poker table turns out to be part of your gang. Now what am I supposed to think of that? Why on earth would a desperado with a price on his head risk coming into town to swindle fifty dollars from a bunch of hayseeds? Unless the real reason he was here was so you could chase after him. You had banks to rob, safes to blow up. You had dynamite you needed to lay out in that canyon."

"Now see here, Two-Trees, let me put my arms down."

"I will shoot you where you stand, LaForge." I throw back the hammer on the Spencer and let him see the unwavering steadiness of the barrel aimed straight at his heart. "Must be a burden, being the only one could set them charges. No one to delegate to. Or maybe that's the secret. Ship don't sail without you."

"You flatter me, friend. If only I had the skill of the Snowman."

"You got skill to a fault. That is what done you in."

"How do you figure?"

"You were stuck in town. A fella as fancy as Avery Willis cannot just sneak out of town, unobserved. So you had to concoct some ruse to get you out. You had a right fun time, playing Willis. Too much fun, I would say. Never quite figured you for the type to get all riled over being cheated. But then you had to jump on that filly. See, the thing is, I seen a fella jump off a railing like that and land full bore into a gallop, but only once. It was when Sheriff got shot. Good horsemanship is hard to hide, especially in the heat of the moment, even if the moment is fake. You were hell and gone." I turn and look at her, fighting back the sickening, dull thud in the pit of my stomach. "All you needed then was someone to cover for you."

"No," she says.

"I don't care how tired a fella is, he don't sleep through a hanging."

"I told you, Avery was embarrassed by that foolish pursuit of the cardsharp. He was too mortified to show his face."

"And I might ought have believed that," I say, "but then Mister Willis did not count on crossing my path at the stables that night."

"As I told you," the dude says, "I could not sleep. I needed some air."

"In your riding clothes? Even in the dead of night, it threw me, kind of like it does now, catching sight of you dressed down like that. And you had a saddlebag with you. Who carries something like that on a late-night stroll?"

"Like you said, I'm fancy."

"Not that night, you weren't. I reckon that set going in my head a whole string of business. But the thing that clinched it was when you had me put my hand on that filly's neck. Poor girl was sweating like a whore."

"So I'd been riding, what of it?"

"Shoulda kept riding. You might got away with all of it, you done that. But no. No, you had to come back to town. That was your mistake. You were free and clear, you had the loot, you had your legend, and you risk it all. For what? Just to watch us squirm in the aftermath? No, sir. That does not figure for the Snowman. He is too smart for that. From that moment on, you were scrambling. You could not have any loose ends and the only folks who saw you that night were me . . . me and Otis Chandler's boy. And when I showed up, he was already dead."

"Oh you are punch-drunk, you know that?" he says.

"You strangled that poor child and tried to make it look like Indians. Except Dineh do not strangle and you should have known that. Mistakes pile up when you get careless. It was not dust on your jacket. It was *flour*." It flashes over his face, a fleeting wisp of a grin, and then he stifles it. But he knows I've seen it. "I will not ask you again. What was his name?"

Slowly, without any hint of subterfuge, he puts down his arms. "His name was Carlyle. Clay Carlyle."

"What are you doing?" she says.

"It's all right, darling. No sense belaboring this."

"Poor old Clay," I say.

"Clay was a loyal soldier."

"Nobody's that loyal. That no-luck sap really thought you were coming to save him."

"Somebody had to swing. Plan don't work otherwise."

"You killed the man what raised me. Gunned him down and made it personal."

"Clay shot the sheriff."

"No, 'cause that would make the sheriff a liar. And that he was not. See, the thing that nobody ever picked up on was the way Sheriff got kilt. 'Twas a forty-four slug they pulled out of his heart. But old Clay, he was holding a shotgun the whole time. Sheriff knew you. Knew your face. And he said with his dying breath, hand to God, that it was LaForge himself what fired the money shot. That means not only did you step in front of Clay to kill Sheriff, but you dropped your mask so he would know it was you. Been gnawing at me all the time until you pulled that forty-four out your belt to go ride off after Jessup."

"Lots of forty-fours around."

"It was you. You looked at me. Same eyes you're looking at me with now."

The snow crunches beyond the rocks behind me. "Someone's coming," she says.

"That would be your partner," I say, without turning to face the newcomer. The air cracks with the distinct, metallic click of a pistol hammer drawn back into readiness. A graveled, venal voice peals from the shadows.

"Drop that rifle." Boone sidesteps into the corner of my vision, the engraved revolver squeezed tightly in two white-knuckle fists. "I'll shoot you dead, son. Neither one of us want that." I lower the Spencer. LaForge swoops in and takes it from me, before reclaiming his guns from the ground. The woman's fingers brush against my hips as she relieves me of the Colts. I watch her, but she will not bring her eyes to mine, so I turn to face Boone. He wears a

long black overcoat, the collar upturned against
the wind.

"I tell you, Boone, I always knew you to tilt the
tables in your favor, but I never figured you had the
sand to bankrupt your own town. Much less have
Sheriff taken out.

"The hell you talking about?"

"Sheriff always did right by you. You let him
bleed out in the street."

"I had no hand in that. Pardell got himself killed
like a dang idiot."

"Let it drift, Walter," LaForge says. "The cat's out
of the bag."

"What?"

"The kid knows."

A spark of stunned wonderment flickers across
the mayor's face. He snuffs it out as quick as it
comes and then his eyes narrow with pitiless scorn.
"Then why the fuck is he breathing?"

"I brought your loot. Every cent of it," I say,
throwing a nod toward the mules and their burden-
some cargo. "That ought to be worth something."

"Maybe it is," LaForge says. "We can talk about it."

"Now you want to cut him in?"

"It's just business, Walter."

"He probably brought the Pinkertons out here.
You check these rocks?" Boone says, jabbing the
pistol out toward the night for emphasis.

"Pinkertons are dead," I say. "All of them."

"Horseshit."

"Ambushed. His handiwork got most of them," I
say, nodding toward LaForge. "Them what was left,
Indians took care of."

"Indians?" LaForge asks, coming closer. "And how did their involvement figure into it?"

"I made them an offer."

"Ha! Well then I guess we're in your debt, Two-Trees," the mayor says, but LaForge cuts him off with an anxious wave.

"And what of my men?"

"Same."

"Dear God," the woman says, a breathy gasp escaping her lips.

"Speak plain, man," LaForge says. "Surely a few of my guns survived the encounter."

"Not a one. You think they would let me ride off with this loot if they had?"

"No, I do not."

"Bad day all around for white men."

"Sweet Jesus," LaForge doubles forward, supports himself with his hands on his thighs. "I will confess, when I saw you ride off with the Pinkertons I had a most uneasy feeling, but I can say with utmost certainty that I did not see *that* coming."

"His share's not coming out of my end," Boone says. "Not after all I been through."

"What—*you* been through?" I cannot help myself. In the swirling black night of winter's first blizzard, the Spirits grant me the true and clear vision of a hawk. I see it all—the greed, the lust, the depths of deceit and depravity. Every errant remark, every incongruous little morsel from the last month unfolds like a map on a table. The unfettered words pour out of me. "The plan don't work without you, do it, Boone?"

"What are you jawing at? I say we waste him right now."

"You had one job and one job only and that was to get every goddamn Pinkerton over to the Bend so them banks would be unguarded. Only two men in the Bend with the power to make that happen— you and Sheriff. And Sheriff was never going to turn. So he had to go. And you bear as much guilt on that as the Snowman. You can add the blood of every last Pinkerton to your head as well. Plus all them what perished along the way."

"This is rich. I suppose you blame me for your whore's death as well. Though I don't think you'd want anybody poking too close around the sudden departure of Jed Barnes, would you?"

"If they did, they'd see he had it coming. And that I did what any man in his right mind would do. It's when fellas start acting in ways outside themself that draws attention."

"Anybody else heard enough?" Boone grips the pistol a little tighter and does his best to steady the quivering muscles in his arm. Cold and fear take hold of him in equal measure.

"Raven. You never should have kilt Raven."

"Raven? That godless *savage*? I got news for you, Two-Trees, the world don't weep for a dead Indian."

"I reckon I thought the same thing. That is why it made no sense. Here you are, a man never so much as drawn on another man much less shot anybody, and then, the morning of the hanging, surrounded by the best hired guns money can buy, you show up with that old commemorative pistol on your hip. That bell rang funny from day one. And then you shot that scout off his horse and showed your hand."

"Everybody was armed that day. We were under siege."

"No, we never were. Was a good story, though. Had to be. But even the threat of the Snowman's gang weren't enough to clear Heavendale and Agua Verde of the Pinkertons, not entirely. So you had to get creative. You're right, nobody cares about a dead Indian, so why kill just one? The smart move, save for doing nothing, is kill 'em both. But instead you shoot the young one and leave his hot-headed brother to start a war. The threat of a red invasion . . . now *that* gets the White Man's attention. Be honest, Boone, I'm impressed you came up with it."

"Who says he came up with it?" Her voice is soft again, soft as I remember it, and that makes the icy calculation in her words all the more bothersome.

"You know, girl. I am not in my right mind after all. Have not been for a while. Just like Boone here stepped out of his self with shooting that boy. And the Snowman? Hell." I turn to LaForge. "You might be the scariest sumbitch in the territory, but you are, by nature, a smash-and-grab man."

"Blast-and-grab would be more accurate," he says.

"A score this big," I continue, "what with all the planning and forethought, not your standard procedure. And this whole business of playing the gambler, well, you would have fared better leaving the playactin' to them minstrels what come through town every summer. Which leaves me thinking, by golly, what's the only thing that could get three grown men to completely lose their minds? Sure enough, that would be a woman."

"You just have all the answers, don't you, boy?"

Boone says. "Had us all fooled, playin' the idiot. You're a real smart crackerjack. Well, bully for you. Ain't no way in hell we're letting you walk out of here."

"Put the gun down, Walter." Her voice is firm, but there is a woman's sweetness to it that warms a heart even as steely and soulless as Boone's. "He brought us our money. He didn't have to do that."

"She's got a point, Walter," LaForge says. "Two-Trees here has a streak in him." LaForge turns to me, his eyebrow arched above a devilish grin. "Damn, boy. You wanted in, you shoulda just asked me."

"Talking ain't my strong suit."

"All evidence to the contrary."

"We'd still have to trust him," Boone growls.

"Being an outlaw is all about trust," LaForge says. "How the hell you think I've stayed alive so long? I had men I could trust. Good men." He trails off, the loss hitting home yet again.

Seeing him grapple with the blow, she offers words of comfort with her own fiendish bent. "The boys didn't die for nothing. . . . It means there's more for the two of us."

"That it does, darlin'."

"She was talking to *me*," Boone says. The finality in his voice—primal, greedy, born from the fiery bowels of hell—follows a quick turn in his pistol hand that levels the barrel square at the Snowman's chest. "Drop it, LaForge."

Garrison LaForge shakes his head, stunned. He lets his gun fall. The snow envelops it. "Well," the Snowman says, "Look who found his calling."

"Step away from the gun," Boone says. "It's over."

"Boone, didn't you hear what I just said? About trust?"

"Now you're the one who's new to the game," Boone says. He points toward the mules. "Go on, darlin'. Bring them mules over this way. They won't bite you."

"I'm scared, Walter," she says, all at once the little girl again.

"It's all right, sweetheart. It's going to be fine, just like we talked about."

"I . . . Garrison . . ." she says.

LaForge turns back to her, the disappointment peeking though his cold, blue eyes. "I guess you better do what he says, darling. If that's what you want."

She exhales and scurries across the snow toward the mules. "Sorry to surprise you like this, LaForge," Boone says. "But she and I have other plans for the loot. And they don't include the two of you." He juts his head in my direction as he says the last.

"Oh, for heaven's sake, Boone. You think I didn't know? She was about as subtle flirting with you as she was with Two-Trees." LaForge finds pause to turn toward me. "Yes, Harlan. I know about you two as well. I know everything." And turning back in Boone's direction, he adds, "I am the goddamn Snowman! I know everything. Just like I know you don't have the sand to shoot me. Now give me that gun."

"Oh, let it go, Garrison," she says, leading the first of the mules by a rope over toward the mayor. "It's over."

"That's right," Boone adds. "Your time is up,

LaForge. I ain't afraid to kill you. I'm afraid to let you live. So I ain't gonna. You got bested. I get the loot. I get the girl. Sometimes life ain't fair."

The woman walks the mule up to Boone, facing him, and then stops. Her eyes narrow and then go wide. I see the movement behind Boone, but by then his fate is sealed. The arrow zings from the darkness. Boone shrieks as the razor-sharp tip slams into the small of his back and punctures clean through his belly. His gun flails uselessly to the side before cascading from his fingertips and down into the snow.

Three Dineh warriors, lead by Ahiga, emerge from the blackness, clubs raised, and descend upon the mayor. His womanly, desperate cries scar the air as they beat him to the ground. Ahiga kicks Boone in the teeth, stifling his yelps to pained, muffled gurgles. The warrior snatches up the fallen pistol and spins it upon LaForge and myself—a menacing display—in case either of us be entertaining thoughts of intervention. Our empty palms extend toward him, cementing our submission.

Ahiga thrusts the pistol toward the Snowman, snarling. "Your life you owe to *him*." He jabs a finger my way to confirm my involvement. I drop my hands and address Ahiga.

"You sure took your sweet time, didn't you?" I say. Ahiga growls at me and turns back toward his captive. Hog-tied and gagged in seconds, Boone finds himself hoisted up through the air and deposited roughly onto the bareback haunch of the palomino for a speedy transport to a slow and miserable death. The woman blows past me and meets the begging eyes of Walter Boone.

"I'd sooner die than lay with you again," she hisses. "I hope they string you up and use you for target practice."

"No," I say, edging up to have my final words with the condemned. "The arrow missed your vitals. That was on purpose. They are going to eat your skin while you burn at the stake." He strains beneath his gag, imploring, in his godless manner, for mercy. But there is none I have for him.

"LaForge asked me how I enlisted the Navajo," I say. "I told him I made them an offer. I gave them what they wanted. And what they wanted was you. You never should have shot that boy." Ahiga throws himself atop the horse and kicks it up. The other scouts mount horses that seem to appear out of thin air. There is some shouting, a cry of victory, and then, as quickly as they came, the Dineh vanish.

The woman stands next to me, both of us staring after Ahiga and his companions as they ride off into the night. "Well, that makes it easy for us," she says.

"How do you figure?" I say.

"This time," LaForge says, "she was talking to me." The gun clicks behind me and I know then and there that he was never going to surrender a penny of his fortune, or his woman, to me. She turns her head partly toward me, but not enough to catch my eye.

"I'm sorry," she says. I lift my hands yet again, but this time believing it is the end. She breaks from me and goes to him.

"You had me going, darling. I'll admit it," he says.

"Oh, honey. How could you ever doubt me?"

She touches his shoulder and moves past him to
retrieve the second mule.

"You were never going to cut me in," I say.

"What can I say? It is my nature."

"I am the fool for thinking you would do otherwise."

"Just think of it as another snatch-and-grab job.
But you did right by me, Two-Trees. I'll make this
quick. Get down on your knees and I'll put a blind-
fold on you." In his eyes I see the steely detachment
that served as the last image on earth for many a
dead man. I think about asking her to intervene,
but then I let the idea go. I drop down into the
cold, wet snow that seeps through my denim as if it
were paper. I think about the Spirits and how I will
soon get to hear their music with my own ears, as
true as morning birdsong. "Darlin'," he says. "Bring
me one of your scarves."

She lets go of the mule rope and walks over to
him, her hands lost inside the inner regions of her
coat. "Here you go," she says.

The Snowman turns to take it from her. She
reaches up with her hand and a little pop explodes
from her fist. The smoky barrel of the derringer—
the best friend of women and gamblers—sends a
gray, wispy trail up into the frigid night.

Garrison LaForge stares down in utter amazement at the tiny, black hole in the center of his
topcoat. As the hole turns from charcoal back to
glistening, liquid red, his legs desert him. The
Snowman drops to his knees and, finding the
strength to look at me, says, "Damn, Two-Trees.
She must really like you." His final breath issues
forth from his lips, which manage a thin, defeated

smile. Then the Snowman falls forward, dead in the frozen powder that bears his name.

"Thank God," she says. "Thank God he's dead." From the corner of my eye I pick up the pearly handle of the Colt peeking from the crystalline blanket of white, maybe ten feet from where I stand. I fancy my odds with the Colt against the stubby barrel and lone remaining bullet of the derringer, but I stand motionless, uninterested in the idea. "Let's go, darling. Let's get out of here."

When I stay put, she turns back to me, her voice pitched with urgency. "Harlan, get your head about you. We have to go. It'll be light soon. Now tie off that mule. We can get a good jump by dawn."

"Look who the real gambler is—playing whatever hand you're dealt right up to the last."

"What are you talking about? Nothing's changed. Let's go."

"You could find the angles on a circle, that's for sure. What's your real name, girl?"

"For Christ's sake, Harlan. Not now."

"All that talk of running off together . . . Hell, you had me believing it. But all you really needed out of me was someone to get you over the Sangres. Come the first thaw, what, you put that last bullet in my head while I'm sleeping?"

"How dare you say that. I love you. Now, please!"

"What brothel he pull you out of?"

"What does any of that matter? I'm just a girl who had a plan. One thing led to another. Nothing more. Are you going to tie off that mule or not?"

"No."

"I wasn't playacting with you. We can do all those things we talked about."

"Boone had plans with you too. So did LaForge. Now look at them. One is dead and the other wishes he was."

"I do not love them."

"That much is quite clear."

"We don't have time for this. Are you coming with me or not?"

"I am not."

"Why not?"

"That money don't belong to us."

"Like hell it don't. I stole it fair and square."

"That's people's lives you got rolled up in there."

"Oh please, don't act like you care about them. Those people sure as shit don't care about you. They hate you. They burnt your house down."

"That don't make me a thief."

"Who you trying to impress? Me?"

"No."

"Oh, why can't you just get on that horse and let's get out of here? It would be so easy."

"Because that's not how I was raised."

"You smug son of a bitch. I'm asking you for the last time. Are you coming with me?"

"No."

"Suit yourself." She raises the gun and points it at me. Her hand quivers, but not enough to miss. "You're leaving here with me, or not at all."

"You going to shoot me?"

"I don't want to. But if I have to, I will. I've worked too hard for this. Years! And nobody's going to stop me. Not you or anybody."

"Then you better do it and get it over with."

"Ain't you going to come at me? Try to take if from me?"

"No."

"I pegged you for more of a man. I guess I was wrong."

"I have no more fight left in me. Not today."

"Have it your way." She steadies the gun, her lips pursed with deep concentration. She takes dead aim. Then she lowers it. "I cannot shoot you. Dammit! I wish I could. I really do! But Harlan, I swear to God, if you come after me I will shoot you dead. Do you understand me?"

"I will not follow you."

"I still can't risk it. You'll go get help."

"No. I won't do that either. If you want to go, you go. I'll stay here till morning so you get a proper jump."

"You would do that for me?"

"When I get to town, I'll tell them you went east. Anybody goes after you, they'll be going in the wrong direction."

She drops the gun and comes to me. I know what is coming and I do not fight it. With a tear dripping from her eye, she kisses me. The kiss is short, final. "Thank you, Harlan. Thank you."

She starts to turn back from me and I grab her, spinning her face to mine. I bury my lips into hers for what seems like eternity, the electricity racing between us, a reminder of what will not be. I break from her. She wipes the tear from her face.

"Mabel," she says. "Mabel Pitts. Of Fayetteville, Arkansas. Nice to meet you, Harlan." She turns from me and sails up onto her horse, the mule rope tied off to her saddle. She leads her horse to the other mule and fastens that rope to hers as well.

"It's cold in the Bloods. You'll need to find wood

before you get too far in." She waves me off, as if she has already thought of this.

"I'll burn money. I've sure got enough of it." She guides her horse out of the rocks, the two mules in tow. "Take care of yourself."

"You too," I say, watching her disappear into the snow.

CHAPTER THIRTY-FOUR

An hour past sunrise, I pull into the Bend and find Merle taking his morning coffee on the back porch of the Jewel. Big Jack is with him, mug in hand. Rico, under Merle's watchful eye, sweeps off the steps. The boy comes over to untie the travois from Storm, who is more than happy to be rid of it.

"What's the matter, Rico," Merle says, "you never seen the way the Navajo wrap their bodies?"

"No, sir. I no like it."

The piss puddle has nearly dried, the stench a mere nuisance. Order seems almost restored. Life, as it does, goes on. The silver star pinned to Big Jack's shirt shimmers in the early light. It is a heavy, proper badge, not the cheap tin he garnered off the mayor.

Jack sees me eyeing it and humbly taps it with his thumb. "Town voted," he says. "It all happened so fast, I guess I never got around to saying no."

"Every town needs a sheriff," I say. "Will be needing a new mayor too, I reckon. How 'bout it, Merle?"

"Not a chance in hell." Merle climbs down off the steps to get a closer look at LaForge. The Snowman's reentry to town, draped over Storm's haunches, is a far cry from the elegant carriage that brought us Avery Willis. Merle pokes him with a finger. "To think this son of a bitch was right under our noses the whole time."

I give Merle, Big Jack, and Rico the whole story of what happened out there in the desert, down to the details of how I watched Genevieve disappear into the snow on her horse, pulling the two well-laden mules behind her.

Rico walks solemnly over to the tightly wrapped remains of the Pinkerton men. He gives one of them a shy poke and immediately startles back. "*¡Dios mío!*" he shouts. He looks down at his hand, dumbfounded by what he discovers there—a solid-gold dollar-piece.

Big Jack bounds over excitedly. "That must be one of them spirit things . . . you need a dollar to pay the ferryman what to take you over to the other side. Like the Pharaohs done."

"This look like ancient Egypt to you?" Merle says, bellying up to the foot of what, by the shape of it, appears to be Delmer. He begins to unravel the sackcloth. After a few turns, the hint of a human form collapses beneath his fingers and a river of gold and silver cascades to the ground around his boots. Merle turns to me. "You son of a bitch. You glorious, fantastic son of a bitch!"

As if the plain truth of what he is seeing is still, somehow, a mystery, Big Jack draws his knife and, approaching the broad chest of the largest mummified corpse, plunges the blade into the center of it.

He slices toward himself, the steel tinkling against metal and paper. Only when Big Jack thrusts his hands into the cavity and opens it wide, revealing the untapped fortune, does the new lawman allow his brain to understand. "Well I'll be a monkey's uncle."

"*¡Dios mío! Santa Maria!*"

"Rico," Merle says, "go get the bottle. The good shit, from my office!"

"Jack," I say, "You will need to get some fellas out to the salt flats straightaway to collect the bodies. You got a few hours till the coyotes find 'em."

"But Harlan . . ." Jack says, "if the loot is all here, then what's the girl got with her?"

"Well, one thing never in short supply around here is sand and rocks. But I would not want to try to make a fire out of them."

Rico hustles down the steps with the bottle and a trio of foggy glasses, which Merle takes from him and lines up on the railing. Big Jack counts out a stack of paper currency and walks it over to me.

"What's that?" I ask.

"A bounty's a bounty. Dead or alive. Ten thousand for this here body," he says, jabbing an elbow toward LaForge. "My first official act. Merle can be witness."

"Hear, hear!" Merle says.

"You keep it, give it them what need it more."

"You sure? You earned it."

"I got the sale of my land. That will be enough."

"Where you gonna go?"

"San Francisco, maybe. Look up this fella what I heard about. Maybe get work on one of them ships passing through."

"A ship? What you know about shippin'?"

"Bout as much as you know about sheriffin'."

"He's got you there."

"You leaving right now?"

"Another storm coming in. Best I get a jump on it." Merle hands me the shot. The three of us clink glasses and drink. Warm whiskey spreads through my body. I feel good, better than I have in weeks.

"How about a beer for the road?"

"No thanks." I pat Storm on his neck. The Spencer rubs against my shoulder. "I got everything I need."

ACKNOWLEDGMENTS

The book you have just read exists because of the contribution of my co-conspirator, Derrick Borte. When the curtain is pulled back on the dark alchemy of collaboration, the process hardly seems any more elucidated. Certainly the craft of fiction writing has been, historically, a solitary endeavor, but in the film business, where Derrick and I learned to swim, collaboration is the name of the game. Several years ago, Derrick told me a brief story, little more than a sketch really, but at its core was a heist, a heist so ingenious, that I wished I'd thought of it. I coveted it, in fact. At the very least, it was gloriously cinematic. Crafting it into a screenplay, however, threatened to be a dubious use of time. The reality is that the shelves of Hollywood's development offices are lined with screenplays of unproduced Westerns. The thought of sentencing such a promising idea to a fate of irrelevance (not to mention the eventual recycling bin) was more than this writer could stomach. And while I have taken great pains to push the words around to the best of my ability as a prose writer, I was, at the same time, transcribing the film that I saw in my head. *3:10 to Yuma, Brokeback Mountain, Django*

Unchained, and the revisionist *No Country for Old Men* are unequivocally great films of the last decade. But to say there's been a resurgence of Westerns pouring out of Hollywood would be over-statement. More often than not, the scant offerings from the genre are either curious anomalies or hard-fought passion projects that managed by attrition, luck, or a combination of both, to get made. Hollywood spits out one or two (rarely three) Westerns a year. Any film desiring to occupy one of those slots better have something new to say. I don't know if this book succeeds in that endeavor, but in trying to figure it out, I could not have asked for a more patient, supportive, and enthusiastic partner than Derrick.

I am deeply indebted to a handful of trusted friends whose advice and early readings of the book proved invaluable, notably Laura Gordon and John Rood. I readily took John's suggestion that I decimate the profanity of that earlier draft and let the remaining *cocksuckers* breathe more. And when I was sure that I had exhausted every imaginable way to describe a horse, Dr. Cindy Rhea, DVM, informed me that I had barely scratched the surface.

Were it not for the gracious support of Mark Ebner, this book would never have found an agent (and I may never have embarked on writing it). That Mark is a fine writer in his own right, makes that support all the more humbling. Mark has been a champion of my prose writing from its adolescence. It was Mark, who all those years ago, invited me into a network of blogs of which he was a part— paving the way for my very first paying, non-movie, writing gig. And it was Mark, in the spring of last year, who ushered me into his very own agency where he is, by his own admission, their smallest client (a ranking in which I have surely now undercut him) and asked Joel Gottler to take a look.

Thanks go to the two representatives who have been with me from the beginning: my film agent Doug MacLaren and my attorney, David Feldman. They have stood by me through the years, even during the lean times when their faith in my abilities was all I had to go on. Thanks to my business manager, Gary Halpert (and the incomparable Nanette), for showing the greatest faith of all. My manager, Alex Lerner, has proved a welcome addition, providing the nurturing encouragement for my ideas when they are good, as well as the insight to know when they are terrible. My television agent, Hrishi Desai, exerts his talents mainly by telling me my ideas are terrible. I will always be grateful for the guidance and support of my book agents, Joel Gottler and Doug Grad. Joel and Doug are longtime veterans of the book world who have escorted this newbie novelist through the intricacies of publication and laid me gently at the doorstep of Kensington Publishing and my editor, Gary Goldstein. Special thanks to Stephen Breimer for navigating the legalities.

My copy editor, Randy Kaplan, and I spent hours discussing everything from the errant comma to the specific color of New Mexico's crystalline dust. Randy knew when to rein me in and when to get out of the way, and had the wisdom to know the difference. I am grateful for his exacting eye and unflagging enthusiasm.

Many fine teachers deserve acknowledgment for

their contribution to this writer's education, including: Drs. Brier, Bendixen, Liu, and the entire English department at California State University, Los Angeles; and from Pembroke Hill School in Kansas City: thanks go to Art Atkison, Bob Del Greco, Dr. Martin-Lester, and especially to my friend Edward Quigley, who taught me we are always students, even when we are teachers. Thank you to Robert Carnegie and Tony Savant from Playhouse West for forcing me to pay attention to what really moves me. I will always owe a debt to my old friends Bryan Singer and Christopher McQuarrie. Those years of heated late-night arguments, fueled by coffee, pastrami sandwiches, and a shared passion for great movies were the curriculum for the finest film school on earth.

Finally, to family, especially my parents, for their love and support. I hope book club is never the same. And to Danielle, for her undying love in the trenches.

Marina del Rey, CA
January 2014